SEE NO EVIL

FIORELLA DE MARIA

See No Evil

A Father Gabriel Mystery

IGNATIUS PRESS   SAN FRANCISCO

Cover photo illustration and
cover design by John Herreid
Individual photos from
istockphoto.com and unsplash.com

© 2020 Ignatius Press, San Francisco
ISBN 978-1-62164-349-4 (PB)
ISBN 978-1-64229-103-2 (eBook)
Library of Congress Control Number 2019947851
Printed in the United States of America ∞

Lead, Kindly Light, amid the encircling gloom
Lead Thou me on!
The night is dark, and I am far from home . . .

"We are in jolly spirits this morning," said Fr Foley, glancing up at the chorister who had just appeared in the doorway. Gabriel was painfully aware of the modesty of his musical talent, in spite of years of chanting in choir, and he had not been singing out loud. He had stepped into the presbytery humming the dolorous tune under his breath, but Fr Foley knew Newman's famous hymn so well he could fill in the words without assistance. "Feeling a little homesick, are we?"

Fr Foley was seated at the kitchen table, where he could make the most of the warmth of the stove as he waged much-needed battle with a mountain of paperwork. Like most men, Fr Foley was not fond of the exercise, but it was one of the few priestly duties he could not cry off on account of his heart condition. Gabriel, never the most practical of assistants, had proved to be particularly hopeless at anything involving sitting at a desk. In a corner, the wireless churned out a chirpy Gracie Fields number, offering the only competition to Gabriel's insubstantial musical abilities.

"Sorry," answered Gabriel, slowly removing his hat and

coat. He had been outdoors only for a matter of minutes, but the church had been so bitterly cold during Mass that he struggled with his buttons now, his fingers numb and stiff. "Thank you for saying the early Mass; the extra hour in bed made quite a difference this morning."

Not as much of a difference as it should have made, thought Gabriel, shuffling into the room, which was at least warm and bright after the chill darkness of the outside. It was one of the many reasons he disliked winter—not so much because of the cold and the perpetual drizzle of rain, but that all-consuming darkness. Rising in the dark and retiring in the dark. It was nearly nine o'clock, and the sun was still struggling to make an appearance through the swaths of fog and gloom. "There's tea in the pot," said Fr Foley, indicating the large, round-bellied teapot half-buried in a much frayed and stained tea cosy. "And I left an egg for you in the saucepan."

Now there was something worth cheering up for. There was tea in the pot and a boiled egg waiting to be eaten with hot buttered soldiers. Except that Gabriel had used up his butter ration for the week, somewhere in all the overindulgence of Christmas, and he would have to eat his toast without. "It's the fog I can't stand," said Gabriel, placing the egg in the chipped white egg cup in the shape of a duck that he had claimed as his own during his first week with Fr Foley. "The way it just descends on one without warning like something out of a horror film. It's always given me the creeps."

Fr Foley chuckled, throwing his friend an incredulous look. "You didn't strike me as the excitable type," he said. "At least it's clean and healthy, not that awful smog you get creeping around you in London. I don't know how anyone grows up with all that muck floating about. Are you all set for your little outing?"

Gabriel groaned, throwing his head back in mock despair. "Do I really have to go?" he asked, like a ten-year-old boy trying to worm his way out of a tiresome visit to a maiden aunt. "I loathe functions like that, always have."

"You might enjoy it once you get there."

"I'd sooner spend a day at the soup kitchen anytime. The people there are worth talking to."

"It will be a perfectly pleasant occasion," promised Fr Foley, his jollity snagging somewhat on his own insincerity. Gabriel was going to the Martin family's ghastly dinner party only because Fr Foley could not bear to go himself and had used his dicky ticker as an excuse to send a substitute. "Think of all the lovely food if the company isn't to your liking."

"Think of the black market it no doubt came from," answered Gabriel, giving the top of his egg an intemperate thump with the back of the spoon. "Think of the farmer making a dishonest bob or two . . ."

"You don't have to eat anything if you don't want to," Fr Foley teased. "If it goes against your conscience, you could always claim a health condition and push away your plate." Gabriel took the hint and said nothing. "There now, you see, there's nothing to worry about. A hearty dinner in a beautiful house, with a roaring fire, some carols round the piano, and who knows, one or two interesting guests."

Gabriel smiled, pouring himself some tea. He stifled the sudden urge for a sugar lump. He had always had a hopelessly sweet tooth, but he told himself it tasted much better

7

this way. "I shan't be a curmudgeon, I swear," he said, aware of his own morose tone. "I'm afraid I've never very much liked the aristocracy. My grandmother was a scullery maid at eleven. She hated every second of it."

"It's all right, the Martins aren't proper landed gentry; they're what you people would call *nouveau riche*. Nothing like the toffs at Lowfleet House."

Gabriel stared at the swirling contents of his teacup. "I suppose I should give them credit for having earned a fortune of their own at some stage in their history," he said, "as opposed to being the by-blow of a lascivious king hundreds of years ago. I just find them all such frauds. The house is fake, a nineteenth-century property built to look as though it were Tudor, a family title they bought to make themselves sound grander than they really are. The twee little folly in the grounds, built twenty years ago to look like an old ruined castle."

Fr Foley smiled fondly at Gabriel as he focused his attention on his breakfast. "You know, if I didn't know better, I'd say the Irish influence was making itself felt. You'll be a proud Republican by the time you go back to the abbey."

Gabriel swallowed hard. "I'm afraid that's where we will always part company, my friend."

"The king's good servant?"

"You could say that."

"Make sure you keep your head then."

Gabriel got up and stacked the breakfast things in the sink for Dorothy when she arrived to tidy up. "If it's all right with you, I'll pack an overnight bag now and leave after I've done my house visits."

Fr Foley tapped Gabriel on the shoulder. "You're not seriously thinking of walking all that way in this weather? It's three miles across country; you'll lose your way."

"Don't worry, I'll be all right. I'll give myself plenty of time."

"They did offer to send the car round," he persisted.

"I do not need to be chauffeured about, thank you very much," Gabriel retorted. "I may have to take them up on the offer tomorrow for the sake of getting home in good time. I'll go under my own steam today if it's all the same with you."

"Pride, my son," teased Fr Foley, causing Gabriel to roll his eyes. "Honestly, you must be careful not to turn your nose up at these people. Snobbery works both ways, you know."

Gabriel nodded wearily. "I know, I know. It's the failing of the social climber. I'll be terribly polite, I promise. I gather Bron's going to be there, and I owe it to him if no one else."

Half an hour later, Gabriel had once again donned his coat, hat and long woollen scarf, ready to take on the worst an English December could throw at him. Over his shoulder, he had slung his old army knapsack, containing his few necessities for a night away. The knapsack put him in the mood for marching, and once he had finished his few house calls, he took the road out of town at a good, steady pace. The air was a great deal clearer than it had been first thing in the morning, and a few pathetic beams of light were forcing themselves through the cloud cover. The one advantage of the overcast sky was that it was a little warmer than it had been a few days ago, and he was grateful for the lack of frost on the ground as he turned off the main road and clambered over a stile into a nearby field.

The previous winter had been one of the most severe in living memory, those long bitter months of deep snow when the whole of Britain had been transformed into Dante's icy hell. Abbot Ambrose had significantly added to the daily penance of that seemingly endless winter by forcing the monks to go out early every day with spades to clear a path all the way from the abbey to the road. When faced with a rare threat of mutiny, Ambrose had told them the story of a bitter winter from his childhood when a boy in his class had died from a burst appendix because the snow blocking the road to the boarding school had made it impossible to get him to hospital in time. Ambrose—who would not talk about the war and the many of its horrors he had witnessed —confessed that he was still haunted by the memory of that child, screaming in agony for his mother, whilst the nuns, unable to offer him anything to alleviate the pain, took it in turns to comfort him. In his delirious state the boy had mistaken Sister Mary Kevin for his mother, and she had played along, knowing he would die happier that way. It was the only time Ambrose ever saw her in tears. Not one of the men in his care, said Ambrose, would ever suffer such a terrible fate if he could prevent it. They had kept the road clear after that without having to be asked.

Gabriel followed the narrow path across the field, hoping the resident cows would not take too much of an interest in him as he squelched his way across land as wet and malleable as a dirty sponge. In the distance, he could just make out the spire of the village church of Palbury, which he knew he had to keep in front of him until he reached the road.

He had been instructed to turn right as soon as he reached the outskirts of the village and to keep on that road until he reached two stone pillars embossed with griffins that marked out the entrance to the Martin estate.

Gabriel smiled to himself, wondering how Florence Martin would feel when he arrived with his boots and the hem of his cassock coated in mud, but he thought he might enter by the tradesman's entrance and ask Molly for the means to tidy himself up before he disgraced himself to his hostess. Molly attended Mass at Saint Patrick's, and it was humbling to consider that she walked all this way before dawn every Sunday, attended Mass and then walked all the way back in time to serve the family their breakfast, probably not breaking her own fast until considerably later. It was one of those quiet, unnoticed sacrifices made by a devout Irish girl while some of his more well-heeled parishioners complained about a journey half that length, made in considerably more comfort.

As Gabriel clambered over the low fence, his feet touching down gently onto a firm stone path, he heard the rumble of wheels behind him and turned in the direction of the sound. An elderly farmer in a mud-splashed trench coat was riding slowly towards him on an old cart pulled by a horse that looked one *clip-clop* away from the knacker's yard. "Morning, Vicar," called the farmer brightly, slowing down as he passed Gabriel. "Where you aff to?"

"The Martin estate," said Gabriel, wondering whether he should correct the man's mistake. He decided he should. "Actually, I'm a Catholic priest."

The farmer smiled broadly. "Nobody's perfect. Hop on. I can take y'as far as the crossroads."

Gabriel clambered up beside the farmer, wedging his bag between his feet. "Thanks. I'd be glad of the lift."

They trotted along, Gabriel holding on tightly as they bumped and skidded down the uneven road. "What would you be doing there? They be nasty folk, all o' them. Never done nothing for no one."

"That seems a little harsh," said Gabriel, trying hard not to think of his earlier conversation with Fr Foley. "I'm sure they're no different to anyone else in the grand scheme of things."

"Cowards," said the farmer. "Paid some doc to say their son had a weak heart."

"You know, that's just a rumour. Perhaps he——"

"Got his reward. Blown to pieces in a raid, living it up in the city. If your time's up . . ."

Gabriel focused his attention on avoiding the prospect of falling off as they swung around a corner. He had never heard that the Martins had had a son, but the charge of cowardice was a serious one to attach to a dead man. Resentment and anger ran high among people who had lost husbands and sons whilst others had sailed through the war, but Gabriel tried to avoid the temptation to assume anything about a man spared conscription. He was old enough to remember self-righteous women handing men white feathers back in 1914, not considering that the men in civvies they publicly shamed had poor eyesight or asthma or some other hidden condition with which they had been burdened in life. "Fine weather for the time of year," was the best response Gabriel could manage.

"None so fine when you're in the thick of it," the farmer

retorted, reasonably. "So long as we don't have another like last one. Damn nearly broke us all."

"Indeed." To his surprise, Gabriel felt a certain relief at the sight of the lichen-covered griffins scowling directly at him as the Martin estate came into view. The cart creaked to a halt. "Thanks awfully," said Gabriel, throwing his bag onto the grass verge before jumping after it. "*Bened*—" The rest of the blessing was drowned out by the metallic crack of hooves as the farmer went on his way.

Gabriel watched the cart as it disappeared down the lane before turning back to the company of the griffins. He braced himself for hours of torture by social nicety and walked the long way around the building to the welcome of the back kitchen.

2

Gabriel felt uncomfortably like a burglar as he tiptoed round to the back door of the Martin residence. Fortunately, he could see Molly through the kitchen window, hovering near a vast range covered in steaming, bubbling pots, while a massively proportioned older woman busied herself at a flour-dusted table, rolling pastry. There was something comical about the pairing—the cook proportioned like Humpty Dumpty next to a young woman with the figure of a beanpole—the two women aware of one another whilst acting completely independently, like a lumbering old planet orbited by a dizzily spinning moon.

Gabriel tapped on the window, causing them both to look up sharply from their work, with Molly throwing him a look of alarm which quickly turned into exasperation. She marched towards the door and threw it open. "Heavens, Father!" she exclaimed, showing him in. He stood on the raffia doormat, indicating his filthy shoes. "You did give us both a turn. Why ever didn't you knock at the front door?"

"I'm so sorry to have startled you, Molly," said Gabriel, nodding in Cook's direction to acknowledge her presence. "I've had rather a long walk across country, and I couldn't bear my hostess to see me before I'd tidied myself up. I wonder if you might give me the wherewithal to clean my boots?"

Molly put her hand on her hips, revealing a thin, angular arm. "Father, take off those boots immediately and hand them over. I'll see that they're cleaned. You go over there and sit by the fire."

Gabriel looked where she was pointing, a small stove which gave some additional warmth to the room, a fire glowing through the soot-smeared glass panel of the door. "There's no need, Molly dear. You've plenty to do without me making extra work for you." Molly did not even grace his suggestion with an answer and simply stood where she was, gesturing that she wanted his boots. He sighed and untied the laces, slipping them off and padding across the room in his socks.

"Those socks want darning too," chided Molly, putting his boots down near him as he sat down by the stove. She stepped into another room, where there was much clattering and shuffling until she came back with brushes and polish and cloths. "Why did you not let Madam send the car for you?"

"Don't be all day about it, girl," said Cook sharply, going back to her work at the kitchen table. "The other guests will be arriving within the hour."

Molly worked with the speed and dexterity of a woman who has been serving others since infancy. Gabriel swallowed his discomfort at the sight of her kneeling before him, cleaning up the mess he had made. He endeavoured to engage her in some conversation. "So, are you expecting a good crowd?"

"We certainly are!" said Molly, struggling to open a tin.

Gabriel wordlessly took it from her and opened it. "There's to be a famous writer and his granddaughter. She is going to be a concert pianist in London. Said she'd play for everyone."

"Now that is a treat," Gabriel agreed. "I haven't been to a concert in ever such a long time."

"I've never been," said Molly.

"Molly, hurry up!" interrupted Cook. Gabriel signalled to Molly to leave the boots to him, and she rose to her feet with obvious reluctance before stepping across to the sink to wash her hands. "While you're over there, fetch me that jar of mincemeat from the pantry. Remember, don't fill them too much; you always overdo it."

Molly had already applied generous quantities of polish to Gabriel's ragged boots, so he let them sit by the stove for a few minutes, watching the women busily preparing trays of mince pies and some sort of fruit crumble, which Gabriel suspected would form the centrepiece of dessert. *Where are they getting all their sugar?* The question nagged him. *Where are they getting fat to make such a quantity of pastry?* He distracted himself by setting to work shining his boots, a task he had always found irksome and pointless. His school housemaster had claimed that a gentleman should be able to see his own reflection in his shoes, which justified the many tiresome hours every Friday evening they had spent on their knees in the boot room, cleaning and polishing until their fingers ached with the effort.

Gabriel was just slipping his boots back on when the lady of the house stepped into the kitchen. Florence Martin was a trim, sprightly woman in her fifties who exuded the easy confidence of a person who has faced few challenges in life other than keeping up her side of a disappointing marriage. Gabriel rose to his feet with as much dignity as he could muster, hoping Mrs Martin would not notice that his laces were undone and that he had traces of black polish in his fingernails. Whatever she had noticed, Florence looked horrified. "Good heavens, Father! What on earth are you doing down here?"

"I must apologise for my unorthodox entrance, Mrs Martin," Gabriel began, aware of Molly hovering guiltily in the background, looking to all intents and purposes as though she had engineered the situation herself. "I'm afraid I wasn't in a state to be seen when I arrived, so I slipped in here to tidy myself up."

Florence gave an indulgent smile that barely concealed her indignation. "You should have let me send the car for you, Father," she fussed, escorting him out of the kitchen and up the narrow stairs. "Hiking all over the countryside at this time of year, you might have turned an ankle, sliding about in all that mud!"

"I was spared a very long walk, Mrs Martin. A kindly farmer brought me part of the way. A little fresh air never did anyone any harm."

That was another maxim he remembered from school, which Gabriel had not believed even then. They had emerged into an impressive, oak-panelled hall, well lit by the large, leaded windows above them on both sides. Gabriel's newly cleaned boots stepped on a fine Persian rug. "Well, you're here now," said Florence, breezily, "and it's jolly good to see you. Let me show you to your room. I'm sure you'll want a little time to recover before the other guests arrive."

"Thank you, you are most kind."

He was becoming a fraud by association, thought Gabriel miserably, as he followed Florence up a staircase wide enough to accommodate four people walking shoulder to shoulder. He was normally hopeless at social niceties, and they were popping out of his mouth now in the absence of anything actually worth saying.

"I trust you had a pleasant Christmas?" asked Florence. "It must be such a busy time for you."

"A blessed time," said Gabriel, and that was at least sincere. "That's a splendid specimen," he remarked, noting the Christmas tree for the first time. It was a glorious monster of a tree, richly decorated in red and gold, carefully positioned at the back of the hall to make the most of the height and width of the stairwell. Standing on the landing, they were at eye level with the topmost branches, a massive gold star perched precariously at the very top, just inches from the ceiling.

The landing led to a short corridor with doors on either side and a large window at the end. A rosewood table had been placed under the window, sporting an aggressive-looking cactus which felt completely out of place, a foreign interloper like himself into this gentrified corner of rural England. Florence opened a door very gently, stepping aside to let Gabriel enter in front of her. "I hope it will be to your liking," she said, as he stood in the centre of a room infinitely more luxurious than any he had ever inhabited before. "Tea will be served in the drawing room at three."

"Thank you, this is splendid."

Gabriel waited until Florence had left the room, closing the door softly behind her, before setting down his knapsack on the bed. The room was more than splendid; he almost felt ashamed of the comfort it offered. The bed, when he sat on it, immediately invited him to sink into a vast luxuriant cloud, promising long, unbroken rest and no prospect of waking up stiff or cold in the early morning. A fire smouldered in the grate, clearly lit some hours before to ensure that the room felt as cosy as possible in time for his arrival. It was an affectation or simply a habit honed in ages past, as the gentle purr of a radiator under the window made it clear that the house had been an early adopter of central heating.

He went over to the window and looked out at the garden below. In summer, it would no doubt be an impressive sight, but in the dead of winter, the garden looked almost monochrome—long rectangles of lawn with sharply defined borders and empty plots of soil where flowers would sprout in the months to come. The bare trees looked black against a grey, overcast sky the colour and texture of blotting paper, but all trees in winter had a funereal quality to Gabriel, as though warning that the spring might not fulfil its promise of new life and prosperity.

Gabriel was overcome by the urge to rest. He suspected it was the unexpected warmth of the room after the bitter chill to which his body had become accustomed during his journey. He still had the best part of two hours before he was expected downstairs and thought it excusable to give in to a Mediterranean habit he had cultivated in the past. It was all Giovanna's fault, he thought fondly, dropping his bag onto the floor and perching on the edge of the bed to remove his boots again. He lay down on top of the counterpane to avoid ruffling the bedclothes too much, his head sinking blissfully into the fattest, softest pillow in England. Gabriel's late wife had introduced all these bizarre traditions into his life, sleeping in the middle of the day and drinking tea black and cold—oh, the horror! As he drifted off to sleep, Gabriel heard a sonata being played expertly on a piano somewhere on the lower floor. The entertainment had arrived then, practising for later . . .

The day was clearly not meant to go well for Gabriel. He had the ill temper of two sworn enemies to thank for the fact that he woke up in time for tea at all, but as it was, he woke with a start to see the clock on the mantelpiece announcing that it was ten minutes to three. Somewhere in his soporific confusion, Gabriel was aware that the exquisite piano music had been replaced by raised voices much closer to him. Two male voices were competing for dominance, overlapping with one another, interrupting, snapping and snarling, right outside his door.

"How you have the nerve to show your face!" came the gravelly voice of a man of mature years.

"I do not recall being obliged to inform my aged father of my whereabouts," answered a deep but weaker voice.

Gabriel lurched drunkenly out of bed, rubbing the sleep out of his eyes. He felt the queasiness of having woken up abruptly just as he was sinking into deep sleep, and the discomfort of having slept fully clothed.

"Let's pretend we're civilised for the afternoon, shall we?" The weaker voice again. "If it's not too much trouble." Gabriel opened his bag and pulled out a comb, hurriedly forcing his hair into some kind of order. "After today, you can return to pretending I do not exist."

"If you think I have any intention of changing my will—"

"Keep it! It profits a man nothing to lose his soul—"

"Don't quote that book of fairy tales to me!"

Gabriel knew the owner of the weaker voice after all. It was Auberon Gladstone, known to everyone as Bron, a recent convert whose father had cut him off without a penny. Gabriel had never had the misfortune to meet Auberon's father, but he was obviously the sparring partner in this unpleasant spat. A more pressing problem suggested itself to Gabriel. The two men evidently did not realise that there was anyone else nearby, or it was unlikely that they would have indulged in a row in the middle of a corridor, and they were showing no signs of shifting themselves away from his door. He did not want to embarrass either of them by stepping out into the corridor and alerting them both to the fact that he had heard them quarrelling, but he could not risk being late for tea either.

Gabriel stood by the door, his ears straining to catch any sound, but there were no more raised voices to be heard; the pair had either moved away to continue their altercation somewhere more private or called it quits for the time being. He counted to ten to make absolutely sure he was alone before he opened the door and stepped out into the corridor, directly between two men glowering at one another in silence.

"Good afternoon, gentlemen," Gabriel ventured, but the sight of Bron and his father on either side of him made him think unhelpfully of the two stone griffins that had greeted him outside—unfriendly, unattractive and faintly ridiculous. "Would it . . . would it be time for tea?"

Bron was the first to recover. He made an elaborate gesture of taking his watch out of his pocket to confirm the time, whilst several clocks within earshot—including the clock tower a few yards away—noisily chimed three times. "It is indeed, Father. Tea calls."

Bron fell into step beside Gabriel. He was the sort of person who might be termed "well-preserved" for his age, a physically imposing man in his late fifties whose black hair showed the early signs of greying and no sign at all of abandoning him. Bron was using his generous bodily proportions now to block his father from walking beside them or overtaking them. Gabriel was fond of Bron, but he felt the awkwardness of being used to isolate an elderly man, forcing him to walk behind them. "I trust you had a happy Christmas?" asked Gabriel over his shoulder.

Victor appeared to notice Gabriel's clericals for the first time. "I see you've found yourself a tame papist, Bron," answered Victor, avoiding Gabriel's glance. "I do hope he won't let us enjoy ourselves too much," he added. "One would not care to find oneself in the fiery furnace under the floorboards."

"Please ignore my father," said Bron calmly. "He lost his manners at the same time as his marbles."

Gabriel heard a series of snorts and tuts and other assorted sounds of disgust before the three men were happily distracted by the sight of a young woman standing on the landing before them, apparently waiting for someone. She was very young, in the first flourishing of womanhood, with soft, mouse-coloured curls that would have looked a little tawdry had they not framed such striking features—eyes almost too dark for her complexion, and a rounded face that spoke of comfort and security. Here was a girl who had been well cared for throughout her young life. Even her dress spoke of a benefactor's generosity and her own good

23

living, a rich red gown made of expensive fabric Gabriel suspected had been salvaged from an older woman's garment.

As soon as she saw the men coming, the girl blushed, giving a shy smile that would have been coquettish if it had not been so obviously genuine. The unexpected attention of three people had unsettled her, but she immediately skipped towards Bron, throwing her arms around his neck. "Uncle Bron! I'm so glad you could come. I was afraid you weren't going to join us!"

"I wouldn't miss a Verity Caufield concert for the world," Bron assured her, behaving in every sense as though the two other men were not there; he probably wished they were not. "I hope you have been hard at work?"

"Rather! The Bechstein's a dream to play. I've hardly been away from the music room for two days. Mrs Martin had to remind me to come and eat."

"Good to hear you're working hard, my dear," said Victor, not wishing to be forgotten.

Verity nodded in polite acknowledgement. She demonstrated all the awkwardness and indifference of a young person, attempting to connect with a man who had enjoyed his own youth in an impossibly bygone age when Jack the Ripper haunted the streets of London. "Good afternoon, Grandfather."

"You haven't met my lovely niece, have you, Father?" asked Bron. "Verity, this is the man who guided me into the light last year."

Victor snorted, quite unable to contain himself. "Yes, Verity, this is the man who dragged your uncle into a church of Irish navvies and Italian waiters. Try not to think badly of him."

Bron shifted position to ensure that he gave his father his back. "Terribly enlightened man, my revered father," he said, making an elaborate gesture of escorting Verity down the stairs, "awfully fond of freedom of conscience, as long as the whole of humanity sees things his way."

I want to go home, thought Gabriel glumly. *Lord, if I can't go home, could I at least be struck down by some mild fever so that I can curl up in bed and avoid having to speak to anyone? Nothing drastic—you don't have to kill me, it's not that bad . . .*

"Verity has a place at the Royal College of Music," said Bron, noticing Gabriel's eyes glazing over. "She's going to be the finest pianist of her generation."

Gabriel smiled. "That's wonderful. Music is a great healer to a troubled world."

They were ushered into a pleasant, spacious room where a mouthwatering tea had been laid out, containing sweet delights Gabriel had not seen in years. Florence was talking to an older man in a white tie who seemed to be directing affairs, whilst Molly, nicely scrubbed up and changed into a smarter uniform, poured the tea. Gabriel moved towards her, intending to thank her for her assistance earlier. "Do sit down, Father," said Molly immediately, indicating the sofas and armchairs on offer. "Let me bring you a nice cup of tea. With or without?"

"Do you suppose it would be very naughty to have half a teaspoon of sugar?" he asked, causing Molly to giggle. The formally dressed older man glared at her.

"Sorry, Mr Trevelyan," murmured Molly, scurrying towards the table. Gabriel groaned inaudibly as he seated himself, counting off the different parts of the day he needed to tick off before morning and the journey home: tea, Verity's little recital (well, that would be jolly enough, especially as he would not be obliged to say anything to anyone) and finally the long dinner with its many little traps, the hundreds of ways he might say the wrong thing and not know how to recover, hear the wrong thing and not know how to respond. A rose-painted plate was pressed into his hands, containing a large, plump mince pie oozing with fruit. A teacup and saucer painted in the same design was placed on the table at his side. "Careful now, it's still quite hot," warned Molly.

"Sorry, I didn't mean to get you into trouble." But Molly smiled and stepped away, glancing about her to see which guest might be in need of tea or sustenance. Gabriel saw that Verity and Bron had seated themselves opposite him. There was a definite family resemblance between them— they shared the same eyes and the same aquiline profile; but if it had not been for those details, Gabriel might have been convinced that they were a courting couple. There was something endearing about the way Bron hovered over her, taking such obvious pride in Verity's talent. "You must be very proud of her, Bron," said Gabriel. "It's rare to see such talent and determination in one so young." He turned to Verity. "Do you practice here often?"

"Yes," said Verity. "I live with Uncle Bron, and he has an upright, but Mrs Martin kindly lets me come here and play her Bechstein. It's so different playing a grand piano, you know."

"I'm afraid I don't play a note myself, but I can imagine."

"It's such a fine specimen, rescued from a grand house somewhere years ago."

Bron shifted position. "Verity has lived with me for a

number of years, Father. Her mother took ill quite some time ago—suffered a stroke. She lives in the nursing home here. Verity can visit her every day when she comes to stay."

Gabriel glanced back at Verity, who had lowered her eyes. "I'm sorry for your loss, Verity. That must be very hard."

Verity sat up sharply. "She's not dead, Father," she said gently, "even though it seemed like that at the time. She always recognises me when I visit. It's just like old times."

"The nursing home is just the other side of that avenue of beech trees one can see from the south-facing windows," Bron explained. "The Martins converted a series of outbuildings and rent them out. It's how they have managed to pay the death duties without selling the estate."

"That's what they tell everyone," interrupted Victor, who had been listening in from an armchair as far from Gabriel's popish vicinity as he could manage. "I wouldn't believe everything you hear about our revered hosts if I were you."

"It is hardly difficult to believe," said Bron as the fingers of his free hand curled into a fist, "given the onerous new taxes on inherited property. If you are so suspicious of the Martin family's finances, one wonders why you accepted to be their guest."

Victor gave Verity a warm smile. "I have come to hear my beautiful granddaughter play the instrument I paid for her to learn. Isn't that right, my dear?"

Verity was out of her depth in every sense of the word. She glanced from Bron to Victor as though calculating which man posed more of a threat, before rising to her feet. Gabriel took the cue and stood up a moment after her. He reached out a hand to her. "I think you should introduce me to this piano you have been telling me about. You'll be wanting to warm up soon, no doubt."

Verity could not take the prompt quickly enough and allowed Gabriel to escort her away from the two men. "I do wish they wouldn't argue in public," said Verity softly. "I hardly know where to look!"

"Do they argue often?" asked Gabriel, walking with her in the direction of the cakes. He thought better of taking her out of the room in case her absence was noticed, but there were enough bodies here now and enough noise to shelter them. "It's a shame to see father and son at war like that."

"No, they don't," answered Verity, helping herself to a teacake. "Argue, I mean. They don't usually talk at all. You must know that Uncle Bron has been disinherited."

"I'm afraid I do."

"It's all so potty, really. My grandfather doesn't believe in anything. I'm not sure why it matters to him so much that Uncle Bron does. If he were desperately religious, he might think his son had condemned himself to hell or something, and one could see that he would be upset about that. But if my grandfather is right and there is no purpose to any of this, Uncle Bron might as well enjoy believing in a kindly God and angels and things."

"And what do you believe, Verity?" asked Gabriel genially.

Verity shrugged her shoulders as though the question were fairly pointless. "Well, I'm probably skating on thin ice talking about this to a man of the cloth, but I suppose I think that, deep down, none of us really believes that there's nothing out there and no point to any of this, not even

Grandfather. If that is what we really believed, I think we'd all top ourselves. Life can be frightfully beautiful and all that, but what's the point of living at all if it's for nothing in the end?"

Gabriel looked over Verity's shoulder and noticed that a young man had entered the room without an escort. He was a fresh-faced, boyish character. Gabriel calculated that he was perhaps in his midtwenties, smartly dressed but in a manner which suggested that he was deliberately trying to look as informal as possible. Gabriel could not help noticing that the seams of his jacket had been restitched several times, either as a result of poverty or parsimony. "Good afternoon," said Gabriel, when the young man moved quickly in their direction. Verity turned around and squealed with excitement, causing a certain silence to descend across the room.

"Paul!" she cried, clapping her hands together. Gabriel suspected she was desperate to embrace the man but was trying to be decorous. "You might have told me you were coming! Mrs Martin said you hadn't answered her invitation."

"I come and go as I please," answered Paul, giving her a wry smile. His voice did not sound right either, mused Gabriel. Like his clothes, the young Paul's voice sounded as though he were deliberately trying to sound less well spoken than he really was, whilst those well-rounded vowels insisted upon breaking through his clipped metropolitan accent. "Only you could entice me to enjoy this bourgeois charade."

"Paul, really!" Verity exclaimed, looking back at Gabriel in mortification. "You mustn't be so rude. You needn't have come."

Paul kissed her lightly on the cheek. "It's all right, darling. I shan't let the side down. I promise."

"This is Paul Ashley," Verity explained, letting out an audible sigh of relief when Paul extended a hand to Gabriel. "He's a . . . a friend of mine."

"Indeed," answered Gabriel, but he was distracted by the sight of Victor coming towards them.

"I see the vanguard of the British Communist Party has arrived," said Victor with unexpected cheerfulness, patting Paul on the back. "What do you think, Padre?" asked Victor, turning to Gabriel with a smile that would have been good-humoured on any other face. Coming from Victor, there was a definite hint of malice about it, and it was certainly not directed at the young Paul. "A good Communist celebrating a Christian feast he doesn't believe in, in a house of privilege he would tear down given half a chance."

"I assure you I would never tear it down," promised Paul, following Victor slowly back in the direction of his seat. Gabriel had apparently been discarded. "I would simply ensure that the wealth was distributed properly. How many bedrooms does a pile like this have? How many families could you shelter here?"

"Really, Paul, I do wish you'd keep your voice down!" chimed Verity, bouncing along behind the two men to remind them both that they were supposed to be there on her account. "You know perfectly well that they did shelter families here during the war. Evacuees."

"Only because they had to," Paul retorted without looking back. "You don't honestly think they would have volunteered to have a whole gaggle of scruffy cockneys on the premises, do you? In any case, they're all back in their slums now. Those who still have homes to go back to."

Verity stood still near the doorway of the room, her former jollity drained away. Gabriel and Bron stood on either side of her, like guardians shielding her from the sight of other guests who might guess that something was wrong. In the midst of the background chatter, Gabriel could still hear Victor and Paul putting the world to rights as they saw it, with what sounded like the beginning of a spat between them on the subject of slum clearances and the relative merits of prefabs to address the housing shortage. "I do hope he won't offend anyone," said Verity quietly. "I feel awfully nervous now, and I wasn't before."

"Don't let him rattle you," said Bron firmly. "Ghastly little man. I don't know what you think you're doing getting yourself caught up with a crank like that."

Verity was prevented from descending into further misery by the sound of a bell tinkling gently, summoning them all to silence. Florence was standing imperiously in front of the fire, which had the unintentional effect of making her look as though she had just stepped out of the *Divine Comedy* —one of its nastier passages. "Ladies and gentlemen," pronounced the shadowy figure, "if you would care to make your way to the drawing room, we have some entertainment ready for you."

"Good luck!" whispered Bron, as Verity dashed out of the room ahead of her audience to get herself settled at the piano. He turned back to Gabriel. "I do hope she's going to be all right; I'm afraid that brute has rather unsettled her. Treats her like an idiot."

"They're only young," reassured Gabriel. "He'll grow out of his politics, and she, I suspect, will grow out of him."

"I do hope you're right, Father," said Bron. "She's talking about marrying the man. Out of the question, of course.

31

They are both of them too young and silly, with or without his Communist pretensions, and she has her studies to consider."

They walked with the other guests into a high-ceilinged, elegantly decorated room, replete with gold-leaf ornamentation and large mirrors to make the room look even larger. A polished grand piano awaited its mistress, and several rows of velvet-seated chairs were quickly occupied by the guests. Bron pointed to two seats near the front, positioned in such a way that the piano would block the musician's view of one of them. "Verity always says she hates to see my face when she's performing. Performing to strangers is one thing; performing to family is apparently very nerve-racking. Can't see why myself. I think everything she plays sounds superb."

They sat down and awaited the performer's arrival. "Verity's young man seems very friendly with your father," Gabriel commented, hoping he would not immediately regret it.

"I suspect the little blighter's just trying to ingratiate himself," muttered Bron, busying himself looking at a copy of the programme that had been strategically placed on every third seat. "He's wasting his time, of course. Even my father would never countenance a marriage like that. Paul fancies himself a Nazi hunter. Couldn't bring himself to shed any Nazi blood in the defence of his country, of course, but thinks he has a calling to bring the few survivors to justice at no cost to himself."

Gabriel offered up a silent prayer of thanks as Verity appeared in front of the small assembled group, prompting a flurry of applause. She looked older as she sat at the piano and began Beethoven's "Moonlight" Sonata. Gabriel was no expert, but he sensed that she played with the maturity of a much-older woman whilst somehow managing to let some youthful impetuosity break through. How ever could she have managed to learn so many notes off by heart? he wondered, watching her fingers dancing effortlessly across the keys with no sheet music to prompt her. Giovanna had been a singer, but Gabriel had never wondered at the sounds that came out of her mouth. In the absence of a visible instrument, it had sounded as natural to him as a bird singing to greet the dawn, and he had always been away at work when she was at home, practising and training.

Now, why on earth was he thinking of her? Gabriel distracted himself glancing around the room at the other guests. He had a clear view of Victor from where he was seated and drew in a sharp intake of breath. There was a miracle indeed, thought Gabriel. The old man had lost his bitter expression and was looking lovingly in his granddaughter's direction, smiling serenely at the sight of her as she enchanted the room. Unaware that he was being watched in a crowded room, Victor had given way to undisguised pride in the talent of another. It was almost as though the man believed that any show of affection was beneath his dignity, but Gabriel knew as he watched Victor that the old man loved Verity, even if he had no way of telling her.

Verity was about halfway through the eerie slow movement, and the room had plunged into absolute silence, as though no one dared breathe too loudly in case he spoiled the effect. Gabriel closed his eyes. He was no more a poet than he was a musician, but he could almost have been walking through that midnight forest in which legend said the young Beethoven had found a blind girl singing and been

33

inspired to write his famous sonata. Gabriel had never walked through a forest at night, but the details were easy to imagine: the dark, sinister branches swaying above his head; the cold, lonely moon hugely inflated in a starless sky; and a voice singing to him from somewhere in the shadows of a past life. Music was not the food of love—the old Bard was wrong about that—but he was sure it had the power to soothe a broken world. The fighting and the bloodshed was over, Gabriel told himself; those battles would never be fought again. It was the turn of the musicians and the artists and the poets to make the world beautiful once more.

3

Gabriel woke up in a state of panic, his heart thumping so fast he could have been persuaded for a moment that he was suffering a heart attack. His body was drenched in sweat as though he had succumbed to a severe fever, but he quickly came to his senses. He was in bed, though in his confusion he could not for the life of him work out what bed, or in what room he was resting. He must have been asleep for hours. The fragments of a nightmare he could not now remember clung to him as though trying to drag him back into the netherworld of darkness and confusion from which he had just escaped.

Bad dream. A dream, nothing more, and Gabriel knew exactly where he was. He did not recognise the room because it was not his own room; he was a guest of the Martin family, and he remembered now that they had kindly offered to accommodate their guests overnight. He had had a pleasant evening, as he recalled, much better than he had expected. There had been conversation, an inspiring recital by a young pianist, and a sumptuous dinner he had enjoyed a little too much. He suspected it was the red wine that had disturbed him; it had been such a very long time since he had drunk a glass of wine, and such a splendid vintage too.

Something fruity and powerful, wine to aid a man's sleep and then torment him during his hours of slumber.

Gabriel shifted position until his head rested on a cool portion of the pillow, and he breathed in and out slowly to let his body settle. Now that his eyes were focusing a little more, he became aware of the room in which he lay and felt guiltily comfortable. Like much of the house, it was a cheerfully fraudulent little room, decorated in a style intended to suggest restrained Regency grandeur. A portrait hung on the opposite wall that looked so familiar he knew it must be a copy of a famous artwork. A Pre-Raphaelite beauty stared out of the painting slightly to one side as though coyly avoiding the gaze of the painter. She had been painted in a pool of light, dressed in soft white and gold clothing, her head unveiled to reveal rippling curls of auburn hair. The whole effect was intended to make the young woman look ethereal, a being not quite of this world and not entirely of the next. An almost saint.

There was a gentle knock on the door, prompting Gabriel to sit up sharply. "Who is it?" he enquired, as his pulse started to climb again. Was someone really attempting to gain entrance to his room?

The door opened very slowly, and Molly stuck her head round, giggling at the sight of Gabriel sitting bolt upright with his bedclothes serving as a kind of untidy shield. "I'm terribly sorry," Gabriel began. "Have I overslept?"

"Not at all, Father," promised Molly, nudging the door open fully with her shoulder. She was carrying a tea tray, which she set down on a small table next to Gabriel's bed. "Just bringing you your morning tea. Let me light that fire."

"There's really no need," said Gabriel quickly, mortified at the idea of lying in bed being waited on. He could see Abbot Ambrose's reproachful gaze across the miles. "I'm perfectly warm."

Molly smiled and politely ignored him, getting on her knees on the hearthrug to stack the fire. It was yet another conceit, thought Gabriel, watching as Molly skilfully stacked the wood and then kindling before striking a light and blowing gently on the glowing timber. Worse than a conceit—an indulgence. He wondered how many frail old people had frozen to death last winter for want of basic warmth, how many little families in those damp London cottages had huddled miserably together during the long, bitter nights when a man might have given up hope of ever seeing the sun rise again. "It's a real pea-souper out there," Molly remarked, as much to break the awkward silence as anything else. "My mammy would have said that the holy souls were tapping on the window, begging for a prayer."

"I'm afraid I've never really got the hang of Wiltshire fog," admitted Gabriel, pouring himself a cup of tea. "I suppose it rains more than I remember in London . . ."

"Ach, it's nothing compared with Ireland, Father," answered Molly. "You know what they say? In Dublin it drizzles on a fine day. But if it weren't so wet, it shouldn't be so green. My brother were in service in Norfolk, and he said it was the bleakest place he'd ever seen. All that flat, dull land. No colour, no hills. I'd rather have green hills any day, even with the rain and fog."

"You're a cheerful soul, Molly," said Gabriel fondly. "Are you happy here?"

Molly shrugged, getting to her feet and dusting down her

hands. "I daresay I'd be happy anywhere, Father. I've a good man, and I'll not be sending him to war."

"Have you everything you need? It's hard to plan a wedding in such times."

"Like I said, Father, I have my man, and no one's going to take him from me. A borrowed gown I shan't mind at all." She moved towards the door. "And by the time I have kiddies of my own, there'll be sweeties in the shops and oranges and bananas. And they'll grow up in a house with a flushing lavatory. Think of that? And carpets on the floor and hot water. Can't think of anything else I could possibly want. I shall cook big, juicy pork sausages every single night!"

Gabriel laughed. "I'm sure you will, Molly. Liam is a fortunate man." There was an air of such easygoing radiance about the girl that would make anyone warm to her, and Gabriel suspected that this was in part why she was so contented with life. It was in her nature to smile at the world, and inevitably the world smiled back at her, giving her every reason to believe that there was goodness everywhere and hope even in a time of austerity. She had grown up in the direst poverty, not owning a single possession, from her hand-me-down clothes to the bed she shared with three other siblings, and she spent her life serving a family who barely noticed her. Yet she was content.

Gabriel became aware of the much-muted, barely audible sound of the piano playing somewhere far off. "That can't be Verity practising already, can it?"

"Oh yes," affirmed Molly. "She's been up and practising the piano for over two hours now. Madam asked her to practice in the little room in the north wing so as not to disturb anyone. She says the piano is not up to much, but it's better than not playing at all."

"I hope she's not overdoing it," commented Gabriel out loud; he immediately regretted it. "I'm sorry; I'm sure she knows what she's doing. I daresay she has to practice for many hours a day."

"Eight hours a day, Father. Just imagine that! My fingers would fall off!"

Gabriel slipped his hand under his pillow to retrieve his wristwatch, noting that it had stopped in the night. "Is that the correct time?" he asked, pointing at the carriage clock on the mantelpiece.

"Yes, Father, I believe so."

Gabriel set about synchronising his watch. "I oughtn't to stay very long," he said, fumbling with the buckle of his watch strap. "Do you happen to know——"

"There's no hurry, Father," Molly chimed in. "Breakfast is served in half an hour. After that, Madam said she would arrange for her driver to take you home."

When Molly had left him, Gabriel went mechanically through the motions of getting ready—washing, shaving, dressing, praying—but he was frustrated with himself that he found it so hard to concentrate with the sound of music rippling through the house, albeit quietly. It was the muffled nature of it that distracted him the most. He found himself straining to make out the different melodies, enjoying passages he remembered even though they threatened to drag him back to the life he had left behind. As soon as he was ready, Gabriel walked out of his room and into the corridor, placing himself back firmly in the here and now.

As he descended the stairs, Gabriel saw Florence, immaculately dressed in powder blue, as she emerged into the hall from the breakfast room. "Good morning, Father," she said brightly, though Gabriel could sense a nervous smile a mile away. "Did you sleep well?"

"Like a top, thank you," Gabriel assured her. "I can't remember the last time I had been made more comfortable. Is anything the matter? You seem a little distracted."

"Not at all," she answered quickly. "I was simply a little worried about the weather. If the fog doesn't lift, I'm afraid it may delay your journey home. I do hope it shan't inconvenience you?"

Gabriel felt that yawning ache in his chest that he remembered from childhood when the train taking him to school had started chuffing down the platform, leaving his mother behind in a cloud of steam. He certainly would be inconvenienced if he could not make his way home, but his feelings on the subject were rather stronger than that. "Please don't concern yourself, Mrs Martin. If the weather is too treacherous for driving, I can always make my way on foot."

Florence looked at him in alarm. "Oh no, Father, absolutely not! You couldn't possibly find your way home in this fog. You'll get hopelessly lost."

Gabriel forced a smile; inwardly, he was trying desperately to imagine himself walking safely through open country without being able to see his own hand in front of his face. "Well, not to worry. I'm sure the fog will clear later. It usually does."

"Come and have some breakfast. I was just going to fetch Verity. She'll forget if I don't interrupt her."

"Why don't I go?" Gabriel volunteered. He was hungry

after a difficult night, but a delay might mean that some of the guests would have finished by the time he arrived, and he could enjoy a little quiet time. "I can follow the sound."

"I'd be grateful, if you don't mind. I hate leaving my guests."

Gabriel waited until Florence had stepped into the breakfast room before walking in the direction of a particularly stormy rendering of the first movement of Rachmaninoff's First Piano Concerto. She really was a fine musician, though even he could tell that the performance was a little unpolished. It held the promise of even greater performances in the future. He walked down a set of back stairs and past the kitchen door, pausing momentarily to savour the exquisite smell of bacon cooking, then knocked on the music room door. Gabriel could not help chuckling at the thought of Florence and her husband working so hard to keep their son's musical enthusiasm at a distance by putting the practice piano in a room in the farthest corner of the house. It was only Verity's passionate mastery of the instrument that made the sound carry so far. He could just imagine a small child belting out "Twinkle, Twinkle, Little Star" for the hundredth time, driving the entire household up the wall.

Gabriel was not sure whether Verity could not hear his knocking over the music or whether she was simply too engrossed to answer, but when she failed to stop and let him in, he turned the handle and nudged open the door a few inches, hoping he would not disturb her too much that way.

Verity was not going to be disturbed easily. She looked the picture of a bohemian musician, unkempt hair swishing from side to side, her blouse hanging over the top of her skirt, having come untucked as she hammered at the piano like a thing possessed. She was nearing the end of the first movement, her face flushed and taut with concentration, causing Gabriel to linger in the doorway, waiting reverently for her to finish.

Suddenly there was a crunch of jarring notes produced by her left hand, and Verity stumbled before coming to an ignominious halt, like a sprinter tripping over her laces seconds before reaching the finishing line. She slammed her fists down on the keys, causing a deafening explosion of discordant noise. "Blast it!"

Gabriel stepped inside, causing Verity to look up from the keys at him. "It looks to me as though you need some breakfast," he said. "You must be exhausted!"

Verity sat back on the stool, lifting her head as though gasping for air. "I need five more minutes," she said, staring up at the ceiling. "I can't stop now. Tell Mrs Martin I shall be up directly."

"I shall do no such thing," Gabriel replied, indicating the door. "You need to get out of this room. How long do you think you've been sitting here?"

Verity linked her fingers together, bending them back until the joints crunched. "I've no idea, but I'm not hungry yet." Verity sighed. Gabriel could not help noticing that he seemed to elicit that sort of exasperated expression from most of the people he encountered. "Were you sent to summon me to the breakfast room?"

"Naturally."

"You're not going to go away, are you?"

Gabriel paused as though thinking deeply about the subject. "No, I don't think so. Come along."

Verity stood up slowly and slipped past him out of the room. "I suppose it wouldn't hurt to take a little break," she continued. "That's one of the troubles with practising so long. I find myself making the same mistakes over and over again, but I'm too tired to correct them."

Florence, Bron and Paul were happily tucking into breakfast when Gabriel and Verity entered the room. "Happy" was perhaps not the right adjective to use for Paul, who looked horribly hung over and was making very little effort to hide the raging headache from which he was clearly suffering. Gabriel smiled in Molly's direction, which she acknowledged before continuing her task of clearing away the used plates from guests who had breakfasted earlier. Gabriel helped Verity into a free seat before going to the side table to inspect the many covered metal dishes waiting enticingly there. He helped himself as quietly as possible, afraid of making too much of a clatter in an otherwise uncomfortably quiet room.

"Where's Grandfather?" asked Verity, amid the faintest clink of milk jugs and teapots being poured. "He was up hours ago. I saw him leaving for his morning walk when I came downstairs to practice."

"Damned fool going out in this weather," Bron retorted. "It's hell on earth out there. At his age he could fall and break his leg."

"The fog was not quite so bad when I was first up," said Verity, "but it was very dark. I shouldn't fancy going out in that myself, but he's always liked to have a walk before breakfast."

Gabriel sat himself down at the table, noticing Florence's

look of anxiety for the first time. "He's not been in for breakfast," she said, looking to Gabriel as though for reassurance. "Do you suppose perhaps he came in and went straight back to his room?"

"No need to make a fuss about it," said Bron, briskly. "If he's not returned by the time I've finished eating, I'll take a stroll myself. Heaven knows," he added grumpily, "he's probably sitting on some tree stump somewhere, contemplating the awfulness of the world."

"There's no need to be quite so unpleasant about him," snapped Paul. "You might think the whole world were pretty awful if you'd seen what he'd seen."

"Here we go again," groaned Bron theatrically. "Molly, would you be a dear and bring me the morning paper?"

There was something unintentionally condescending about the question, phrased as though Molly had any real choice in the matter. Minutes later, she had done as she was told, and Bron was safely hidden away behind the *Times*, leaving Paul with no further vent for his righteousness. Florence got up and put her hands on Verity's shoulders. "Come on, my girl, let's get you a proper breakfast. You've always eaten like a little bird."

"Mummy always said it was unladylike to eat too much in public," said Verity, allowing herself to be chivvied to her feet.

"You don't have to stand on ceremony here, my dear," answered Florence. "Cook likes to see her food appreciated. Here"—she began placing hot buttered kippers on Verity's plate. "Your favourite, if I remember rightly?"

Verity giggled. There was an easy, mother-daughter relationship between them which they both clearly enjoyed.

44

It was a scenario Gabriel had seen many times, a woman without a much-longed-for daughter naturally gravitating towards a young woman who was still feeling the absence of an adored mother. Each effortlessly filled the void the other woman was carrying without perhaps even knowing it. As Verity sat down, Florence ruffled her hair lightly and went back to her place. "You'd better move back upstairs and use the Bechstein once everyone's safely out of bed," suggested Florence. "It must be frightfully cold down there."

"It's not at all bad," promised Verity. "There's some heat from the kitchen, and Molly has kindly been keeping the fire burning nicely. But I daresay it would be a lot less trouble for her if I came upstairs. I do so love the Bechstein."

"Nasty German invention," Paul put in. "Ought to have been burnt."

Verity rolled her eyes. "I suppose you'd stop me playing Schubert for the same reason? That's just silly."

If Paul had intended a retort, it was lost in the excitement of the telephone in the hall ringing, sending jarring, tinny chimes into the room. Molly dashed out of the room to answer it but must have arrived too late, as they heard the booming voice of Horace Martin announcing his presence. None of them could make out what was being said, but they remained silent nonetheless, waiting for the moment Horace would put down the phone and come to tell them the news. For several minutes, the eavesdroppers heard nothing but grunts and noncommittal words, "I see" and "yes"; then there was the sound of the receiver being replaced, and Horace appeared in the doorway like the Grim Reaper.

You had a skinful last night too, thought Gabriel, noting the

45

purple, sagging bags under Horace's eyes and a greater-than-usual ruddiness about his cheeks, as his blood pressure had risen. His appearance suggested that he had dressed in a hurry and had not seen fit to comb his hair or moustaches, which gave him a comically windswept look. His eyes fell on Verity, causing her to rise to her feet. "What is it, Mr Martin?" she asked, shrinking a little away from him as though he always made her fear the worst.

"Verity, my dear, that was the nursing home." Now they were all sitting up in their seats. It was not like Horace to sound so gentle and sympathetic to anyone. "They telephoned to say that your mother appears to have gone missing. She was not in her room when the nurse went to wake her this morning, and her window had been forced open. She appears to have wandered off."

Bron jumped to his feet, the paper sliding off the edge of the table. "Wandered off? That's ridiculous; they're supposed to keep her safe. How could she possibly have just walked away like that?"

Horace shrugged his shoulders wearily. "That may be a question for another time. The fact of the matter is, she has wandered off, and she does not appear to have taken a thing with her. Not even her shoes. Wherever she is, she's in her nightdress and slippers."

Verity looked around the room for support. "Whatever are we to do? Should we go out and search for her? She couldn't have gone far on foot."

Horace motioned for her to sit down and sat beside her. "The nursing home wishes to know whether you would like to call the police. The trouble is that she may be in some danger. It's bitterly cold, and she hasn't so much as a cardigan with her. If she is not found soon—"

"Of course they should call the police," answered Verity. "They should have summoned the police as soon as they noticed she was gone."

"Verity, they had to ask you first," Bron put in. "You're her next of kin. And now that you're twenty-one, she is legally your responsibility. That's why they're asking."

"Of course they must call the police," Verity repeated, but she sounded out of breath. "We should all go out and look for her. She might be hurt; she might have frozen to death." She got up and made for the door, but Horace blocked her way. "There's no time to lose! She could be anywhere."

Bron and Paul got up and went over to her. "Darling, it's not that simple," said Paul. "It'll be like finding a needle in a haystack out there in this weather. Even the police will struggle to find her."

Verity's eyes welled up. "Well, they'll have to try, won't they? That's what they're there for." She turned to Horace, who was standing behind her like an old retainer. "Mr Martin, please ask the nursing home to call the police immediately. I shall go and search for her myself."

Paul put an arm around her. "I really wouldn't, Verity, not on your own, at any rate."

Verity shrugged him off, which Gabriel somehow found encouraging. She was more independent than she looked. "The fog looks to me as though it's clearing. It always goes as quickly as it comes. I do wish Grandfather would hurry back. I'd feel a lot happier if he were here."

Paul followed her to the door, but Verity indicated that

she wanted him to stay where he was. "Darling, it really would be better if you stayed here," said Paul. "The rest of us can go out in a group and search."

"Give me five minutes to change into something more suitable," said Verity, by way of an answer. "If she's out there, I'll find her."

Paul waited until Verity had disappeared upstairs before turning back to the others. "I suppose I should get ready too. I won't leave her to go out alone in the state she's in."

"We'll join you," volunteered Bron. "It would be safer all round if we stuck together."

Paul nodded, then left. Gabriel got up from the table, suppressing a sense of regret at the breakfast he was leaving behind and a nagging feeling of guilt that he was even thinking about a rasher of bacon at a time like this. Molly was at his side in an instant. "It's all right, Father," she whispered. "I'll have it kept warm for you. Wouldn't want it to go to waste with all the hungry people in the world."

Gabriel smiled guiltily and turned to Bron for instructions. "Are we to meet at the front door?"

"I should probably stay here in case there's news," ventured Florence, who had taken one glance into the gloom outside and evidently decided to remain in her proper place.

"Yes," said Bron, cordially. "Father, let's go and wait for the others."

Mr Trevelyan was waiting in the hall to assist them in putting on their coats and hats. "I'm not sure Verity should be going out at all," Gabriel suggested, taking the hat Trevelyan had handed to him in mild distaste. "She looks awful. With two people missing, we've no idea what we'll find."

48

"I wouldn't waste your time trying to persuade Verity to do anything," said Bron. "She'll be quite determined. She was always very close to her mother; the news will have brought back all kinds of memories."

"How long has she been in the home?"

"This nursing home opened only a year ago, but my sister has been in nursing homes for seven years now. Verity was fourteen when my sister collapsed. It's a bad age to watch one's mother decline so suddenly. Not that there's ever a good age."

"Is that why she's going to music college only now?" asked Gabriel. "I mean . . . that is, at twenty-one, not eighteen."

"Well, the war rather got in the way, but yes, it took Verity well over a year to return to some kind of equilibrium after that. She lost interest in everything, even music."

Gabriel noticed a flutter of activity at the top of the stairs and signalled for Bron to stop talking. Verity hurried down the stairs towards them, almost tripping as she went. "I'm ready!" she called. "Where's Paul?"

"Here!" came a call, as though someone were answering a school roll call, and Paul descended the stairs. "Why don't we split into pairs?" said Paul, in what was more an instruction than a suggestion. "Verity and I can go together, and you can search with the priest."

"Actually, old boy, I think you and I had better search together," Bron retorted. "Verity can search with Fr Gabriel."

Paul flushed with embarrassment but clearly knew better than to start an argument with his beloved's uncle at such a moment. "Very well, the priest can protect Verity's virtue. Let's not waste any more time, shall we?"

4

The mist was slowly clearing as they left the house, much to Gabriel's relief. Bron and Paul took the more direct route across the lawns which led to the nursing home, whilst Gabriel suggested that he and Verity cut through the woods on some instinct that it was the most likely place for a wandering soul to hide. "I hope you're not superstitious," said Verity, as they were slowly swallowed by the ancient woodland. "Or is that a silly question?"

"It is a silly question, but not for the reason you mean, I suspect," answered Gabriel, glancing about him more anxiously than he ought. "I daresay there are many legends surrounding a place like this, none of them true."

The path was leading them through the twisted ranks of ancient trees, dark and threatening in the residual mist like some demonic army awaiting the signal to come to life. Some of these oak trees, groaning under the weight of centuries, had been saplings before Roundheads and Cavaliers had fought for England's soul, before Shakespeare wrote *Hamlet*, before King Henry had demanded his divorce. Gabriel could understand why ancient woodlands attracted so many myths and superstitions—there was something inherently mysterious about dark places and natural life rooted so far into history. There were woodlands in England that were far older than this one, stretching back so far into the mists of time that they might have greeted the Romans when they came as conquerors. This woodland, by comparison, cultivated to look as though it dated back to the time of the druids, was practically a young pretender—a folly, like everything else about the estate.

"Did you hear something?" whispered Verity, stopping in her tracks. "I swear I heard a moan!"

Gabriel stopped in his tracks and strained to hear anything of interest. There was a persistent background whisper he had all but blocked out, the sound of a light breeze shivering across the bare branches of the trees. To a nervous ear, it could so easily sound like a moan. "I think it's just the wind, Verity," Gabriel reassured her. "It's all right; a breeze should help our search. The mist will clear much more quickly that way."

Gabriel could see light attempting to pierce through the trees ahead, signalling to him that the density of the trees was thinning. He walked on, with Verity stumbling reluctantly behind, still looking round her for the owner of the moaning voice she thought she had heard. "What's that up ahead?" asked Gabriel to distract her.

"Mr Martin calls it a Pen Pit," she answered with a nervous laugh. "Nonsense, of course; you don't get them hereabouts. It's just a big hole in the ground. Watch your step —the ground gives way quite quickly."

"What on earth's a Pen Pit?" asked Gabriel, walking more carefully towards the fringe of the trees. It would be easy enough to fail to notice the ground disappearing beneath his feet in this weather.

"I've no idea. Some Iron Age feature or something, but they're much shallower—"

Gabriel heard the sound too. A thin, sad exclamation of mourning found its way to them—an unmistakably human noise. "Don't worry, Verity. Stay close."

But Verity had ideas of her own and scampered ahead of him, coming to an unsteady halt at the edge of the ravine. "It's my mother," she said quietly. "I knew it was her voice the first time I heard it."

Gabriel stood beside her and looked down. The fog was a little thicker lower down, but he could clearly make out a steep drop of some twenty feet and a cavernous space large enough to build a house. Cowering against the opposite side of the space was a ghostly figure in white, shivering and bare-foot. Gabriel held Verity's arm. "Don't try to climb down there on your own—you'll fall. Go back and see if you can alert anyone. I don't think she's hurt."

For the second time, Verity brushed him off and walked carefully along the edge of the drop, looking for a way down. "It's all right, Mummy; I'm coming!" she called down. "Stay where you are. I'm coming."

Gabriel watched as she reached a steep, narrow downward path and began her descent, clinging to the inner wall of the ravine as she went. The ghostly figure noticed Verity and watched as she moved towards her without making any effort to go to her. A minute later, Verity was embracing her mother, and the older woman allowed herself to be embraced without returning the show of affection. "Verity, is she all right?" Gabriel called down. "She looks stunned. Has she had a fall?"

Verity drew back from her mother and took a look at her

before calling back. "There's some blood on her nightie, but it can't be more than a scratch. It's all right, we just have to get her back to the . . ." Verity did not so much stop talking as sound as though the words had been strangled out of her. She gave a gasp and a whimper, then froze.

"Verity, what is it?"

"Father, please come down here," she said tonelessly, her face barely moving. "There's something . . . there's someone else here."

Gabriel immediately began walking down the path towards her. "Don't move!" he ordered her. "I'm coming."

Verity's gaze was fixed on a point Gabriel could not see from where he was descending, and she dashed towards it, momentarily disappearing from view. A second later, Gabriel heard a shriek, followed by a prolonged, blood-curdling scream so terrible, Verity's mother collapsed onto the ground in panic. The older woman's wraithlike figure seemed to be trying to bury itself among the detritus of the forest floor, her hands clutching her grey head as she howled with shock. Gabriel scrambled the last few feet down the path before he was able to jump lightly onto the ground and turn in Verity's direction. He could see the girl clearly now, kneeling next to a heavily coated figure lying prostrate on the ground. Even from where Gabriel was standing, he could see that the man's head rested at an awkward angle where his neck had broken with the force of the fall. It was Victor Gladstone.

Gabriel tried to chivvy Verity to her feet, but she was screaming inconsolably and fought him off. "Get help!" she screamed. "Go away and get help!"

"Verity, he's dead," said Gabriel, making a renewed attempt at getting her away from the body. "Please, you must move. We shouldn't disturb——"

Above their heads, Gabriel could hear the thunder of footsteps as Verity's screams drew the attention of the other searchers. Verity's mother had curled up in the foetal position, but even with her huddled up like that, he could see the smudges of blood on her sleeve. There were policemen hurrying down the path towards them. Gabriel looked up at the sergeant and shook his head to indicate that the man was dead; the sergeant nodded and signalled for the other men to fall back, before walking over to where Gabriel was standing.

"What's happened here?" he asked, glancing from one crumpled figure to the other. The sergeant was a short, thickset man with eyebrows that looked as though they might crawl away and hibernate at any moment.

"That woman left her nursing home early this morning," said Gabriel, as calmly as he could. "We found her wandering down here near the body. The dead man's her father."

"Did you see what happened, sir?" asked the sergeant.

Gabriel was about to answer that he hadn't when Verity's mother blurted out between her sobs, "I've killed him! Sweet Jesus, I've killed him!"

Gabriel felt as though some unnamed individual had hurled a bucket of cold water over him. By rights he ought not to have been surprised, but he gasped for breath. This was nothing to the effect on Verity, who leapt to her feet, too stunned to cry any longer. The sergeant was hauling Emma to her feet. "Don't arrest her!" pleaded Verity. "She's out of her mind. Even if what she says is true, she's not capable——"

"I think you'd better get that young lady away from the scene of the crime," answered the sergeant coldly. "It looks like we have a murder enquiry on our hands."

Verity was never going to go quietly, but the cold enunciation of the word "murder" unsettled her again. "She's not a murderess—she doesn't know what she's saying!" shouted Verity as Gabriel led her back to the path. She hurried over to where her mother was standing, flanked now by two policemen. Emma had slipped into the catatonic stage of shock and hardly needed the long arm of the law to keep her in check. Verity threw her arms around her mother, a desperate gesture that elicited no response whatsoever from Emma. "It's all right, Mummy, it's all right," cooed Verity. "You've done nothing wrong."

Gabriel almost felt relieved when the policemen began to escort Emma from the scene. There was something so distasteful about a woman standing before a group of men like that—stunned, dishevelled, barefoot and wearing only a shapeless nightdress, with none of them taking any care to protect her dignity. "If you have to take her into custody, please be gentle with her," pleaded Gabriel. "She's ill."

"I can see that," snapped the sergeant, signalling to one of the men not to shackle her. "We won't be placing her under arrest at the present time. She'll be returned to her nursing home."

Verity accompanied her mother up the path, giving Gabriel a moment to look back at Victor's body. It was undeniably him; his face in death looked as disgruntled as it had when Gabriel had been introduced to him the previous day. He lay so awkwardly, Gabriel wondered if his back had broken along with his neck as he fell, and there were various abrasions and grazes on his face from where he had scraped along the jagged ground on his way down. A long wound across his right temple was still bleeding lightly. There was not much else to notice: Victor was dressed in the manner of an older man accustomed to taking long lonely walks to collect his thoughts—his coat was thick and of good quality, his boots similarly so, if a little worn around the heels from long use. There were two thin, short green threads caught in the creases of his coat sleeve.

"Do you want us to wait while you anoint him?" asked a young male voice behind Gabriel.

Gabriel turned to see a police constable standing in respectful silence, watching him. "No, no thank you. We don't anoint the dead," he answered, stepping away from the body. "I was just paying my respects. I'd . . . well, I'd better get his granddaughter back to the house."

Gabriel ascended the path, which was a harder exercise than he had anticipated, both because of its steepness and Gabriel's natural aversion to heights. He would not have admitted it readily, but he felt such a sense of horror at the prospect of losing his footing that he was forced to inch his way up, facing the wall of earth to avoid any awareness that he was climbing higher and higher from terra firma than felt entirely sensible. It really was a hazardous place; he could so easily see how a man unfamiliar with the lie of the land, disoriented by the fog, could have lost his footing and plunged into that cavern to his death. It was hardly the Grand Canyon, but the fall would be far enough if a man were hurtling down head first.

By the time he reached the top, Gabriel found that he was redundant. Bron and Paul had heard Verity's screams and arrived at the scene in time to take over her care. Gabriel watched from a distance as the two men jockeyed for position as Verity's principal comforter, rivals even in this most desperate of situations. The idea was forming in Gabriel's mind that poor Emma had stumbled upon her father's body as she wandered aimlessly through the fog and convinced herself that it was her fault. She might perhaps have tripped over him, discovered his blood on her white nightdress and jumped to that conclusion, simply because she was too confused to remember how she had come to be in that place and what she might have done. He would have to go to her as soon as he possibly could and make some attempt at finding out what she remembered. Gabriel knew she could never stand trial even if the police found enough evidence to incriminate her, but he felt the need to help her in some way, even if it was only to comfort her. Gabriel's worst fear was losing his memory, the only detail of old age he dreaded. He shuddered simply imagining what it must be like for a relatively young woman all of a sudden to have her mind shattered the way it had been—one minute to be pottering around the house, lucid, fit and healthy, the next moment to be collapsing into a void of night and fog from which she could never entirely return.

Gabriel cleared his throat to call out to the others, then thought better of it. He had a little task for Molly before he met up with the others, and he thought it best that none of them noticed him slipping round to the back of the house and the welcome of the kitchen door.

"Is it true?" asked Molly as soon as she had opened the door and let Gabriel in. "I heard Miss Verity crying in the hall about her grandfather. Is he truly dead?"

Gabriel nodded slowly. It was only now, with the warmth of the kitchen enveloping him, that he realised he was trembling. "I'm terribly sorry, Molly, I'm afraid he is. It looks as though he took a fall. The fog was terrible, and he did not know the lie of the land."

Molly stepped back and clutched the table behind her for support. "Oh, but that's terrible, Father, and so close to Christmas. Whatever can he have been thinking, going out in this terrible weather? And at his age?"

"I fear a fall like that might have killed a much younger man, Molly," said Gabriel, "but at his age the shock might have been enough. Listen, I must go back upstairs and attend to the others. There's a man there who has lost his father, and a young woman who has lost her grandfather. I wanted to ask you to do me a little favour, if you don't mind?"

"Anything, Father," said Molly, immediately. "Is there something you'd like me to take upstairs? I daresay they'll be needing some refreshment."

"You'll certainly have to make yourself useful upstairs," said Gabriel. "I suspect the police will pay us a visit later, if for no other reason than to advise as to how Mrs Caufield's faring."

"Mrs Caufield?"

"Nothing; I'll explain later." Gabriel glanced over his shoulder, half expecting to find Inspector Applegate breathing down his neck already. "I probably shouldn't be asking you this, Molly, but I wonder if you could take a look round the wardrobes upstairs before the police start crawling all over the house?"

Molly looked at him in alarm. "Whatever for? I'm not supposed to go snooping about."

"It's all right. I just want to know if anyone owns a dark green garment of any kind. Perhaps a coat or jacket."

"A green jacket?" Molly echoed. "Why?"

"It's probably not important, but I should like to know," Gabriel answered. "Satisfy an old man's curiosity."

Molly smiled uncertainly. "You're not old, Father," she said kindly, "and I don't think you're ever just curious, but of course I'll check."

"Thank you."

Upstairs, Paul, Bron, Verity and Florence were seated in the drawing room, holding a council of war. "Come and join us, Father," said Bron, rising to his feet as Gabriel stepped through the door. Gabriel nodded and sat next to Bron, trying hard to avoid the thought that Florence bore the look of a woman whose dinner party has been ruined by a clumsy cook burning the roast chicken. It was unreasonable to think ill of the woman under the circumstances. It could hardly be edifying to discover that a formerly distinguished writer has been found dead on the estate.

"I do hope the police won't go around telling everybody about it," fretted Florence. "You don't suppose it will get into the papers, do you?"

"I'd be surprised if it didn't," answered Paul, glancing coldly at her across the table. "It's a story. You may brace yourself for a storm, Mrs Martin."

"I very much doubt it," snapped Bron. "Old man falls to his death whilst walking on a foggy morning. It's hardly front-page news."

"You're very sure he fell," said Paul. "Awfully clumsy of him, losing his footing like that. Awfully convenient."

60

Gabriel could almost feel the temperature rising in the room. "I'm really not sure you ought—" His halfhearted call to order fizzled out at the sound of Verity bursting into renewed tears.

"Please tell me it was an accident!" sobbed Verity. "She would never have done anything to hurt him!"

Bron got up angrily, causing an ugly screeching of chairs and thundering of boots as he moved behind Verity, putting his hands on her shoulders. "No one is suggesting anything like that, my dear. Please don't let him upset you."

"But what will happen to her?" Verity persisted. "What if they think she pushed him?"

Bron made an elaborate gesture of cradling her weeping head, gently pushing the damp curls out of her face. He ignored Paul's cold glare. "Please don't cry, Verity. Nothing is going to happen to her. Even if it did turn out that she had something to do with this ghastly business—and frankly I can't see how—she's not in her right mind. She would never be held responsible."

"They will lock her up, though, won't they?" Paul retorted, without apparently realising that his hostile manner was making Bron's work very much easier. "Even if she didn't give the old man a shove, they'll put her in an asylum now just for wandering off like that. She could have killed herself, going off in the bitter cold in her bare feet."

Verity looked up at Bron in horror. "You won't let them lock her up, will you?" she pleaded. "They must have made a mistake, left the door open or something. Someone should have noticed. She's . . . she's not supposed to be left on her own."

"You needn't worry yourself about that," Bron promised,

still holding her close to himself. Gabriel suspected that Bron had been guardian angel to a few hapless individuals in his life but that no one had mattered to him quite so much as the substitute daughter he had been granted in the person of Verity. "You are quite right; it was a dereliction of duty. I'm sure there will be no reason at all for her to leave the home."

"I think you need to get to bed," said Florence, rising authoritatively to her feet. "You've had a terrible shock, Verity. Let's get you away from all these awful men."

Verity had calmed down, but she was trembling all over and swayed unsteadily on her feet as she left the table and moved towards Florence. Her teeth chattered as though she were freezing to death. "Are you cold?" asked Florence anxiously. "Is anyone else cold?"

"She's in shock, Mrs Martin," said Gabriel. "I daresay her blood pressure's a bit low. Is there any brandy in the house?"

"Excellent idea," said Florence, chivvying Verity out of the room, but Verity turned around to look back at Bron. "It was so horrible to see her like that, Uncle," she whimpered. "It was almost as bad as seeing Grandfather dead. She almost looked dead too. I keep trying to remember what she looked like before she took ill. She was so beautiful—" Tears overcame her again, and she let Florence lead her in the direction of her welcoming bed.

As soon as the two women were out of the room, Bron sat down again and stared down at the damask tablecloth. "Perhaps you should get some rest yourself," ventured Gabriel. "Verity's not the only one to have had a shock."

"Yes," agreed Paul, "go and have a nice rest to calm your nerves. We all know how devoted you were to the old man."

Bron jumped up, causing Paul to raise his hands in front of his face in self-defence. "Bron . . . ," Gabriel began, but Bron had already dropped his clenched fists to his sides and stepped back from Paul's cowering body until he stood several arm lengths away from him. "For God's sake, get out!" hissed Bron. "My father did very little to endear himself to anyone, but that is absolutely none of your business. Get out of this house, and stay well away from my niece."

Paul got up and sauntered towards the door with deliberate slowness. In the absence of an immediate threat of violence, Paul's courage knew no bounds. "Out of respect for Victor Gladstone, I'll leave you to sulk, old boy," he said, an unbearable smirk crossing his face. "But don't tell me to leave a house that's not yours. And I'll go as close to Verity as she lets me. She's a grown woman now, in case you hadn't noticed."

Bron grabbed the nearest available missile, which happened to be an unused teacup—an unfortunate choice of weapon, all said and done. "Just get out!" snarled Bron.

"I wouldn't throw that at me if I were you," Paul retorted. "It was probably looted at great expense from some French toff's house while the revolutionaries were cutting off his head."

With that, he was gone. Bron set down the teacup on its saucer with a ludicrous level of care before sitting down again. He looked steadily downwards, taking several deep, long breaths, as he had no doubt been taught to do long ago under such circumstances; then he sat up straight, looked across at Gabriel and said, matter-of-factly: "I shall have to discuss the situation with my sister's solicitor. It may be that this nursing home is no longer suitable for her after all. As to my father, there will have to be an inquest, of course. Until we know the official cause of death, there's not much more we can do."

"It may be some weeks before there can be an inquest," warned Gabriel, "though they may work more quickly if they suspect foul play."

"You don't honestly believe he was bumped off?" asked Bron. "Who on earth would do a thing like that?"

"You would be in a better position to tell me that," said Gabriel, directly. He had not intended to sound so accusatory, but if Bron had noticed the unfortunate choice of words, he did not respond. "Did he have any enemies?"

"Besides me, you mean?"

The two men were mercifully interrupted by Florence reappearing in the doorway. "Verity's safely tucked up in bed," she announced. "I tried giving her a sip or two of brandy, but the poor dear said it burned her throat."

Bron smiled for the first time. "I'm pleased to say she's not used to it. Is she all right?"

"She's calmer now, but I might call a doctor for her, if you don't mind."

"Of course, if you think she needs one."

"She's still ever so shaky," said Florence. "I thought a doctor might be able to give her something for her nerves. It was so sad—she kept crying, saying she wanted her mummy back."

Florence's words affected Bron more powerfully than Gabriel would have expected. His eyes became red and glistened with tears; he would die rather than shed them in public. "Please do call a doctor for Verity," he said hoarsely. "I'm afraid we may have to trespass upon your kindness for a few more days until she is well enough to return home."

"You know you needn't ask," promised Florence, warmly. "You must both stay until this horrid business is cleared up. I can help you with Verity." She turned to Gabriel. "What about you, Father? You are most welcome to stay on too, of course."

Gabriel smiled politely and shook his head. "It's most kind of you, Mrs Martin, but I must get back to the parish. If it's not inconvenient, however, I will return as soon as I can to visit Verity. I would like to visit her mother to see how she is recovering, and I'm sure Verity would like to know how she is recovering."

"That would be splendid, Father," said Florence. "I'm sure it would put Verity's mind at rest to know that her mother is being looked after. I'll ask Horace to drive you home."

"It's really not necessary, Mrs Martin," Gabriel demurred. "I'm perfectly happy to walk. Please don't trouble yourself."

"Father, I shouldn't dream of letting you walk all that way in this cold weather when you have had such a time of it. You can't have had any breakfast with all the commotion."

"I think Molly was keeping it warm for me," said Gabriel, hesitantly. "It's really not——"

"Well then, you can have your breakfast whilst Horace gets ready."

Gabriel groaned inwardly as he headed for the dining room. He was desperate for some peace and quiet in which to collect his thoughts, and a brisk walk home across the fields would have been absolutely perfect. He could see out a window that the sun was making brave attempts at shining; the lawn was shimmering with gossamer. This little corner of Wiltshire would soon be turned into the sort of arcadian vision Gerard Manley Hopkins might have described during his moments of ecstasy. Instead of enjoying God's grandeur outdoors, however, Gabriel endured the company of the most belligerent member of the English upper classes as he shared his many opinions on the Labour government, the future of the Empire and what-on-earth-did-we-fight-for? Not that Horace had ever fought in a war—he was too old for the last one and too anaemic (apparently) for the first.

After he had finished breakfast, served at table by Mr Trevelyan, Gabriel went upstairs and found Molly waiting nervously outside his room. "I've just been packing your bag," she said, by way of explanation, opening the door for him.

"Oh Molly, you needn't have bothered," Gabriel protested, but there on his bed was his knapsack, with not another trace of his presence left in the room. "But thank you anyway." He searched in his pocket for his purse, but Molly shook her head.

"Please don't, Father," she protested. "I'm paid enough." She glanced towards the door before saying more quietly, "I took a look for green clothes for you. I couldn't find nothing that colour. I didn't have time to search the master's and the mistress' clothes, but I'm sure neither of them wear that colour."

Gabriel nodded. "Are you sure about that?"

"Quite sure. I've been washing and mending their clothes for over a year, and I never saw nothing that colour green."

"Thank you, Molly." *The threads were important then*. Gabriel noticed that Molly seemed to be hesitating to speak again, looking over her shoulder to check that the door was closed. "Was there something else?" he asked gently. "There's no need to be nervous; we're a fair way from everyone else up here."

"It's probably nothing," she began, apologetically, "but I took a little look in Mr Gladstone's room. I'm not sure it were proper, but I thought that maybe he had something green. I didn't dare stay too long. You shouldn't touch a dead man's clothes anyhow. There was something strange in his case. He had a mishap with his clothes the night before."

Molly slipped both hands into the large pockets in the skirt of her pinafore and pulled out a man's belt. There was nothing especially unusual about it—it was made of good-quality brown leather with a star-shaped buckle—but as soon as Molly handed it to him, Gabriel noticed that the leather had been torn right the way through about a third of the way round, and the belt was in one piece only because the buckle was still done up. Gabriel chuckled. "I wonder if the old man overindulged a little over Christmas."

"But wouldn't the buckle've broken before the leather gave way?" asked Molly. "I'm not even sure it's been worn recently. Look—there are little bits of dust in the creases."

Gabriel looked at it a little more closely. The place where the belt had broken was torn through in a ragged line. It must have broken the previous evening; or else it had broken on a previous occasion, and Victor had thrown it into his case in annoyance and simply forgotten to take it out again. Sensing that Molly was watching him intently, Gabriel rolled up the belt and put it into his own knapsack carefully. "Thank you, Molly," he said, "that's very interesting. I'll take a closer look at it when I get home."

He knew he had asked Molly to do something that had made her extremely uncomfortable. There was nothing particularly wrong in telling a guest what clothes a member of the household did and didn't wear, and Molly was used to having undisputed access to the bedrooms and personal belongings of the entire household; but he knew Molly would have felt that she was snooping and telling tales about the people she served—and now possibly stealing, even if the owner in question was dead and neither of them could see the use in a broken belt. Gabriel found sixpence and pressed it into her hand. "No, please, I insist. You have gone well beyond the call of duty."

Gabriel had a nasty feeling he had insulted Molly by forcing her to take his money, but he had no further opportunity to ponder his mistake. Horace Martin was waiting for him in the car. He was already seated behind the wheel, which Gabriel suspected was a deliberate attempt at avoiding the need to assist his passenger. Swathed in a thick dark overcoat and hat, his vast moustaches poking out from beneath a grey scarf, Gabriel tried hard to avoid the thought that he was being driven home by an enormous walrus. "Home, James, and don't spare the horses!" chimed Gabriel with forced cheerfulness.

The Walrus stared back at Gabriel. Gabriel could not see his mouth, but he suspected he was not smiling.

5

Horace Martin drove a car in the style of a man who had spent the greater portion of his life being chauffeured about by others. "We lost our driver during the war," Horace explained, taking on the narrow stone bridge they were crossing with the level of patience Gabriel might have expected from a man convinced that half the world was against him. "Impossible to employ another now, of course. Bunch of Reds in Westminster bleeding us all dry."

"Well, you've kept your home, thank God," said Gabriel, fixing his attention on a gaggle of children playing on the riverbank. They were poorly dressed with thin, ill-fitting coats offering little protection from the elements, no gloves to protect their raw fingers and only thick knitted scarves to give them some warmth. They ran after one another, perilously close to the river's edge, the sound of their shrieking laughter magnified by the water. "It was a good plan to convert those outbuildings."

"Damn silly idea, if you ask me," Horace growled, "even if it brings in money. Bringing a crowd of lunatics to the estate—and now one of them a killer. No doubt they'll close the wretched operation down and bankrupt us."

"Do you truly think Emma killed her father?"

Horace snorted with mirthless laughter. "Plain as a pike-staff, I would have thought," he said. "Crazed woman mysteriously disappears from clink and turns up wailing over the dead body of a hated father. If he died at anyone's hand, it would have been hers."

Gabriel bristled at the man's brutal tone. "Look here, Martin, it's hardly a foregone conclusion. Plenty of people, sadly, grow up to hate their parents, but they don't turn into murderers."

"Listen, Padre," Horace continued without softening his tone one iota, "I've heard you fancy yourself as a bit of a Sherlock Holmes. Word gets round these parts very quickly. But I wouldn't waste your time with this. There are only two things that could have happened this morning. Either Victor Gladstone, being the blithering idiot he always was, took a stroll in blind fog and broke his own neck, or his ghastly daughter gave him a necessary push. She was always wayward even before she went gaga, head full of silly ideas. And old man Gladstone too full of his own vanity to notice."

Gabriel closed his eyes. Conversation with a man like Horace Martin was rather like finding oneself wading waist deep through an open sewer. It would take a hot bath and several decades of the Rosary before Gabriel felt clean again. "I do hope you're wrong."

"Padre, you needn't play the innocent with me," said Horace, taking a hand off the steering wheel to remove his pipe from his coat pocket. "You know it was murder as well as I do. I was standing with the others when the police arrived, and you were giving that dead body a little too much attention for a man who thinks it was an unfortunate accident. I can't tell what you were looking at, of course, but you clearly saw something out of place. And if I noticed, I shan't have been the only one."

Gabriel watched in some fascination as Horace deftly filled his pipe with tobacco, controlling the steering wheel precariously with his elbows as he struck a match and lit up. Gabriel distracted himself from the obvious threat to which he had just been treated by marvelling at the nerve of the man. If that lighted match fell between his legs . . . "Forgive my morbid curiosity," said Gabriel. "Until we know more, let's give humanity the benefit of the doubt and hope it was an accident."

Horace snorted again, happily distracted by his pipe. Gabriel felt the tendrils of fruity pipe smoke curling around him in the car and let his mind wander back to the abbey and the sight of old Brother Cuthbert sitting on his favourite bench in the apple orchard, surrounded by pipe smoke and the many decades of memories he had collected. He had gone to his eternal reward earlier that winter, but Gabriel felt a painful urge to be able to sit with him and ask the advice of a wise old Victorian. But then, Gabriel always felt homesick for the abbey when there was danger about.

I have made my first mistake, thought Gabriel, looking out of the side window to hide his face from Horace. *Two mistakes, if Molly's snooping is discovered by the murderer. Assuming it really wasn't Emma . . .* It was the first time in Gabriel's life that he had willed a person to have been a killer.

71

"I'm not sure I should let you out," commented Fr Foley, when Gabriel had explained what had happened. "I'm sure there would have been no dead bodies found scattered about the estate if I'd gone to the dinner party."

"Well, next time you go," wailed Gabriel, "since I seem to be such a harbinger of doom!"

Fr Foley smiled, his attention drawn to the sight of a twelve-year-old boy hard at work in the courtyard, mending a bicycle. "Are you sure you want to ride that thing?"

"I need to get about more efficiently," Gabriel explained. "It was one thing ambling about when I was at the abbey since I only ever walked between the abbey and the village, but I'll be a good deal more use to you if I can get from one place to another in good time."

"Aye, and you'll do anything to avoid getting in a car."

"It can be perfectly pleasant to take a ride in a motor with a friendly driver," Gabriel protested, "but getting stuck in a car at the mercy of a time traveller from Calvin's Geneva was unbearable!"

"Gave you a hard time, did he?"

"Abominable. When he'd quite finished treating me to the most appalling gossip about a woman too ill to speak for herself, Horace Martin then treated me to a condensed version of every anti-Catholic myth a good reformed Englishman could possibly believe. Did you know there was even a Pope Joan?"

Fr Foley laughed. As an Irish priest living in a rural parish where suspicion of Paddies and papists was an accepted part of life, he had learnt to laugh at the absurdity of it all where his younger self would have needed to be physically restrained from retaliating. "If it helps, Horace Martin's not desperately friendly to anyone," said Fr Foley. "I shouldn't fancy being a Jew or an Indian in his presence either."

Gabriel sighed. "In a way, it's not the Horace Martins of this world who trouble me—it's the men and women who pride themselves on being terribly modern and tolerant. Five minutes into the conversation, they're frothing at the mouth over the latest Popish Plot to breed them out." He joined Fr Foley at the window. Outside, the boy had the bike upside-down and appeared to be oiling the chain, which Gabriel assumed meant that he had nearly finished. "I should see how Freddy's getting on."

"You know, that bike's been rusting in the shed for years," warned Fr Foley. "I wouldn't trust it meself."

"Freddy's good with bicycles," said Gabriel, walking over to the coat stand to get himself ready to brave the cold. "He won't let me go speeding off without brakes. I don't suppose you could lend me a shilling, could you? I gave my last sixpence to Molly."

"You shouldn't be handing out coins like that," Fr Foley admonished, but he reached into his pocket in search of the required cash. "Heaven knows we're all feeling the squeeze."

"He's been working hard out in the cold for hours," said Gabriel. "A workman deserves his wage. The poor kid's hardly going to spend it on a life of debauchery." He took the shilling from Fr Foley gratefully. "He's not even going to be spending it on sweeties. Now if I could have given him a bar of chocolate . . ."

Gabriel stepped outside in time to see Freddy righting the bike and sitting astride it, giving the brakes a squeeze. He was a big lad for twelve and would no doubt be a powerfully built man one day, but Freddy already had a reputation as a gentle giant, the bighearted youngest child of a local poultry farmer. God had a sense of humour and had blessed Freddy's parents with seven daughters, meaning that Freddy was growing up under the watchful eye of a regiment of indomitable females. The attention did not appear to have done the boy any harm, and he smiled happily at Gabriel when he looked up and saw him coming.

"I'll reckon she's about ready to go now, Father," he said, hopping out of the saddle. "She weren't hardly moving when I got her out the shed."

"Well done, Freddy," said Gabriel, holding out the coin to him. "I shall speed around the town now, thanks to you."

Freddy took the coin eagerly, giving Gabriel a nod of thanks. "Can you ride a bike in a cassock?"

Gabriel had not actually given this any thought, but he shrugged. "Well, ladies manage in skirts, so I daresay I'll manage with a bit of practice." He was aware of Fr Foley's uneven footsteps behind him. "I shall get about so much more quickly than I would have done walking."

"At least on foot you'd be sure of getting back," said Fr Foley dryly, causing Freddy to giggle. "Freddy lad, you'll have to teach him how to ride."

"I cycled everywhere as a child," Gabriel assured him. "I was a telegram boy."

"That was about a hundred years ago, and that was London," answered Fr Foley. "They have things like roads in London, I hear. You going to try this thing out?"

"Absolutely."

Gabriel took the bicycle from Freddy and seated himself as comfortably as he could. Freddy had been right—

the cassock was going to be a complicating factor. He tried hitching it up and sitting on the surplus material, but the presence of a bemused audience of two made him clumsy, and he could feel the heavy black folds slipping down over his knees as soon as he shifted position. "Are you sure about this, Father?" asked Freddy unhelpfully. "Would a couple of safety pins help?"

Please, God, don't let me fall off until I'm out of sight, Gabriel prayed as he skidded out of the courtyard, leaning dangerously as he turned left onto the road. He gritted his teeth to steady his nerves and let himself speed up, allowing the steady downward camber to carry him faster and faster along the mercifully empty road. As long as he remembered to slow down a little before the road began winding into a series of blind turns, he would be perfectly safe.

Fr Foley was right, of course; cycling along a country road was worlds apart from weaving between omnibuses and pedestrians wandering into his path without looking. But then, as a telegram boy he had travelled to every destination with a knot of anxiety in the pit of his stomach about the details of the missive he was about to deliver. It had horrified him as a young boy that one or two cold sentences had the power to shatter a woman's world forever: REGRET TO INFORM YOU PRIVATE HENRY JACKSON KILLED IN ACTION FRANCE MAY 26. Then there were those ghastly form letters, no doubt produced to save time as the thousands of fatalities had to be processed, in which the blanks were filled in with the young man's name, date of death and the cause: "killed in action" or "died of wounds". Sometimes a death caused by illness. Gabriel remembered the terrible summer of 1916, when he had visited the same little terraced house no fewer than four times. Four sons, four telegrams. Four formal expressions of regret. On the fourth and last time that Gabriel had slowed to a halt outside the woman's door, he had seen her ashen face through the kitchen window where she had been standing, praying he would pass her by. By the time she had thrown open the door, she was in a blazing rage, snatching the telegram from his hand and spitting directly in his face.

"Why are you alive, you dirty little swine!" she had screamed at him, lunging at him, fingernails poised to scratch his face. Gabriel was bigger and stronger than the woman and grabbed her arms reflexively to protect himself, pushing her away as she shouted, "Why cannot you be dead? Why? Why should my Adam be gone and you live?"

Gabriel had seen so much grief by then: the sudden rush of tears as the telegram was torn open; the coldly mechanical nod as the recipient of the worst news slipped into the dark void of despair and retreated from him; the shriek of horror. He had picked a few women up off the ground when they had fainted with the shock; but never had he seen a woman so consumed by despair and rage. "Please . . . ," he said, but she could not hear him; she was screaming her dead sons' names over and over again like a litany, willing them back to life—willing him dead. Gabriel felt so overwhelmed with pity for her that he let go of her and made no further effort to defend himself as she slapped and punched and spat at him.

Two days after that, when Gabriel's nerves had recovered, he had arrived at the post office to start work and found the woman waiting for him with the inspector, Stan Waldron. "This lady would like to speak with you," said Stan.

Gabriel stood in mortified silence as the woman got up in front of everyone and embraced him, pressing a tin of chocolate into his hands. Her face was so pinched and devoid of colour, she might have been twenty years older, the life having drained from her with every loss she had suffered. "Forgive me," she said, in a thin, weak voice he never forgot. "I should never have said those things. Do something good with the life you've been given. Suddenly, it will be gone."

Suddenly, it will be gone . . . It had been the sight of Gabriel bruised and bloodied that had convinced his mother to send him back to school, ignoring his pleas that he ought to be helping the war effort, not going back to a world of classics and cricket. She had thought otherwise.

Suddenly, it will be . . . Gabriel lifted up his head so that he could feel the breeze rippling through his hair. There was so much to be joyful about, he told himself, though he had never been the greatest master of the art of optimism. The hedgerows lining either side of the road blocked his view, but he knew he was surrounded by dormant beauty, the whole of creation poised for the first sign of spring to come. *Glory be to God for dappled things . . .* He was travelling through one of the loveliest places in England; he ministered to a kindly, welcoming people; he was on his way to comfort a woman who might have inadvertently murdered her own father; he had just seen a man dead under suspicious circumstances . . . No, he was not a man for whom the glass was half-full.

His rear tyre began to slide on a patch of mud, causing Gabriel to skid sharply into the middle of the road. Instinctively, he turned the handlebars towards the verge to try

77

to right himself, only to send himself into a flat spin. He panicked and gave the brakes a sharp squeeze. Freddie had been right, the brakes were fine—the front brakes at least. The front wheel stopped abruptly, and the back wheel continued to spin, making the bike buck like an out-of-control horse. Gabriel felt himself being catapulted over the top of the handlebars; he saw the ground beneath him, then the sky, then the dank, waterlogged verge lurching towards him in slow motion before he made a soft and very damp landing.

At least there's no one to see, thought Gabriel gratefully, as he scrambled to his feet with what was left of his dignity. His thick clothing offered him some protection, but he could still feel the icy rainwater seeping through to his skin, and it would be a very long time before he could go home to change. He looked down at his mud-splattered coat. More than mud-splattered: there was a thin film of dirt painted across his legs and torso. His hand went up to his face, and he brushed away a few blades of wet grass that had attached themselves to the end of his nose.

The good news was that the bicycle appeared to be intact, even if the edge of the handlebars had scraped against the road momentarily, leaving a small tear. It was only as he attempted to ride the thing again that he realised the chain had come off, and he groaned loudly. It ought to have been a fairly straightforward procedure to put it back in place, but Gabriel could not remember for the life of him how to do it. He stared down at the slack, useless chain, wondering what to do.

"Everything all right, Your Holiness?" called a familiar, clipped voice from a little further down the road. Gabriel looked in the direction of the sound to see Paul walking briskly towards him. Gabriel remembered now that he had passed a man walking as he had sped along, but he had been too focused on the summer of 1916 to register who he was. "You look as though you've been dragged through a hedge backwards. I think perhaps you actually have!"

Gabriel smiled sheepishly. "Caught in flagrante delicto, I'm afraid," he said. "It's rather a long time since I've been on a bicycle, and I was barely out of short trousers then."

"Well, if they *will* make you wear period costume," answered Paul, swaggering to his side. "Chain come off, has it?"

"So it would seem," answered Gabriel, "and you're under no obligation to approve of the way I dress, though who 'they' are is anybody's guess."

"No offence," said Paul, and Gabriel noticed that he was rather humbler in private than he had been before an audience. "Here, let me help you with that."

Gabriel watched as Paul crouched down, removed his gloves and set a package down carefully beside him before deftly replacing the chain. Then he wiped his oily fingers clean on the nearby grass, replaced the gloves and picked up his package. "No offence taken," said Gabriel. "Thank you. We must be going the same way."

Paul held up his parcel for Gabriel to examine, not that there was much to see other than a large rectangular prism wrapped in brown paper and string. "It's a tin of biscuits for Verity's mother," he explained. "Verity wanted to see her, but the doctor said Verity was in no fit state to visit anyone, especially her mother. I told Verity I'd go and check up on her."

"Awfully decent of you," said Gabriel. "I thought I'd pay

her a visit too. We can go together." He was sincerely impressed that Paul would be kind enough to visit Emma when many young men might shy away from such a task. Neither of them said anything, but they were both aware of the harrowing scene that might await them. Gabriel's greatest fear was that the police might attempt to question Emma, even take her into custody; he suspected they would not be allowed to do so on account of her illness, but he had no idea what the law stated on such matters. "You're very fond of Verity, aren't you?"

Paul laughed a little too forcefully. "I'd marry her tomorrow given half a chance. Well, frankly, I'd elope with her tomorrow if she'd accept it, but she's far too much of a good girl for that."

"I should hope so too."

"It's all right, I'm not against marriage as a principle," he assured Gabriel, who was not reassured in the least. "It's of socioeconomic benefit to society and therefore a good thing, in my opinion."

"How romantic, old chap," mused Gabriel. "We'd call it a sacrament."

"Well, you know what I think about all that."

"I suspect I can guess."

"Look, even Verity's not entirely sold on all that stuff, you know. She's talked about crossing the Tiber only to please her uncle Bron. She'd park herself in any church if the choir sang sweetly enough."

The two men had stepped off the road onto a narrow lane that temporarily required them to walk in single file between tall rows of trees. This was an orchard—not the darkly chaotic woodland they had had the misfortune to visit that morning but a large, cultivated square of bare trees that would have heaved with cider apples just a few short months before. "I couldn't possibly comment," said Gabriel over his shoulder, "but I do know that Verity's uncle will never consent to the marriage, and it's his opinion that matters."

"He's no right to stand in our way. She's twenty-one, not twelve!"

"He cannot stop you from marrying her, but he might well cut her off. Think what that would mean for her musical training. She's supposed to be going to London."

Gabriel was aware that the footsteps behind him had stopped. He turned to see Paul standing still, some way back, and stopped himself to wait. "Look here," said Paul, hurrying over to him, "I don't suppose you could have a word with him, could you? I know men like that only ever listen to their priests."

Gabriel felt his good humour falling through the floor. There always had to be a catch when the enemies of the Church started trying to be polite. "You want me to put in a good word for you to Verity's uncle?"

"In a word, yes. Please."

Gabriel waited until they had walked the last few steps onto open ground and could walk side by side with the bicycle between them. "Would you be prepared to renounce your current creed?"

"Never!" answered Paul with spirit. "I will never stand against my own conscience."

"Even for Verity?"

"You wouldn't expect me to."

"Would you be prepared to raise your children Catholic then?"

Paul started making disagreeable tutting noises. "Honestly, Father, you know I couldn't bring up my children believing in some fairy story I don't believe myself! Are you really heartless enough to expect me to renounce my beliefs?"

"Yes," responded Gabriel calmly, "that is precisely what I pray you will do, whether or not you marry Verity."

"Now just a minute—"

"Marxism is the most dangerous fairy story of them all, Mr Ashley. A system that can never be attained on this earth but that concerns itself only with the here and now. Can't you see a flaw in there somewhere?"

Paul threw Gabriel a look of absolute contempt. "You know, for a moment I thought you were different from the others." He handed Gabriel the package, so violently that the heavy metal tin slammed against the palms of his hands. "My mistake."

Gabriel had had plenty of moments like this in the past, but it would not stop him agonising for days over how he might have conducted himself differently to make his words more palatable to a young man searching for the truth in all the wrong places. But he doubted anything he might have said would have made a difference.

There was very little from the outside of the house to suggest to Gabriel that he was entering an institution. The nursing home must have been the old coach house and stables once, but it had been so expertly transformed that Gabriel could have believed he was going to visit the comfortable private residence of some dowager or retired brigadier. During the summer months, the residents would no doubt make use of the pleasantly cultivated garden, but no one was venturing out in the cold. It was only as he stepped through the entrance that Gabriel was assailed by the odour of carbolic soap, and a matronly woman in uniform appeared before him, the guardian of the nursing home's inner sanctum.

"Good morning," said Gabriel, removing his hat. He tried to ignore the look of distaste the woman was giving him. She had clearly thought for a moment that he might be a vicar, then realised her mistake. "I've come to visit Emma —Emma Caufield."

"She's not one of yours," answered the nurse tersely, "and she's very unsettled today. She's—"

"Yes, I know, I was one of the people who found her." He held up the package. "I've brought something for her from her family."

The nurse indicated a discreet door to one side of the hall. "Might I suggest that you tidy yourself up before you go before one of my patients," she said, in a tone that was very definitely an order. "When you are in a more suitable state, I will take you to her."

Gabriel blushed, fleeing into the Gents like a bat out of hell. It might not have been his Romish tendencies that had caused such a cold response after all. He had forgotten the mud all over his clothing, and when Gabriel looked in the small square mirror over the sink, he noticed that there were still traces of ditchwater on his face. Paul might have had the decency to tell him . . . He turned on the tap and bathed his face in the freezing cold water, making use of the squares of cut-up newspaper to clean off as much of the mud as he could.

"I'm afraid I fell off my bicycle on my way here," Gabriel

volunteered, when he emerged into the hall, looking only partially tidier than he had before. The nurse was not as interested as she might have been and turned away as soon as she saw him, leaving him to follow her to a magnolia-painted door with a brass number three on it. She rapped on the door before opening it and walked away, leaving Gabriel to step inside alone and unannounced.

Gabriel half expected to enter the room and find Emma fast asleep in her bed, drugged up to the eyeballs by doctors who could not think of any other way to help a woman in that level of distress, but the opposite turned out to be the case. Emma had been helped to wash and change her clothes and was seated in an armchair near a large bay window. She did not turn to face him as he closed the door softly behind himself; she was apparently mesmerised by the view.

"Mrs Caufield?" said Gabriel, but she did not stir. Gabriel looked around the room for inspiration. It was a small but cosy room which the staff appeared to have gone to some lengths to decorate in a way that might provoke some memories. The counterpane and cushions on the bed looked as though they had belonged to Emma before she came to the home; on the desk in the corner, there was an embroidered spectacles case Emma might have been given to make as part of a needlework class. On the wall facing the bed, there was an oil painting of a little girl aged around ten. Verity. Obviously a younger version of Verity, her hair tied up in pigtails decorated in blue ribbon, wearing her best frock. "Emma?" he tried again. "My name is Fr Gabriel. I was with Verity this morning—"

"You don't belong here," said Emma tonelessly, without

moving her gaze away from the window. "I'm a Protestant. At least I was."

"I know. I've brought you a present from Paul."

Emma turned slowly to look at Gabriel. He knew she was not yet forty years of age, but her hair was already streaked with white, and she had the gaunt, weary look of a woman nearing the end of her life. "I don't know a Paul."

Gabriel handed Emma the parcel, but she let it sit in her lap without showing any interest in opening it. "Paul is a . . . well, a friend of your daughter. Your daughter, Verity."

The name brought a smile to Emma's lips. "My lovely baby." The pleasure the name brought her was quickly overtaken by a look of panic as Emma's face clouded over. "What will happen to my baby, Father? What will happen to my child when they hang me?"

"Emma, they won't . . ."

"I'm going to hang, Father. I'm going to hang. That's why they sent you to me, isn't it? To confess."

"No," said Gabriel, pulling up the chair from the desk so that he could sit at eye level with Emma. "You're not going to hang."

"But I have killed a man. Of course they'll hang me. They'll have to hang me."

"Emma, it doesn't work quite like that."

"I wish I were a Catholic," Emma continued, staring back at the window. "I should like to confess. Just to be able to say it."

Gabriel sat forward in his chair. "Emma, I can't hear your confession, but I can listen to what you have to say if it helps, and I may be able to offer some advice."

85

"I couldn't confess anyway, not the way you'd see it," continued Emma, as though he had not spoken. "I'm not sorry. One has to be sorry, doesn't one?"

Gabriel nodded. "Yes. Would you like to talk to me? It might help if you can unburden yourself."

"He was a bad man, you know," she said, "a bad father, a bad husband. All he ever cared about was his wretched books."

"Did you kill him, Emma? Did you kill him for being a bad father?" Gabriel had not intended to be quite so direct, but Emma had immediately fallen into the trap so many penitents fell into, of confessing somebody else's sins. "Do you remember what happened?"

"I didn't mean to," she said, and Gabriel was sure that that much was true. "I didn't know he would be out there."

"Why did you leave? It was very dangerous to wander off like that."

"I've no idea. I can't remember a thing. One minute I was fast asleep in my bed—at least I think I was. Then I was wandering around in the fog. It was so cold. I was so cold. I think I've wandered off before. I've found myself in strange places, and I can't remember. Why was he there, Father? Why was he there?"

Gabriel reached out and placed a hand on Emma's. She was trembling with the effort of trying to recall what she had done, but a picture appeared to be emerging somewhere in her confused mind. "I killed him so many times in my imagination, and then I did it. Fate placed him in my power."

"How did you do it?"

"I pushed him. It wasn't even hard. It's how I always imag-

86

ined I'd do it. I always imagined myself pushing him down the stairs. In my childhood home, there was a great staircase, a great wide, dangerous staircase. I think that's where I got the idea." Emma looked distractedly at Gabriel. "I do wish there were a God. I wish there were a God to damn him to hell. I should so like to think of him burning. I wish there were a hell, Father; you can keep heaven to yourselves, but let there be a hell."

Gabriel shuddered at the woman's cool, unremitting flow of hatred. He had no idea what to say to her. He knew that her mind was broken, that she might not even remember this conversation in an hour's time or might not even know what she was saying at all, but he suspected that these were no mere ravings. Hatred as terrible as this took years to nurture and refine, years of resentment and brooding and the refusal to make peace with the past while it was still possible to do so. Emma's mental infirmity had simply removed any ability she had once had to hide it, and she sat before him now with no mask, no guile, no willingness to conceal her true feelings. Yet, he did not know what to say to her. He could not discern the point at which the years of bitterness ended and the years of illness began.

Gabriel got up as though to stretch his legs and took a closer look at Emma's desk. He doubted she had sat and written down anything in years, possibly ever; the blotting pad was fresh and had never been used, there were squeaky-clean pens and an unopened ink pot. The whole arrangement was an affectation, a strange attempt at making the room look as though it belonged to a much-younger person, even a child who might come home with a satchel full of prep to do before the morning; or perhaps it was supposed to make the bedroom look more like an old-fashioned lady's boudoir. Either way, the desk was almost insulting. Gabriel could hardly imagine Emma sitting there copying out a Latin exercise or writing a carefully crafted letter of thanks for an invitation to a dinner dance.

"Who will care for my baby if they hang me?" asked Emma to Gabriel's back. "I'm still nursing."

"Emma, I think you should label that tin," suggested Gabriel, turning to look at her. "You wouldn't want anyone to take it by accident, thinking it belongs to someone else."

"Yes, I suppose I should," answered Emma, moving effortlessly from the subject of babies to biscuits. "I like biscuits."

Gabriel went back to the desk and inked a pen for her, then offered it to her. Emma took the pen in her left hand and scrawled her name untidily across the top of the package, the brown paper absorbing the ink messily so that the letters spread out in thick, spiky lines over the fibres of the paper. "Thank you, Emma," he said, taking back the pen. "Let me help you with that."

"It wasn't a sin, it was justice," said Emma softly, as Gabriel prepared to leave. "I only married to escape."

"Emma, where is your husband?" asked Gabriel.

"Waiting for me at home," Emma explained. "I'd best be getting home, really. It's nice to chat, but I've so much to do before Reggie gets home from work."

Gabriel gave Emma a little bow and left, hoping he had not unsettled the poor woman too badly. He thought he might not tell Verity anything about their meeting, other than that she had liked Paul's biscuits.

6

Gabriel was going to have to find himself another mode of transport. If it had been hair-raising skidding down the winding roads to the nursing home, it was a purgatorial nightmare trying to cycle up them again, especially when the heavens opened near the top of the hill, where there was absolutely no shelter, and he was soaked to the skin. By the time he reached something resembling civilisation again, Gabriel could almost see Dante's avenging angels queuing up to hurl stones at him to purify him of his pride.

Not that it was easy to hold on to one's pride—or dignity, or self-respect—for very long in the presence of His Majesty's police force. Gabriel left his bicycle propped up against the railings outside the constabulary and staggered inside, dripping wet and out of breath. "Good God, you look like you've been dragged through a hedge backwards!" boomed PC Stevens from behind his desk.

"It's always backwards, isn't it?" puffed Gabriel, leaning against the counter for support. "I might have been dragged through the famous hedge forwards, resisting volubly."

Stevens grinned amiably. He was a good-natured man in his forties who had spent a quiet war mostly in barracks in Aldershot, with just enough time spent shooting at various

Germans in France to earn himself a medal and a few good stories at the pub. "You'll catch your death like that, you know."

"It's all right, Stevens, I'll go straight home and get a change of clothes," said Gabriel. "I just need to take a look at Victor Gladstone's file. It's quite urgent."

"Victor who?"

"The man who was found dead early this morning. I need to check something."

"You'll be lucky, Father; they're only now finishing their report. Inspector—"

"Oh no, is Inspector Applegate on the case already? I rather hoped . . ."

Gabriel was distracted by the clang of a door opening, and almost on cue, Inspector Applegate swept into view. "Walked into a bog, have you?" asked Applegate, which made a nice change from references to hedges.

"I didn't expect to see you here," said Gabriel, and he was trying hard to pretend he really didn't mind.

"I wish I could say the same of you," Applegate retorted. "I'm presented with a nice open-and-shut case of a deranged woman bumping off her old man, and Count Dracula jumps in to wreck everything. What do you want?"

"Nothing," said Gabriel, calmly. "I simply wanted to tell you that Emma Caufield is innocent."

Applegate maintained his poker face with admirable professionalism. "What?"

"That's it; Emma Caufield is innocent."

"I know she is; she's insane."

"That's not what I mean. She couldn't possibly have done it."

Applegate's calm demeanour never held up for very long; he grabbed Gabriel by the arm and propelled him in the direction of his office. "Five minutes, mate, all right? Five minutes. That should be long enough for you to hurl a few grenades in the direction of my case."

Gabriel brushed Applegate off and walked into an office that had become quite familiar over the past few months, though not familiar enough for him to risk sitting down. "If it's such an open-and-shut case, why are you investigating at all?" asked Gabriel. "You must have your own suspicions."

"None whatsoever," answered Applegate, settling himself at his desk. He snatched up a couple of sheets of paper that were lying in wait for him in his tray and gestured for Gabriel to take a seat, observing him warily as he sat down. "I'm just here to cross the t's and dot the i's. A violent death is still a violent death, and it has to be investigated."

"Good, an investigation. I could help you with that."

Applegate glanced over the report. "It's all exactly as I was informed," said Applegate casually. "The woman was found in the near vicinity of the body. There was blood on her clothing. Just in case she couldn't make it easy enough for us, she was heard shouting, 'I've killed him! Sweet Jesus, I've killed him!' You were one of the witnesses, I gather?"

"You haven't taken a statement from me yet," answered Gabriel. "Would you like to interview me now?"

Applegate looked steadily across the desk at Gabriel. "What do you want? If you're worried about Emma Caufield, you needn't be. She'll not be brought to trial; she'll go nowhere near the hangman. We'll find her a place in an asylum, and no one will ever trouble her again."

"Inspector, that's all well and good, but she didn't do it."

"She confessed to it, she was found at the scene of the crime and she had motive."

Gabriel sighed, wondering if Emma had repeated the same feelings of diabolical loathing to the inspector as she had to him earlier. He repeated an earlier observation in the hope it would lend some support to his position. "Sadly, there are many men and women in this world who grow up to hate their fathers. Most do not turn into murderers."

"Most," repeated Applegate. "Emma is the exception to the rule then."

"I don't believe she is, Inspector," said Gabriel cautiously. "I think she was wandering around, lost and frightened. Somehow or other, she stumbled upon her father's body, and in her confusion, she imagined she had killed him. Perhaps she had imagined killing him before, many, many times, and when she saw him it was easy for her to think herself responsible. Remember, she is an extremely impressionable person."

Applegate shifted in his chair, a sure sign that the interview was nearing its end, whether Gabriel liked it or not. "Don't you think it rather a coincidence that a woman walks out of her nursing home on a morning she knows nobody is likely to find her quickly, then an hour later her hated father is found dead? Even if she hadn't been found howling the place down, it doesn't look very good for her, does it?"

Gabriel shook his head impatiently. "How could she have known her father was there? She barely knows what day of the week it is! When I spoke with her this morning, she thought it was years ago and her daughter was still a nursing infant!"

"You've been to see her?"

Gabriel chose to ignore the accusatory tone. "Yes, and that's why I know she didn't do it. She said she pushed him, but that's not how the killer brought him down. It was a blow to the head."

"Father, there's been no postmortem—"

"I saw a gash on the side of his head that looked different to his other injuries. Of course, he might have struck his head on a stone or a branch on his way down, but I thought—"

"Yes, he might have done. None of this makes any sense."

"And the injury was on his left-hand side. It was dealt by a right-hander. Emma's left-handed."

Applegate looked impassively at Gabriel for what felt like an age before answering. "Father, until I have substantive evidence to the contrary, I can neither confirm nor dismiss anything you say. There is simply no point in speculating like this until we have the results of the postmortem."

It was the answer for which Gabriel had the least respect, so slippery, so unwilling to take sides. "How long will it be before the postmortem?" he asked.

There was a thunder of feet and muffled voices some distance away, causing the two men to stop talking. The door flew open, revealing Bron looking very much the worse for wear. "Has my sister been accused?" he demanded, completely ignoring Gabriel's presence in the room. "This is not a police matter. The woman is seriously ill, has been for years. If you have any doubt about that at all—"

"I'm well aware of that, sir," Applegate broke in. "I can assure you that my constables were very gentle with her, and there was no attempt made to have her taken into custody.

She has been returned to her nursing home for the time being."

"For the time being?" echoed Bron. "Please tell me you're not suggesting Emma could be held to account for this? She might not have had anything to do with it!"

"Bron, is your sister left-handed?" asked Gabriel. "Sorry if it sounds like a silly question."

"It's a ridiculous question!" blustered Bron, looking at Gabriel as though he had two heads. "What on earth are you doing here?"

"Exonerating your sister, possibly," he answered. "Was she left-handed?"

Bron shook his head in confusion. "Well . . . well, as a matter of fact she was, Father, and extremely bitter she was about it too. She never let the rest of us forget that she was forced to write with her right hand all the way through school. No other child has ever been forced to write with the correct hand in the history of education. She made a huge fuss about writing as she pleased ever after. Why do you ask?"

Gabriel gave Applegate the sort of smile that was as close as he could get to saying "I told you so," but Applegate had other matters on his mind. "I don't wish to be rude, gentlemen," said Applegate wearily, "but I wonder if I might get on?"

"Without wishing to be rude, Inspector," countered Bron, "I should like some assurance that my sister will not come to any harm as a result of this unfortunate business."

Applegate gave Bron his very finest professional smile, the effect of which was completely lost on Bron. "Sir, I can give you that assurance. In spite of what was said at the scene, there is no reason to believe that your father's death was anything other than a tragic accident. Until the results of the postmortem are available, I will continue to treat this as an accident."

"Thank you, Inspector," answered Bron, before leaving the room without pausing to close the door behind him. Applegate got up and moved towards the door, watching until he was sure Bron had left the police station, and then turned on Gabriel so aggressively that Gabriel crossed his hands in front of his face to shield himself.

"You blithering idiot, he might have done it!" growled Applegate. "Didn't it occur to you that if your own ridiculous theory is true, then we have no way of knowing who killed Victor Gladstone?"

"I thought you didn't really think anyone killed him," said Gabriel, lowering his hands. "Frankly, you didn't seem to think very much of my theory at all."

"This may come as a surprise to you, Father, but I like to keep an open mind, and I was as unwilling to dismiss this as an unfortunate accident as you were. I'll thank you not to go around blabbing to suspects."

"You don't honestly think that a man like Bron would be capable of murder?"

Applegate snatched a file from his tray and threw it open, giving every possible signal that he wished Gabriel to leave. "In my opinion, if there is no obvious suspect, then everyone's a suspect, including terribly nice gentlemen who have just bent the knee to Rome." Gabriel winced. "No need to pretend you don't have an ulterior motive; I've heard that the charming Auberon Gladstone has been dragged kicking and screaming into your church. It counts for nothing."

"I would never be foolish enough to pretend that no Catholic ever commits a crime," said Gabriel quietly.

"Except, of course, if he *had* committed a murder and confessed to you, you wouldn't tell me, would you?"

"Couldn't, no."

Applegate gave Gabriel the benefit of his favourite smirk. "Let's hope he doesn't confess to you and then frame you for the crime—you wouldn't be able to defend yourself, would you?"

Gabriel smiled. "It's an old conundrum, Inspector. It would depend upon whether it were a bona fide confession, of course. A lot of people forget that; but if it were, and the only way to save my life was to break the seal, then yes, I would have to surrender my neck to the hangman. But if it were a genuine confession, the penitent would be unlikely to allow me to hang."

Gabriel waited for Applegate to respond, but he had lost interest in the conversation and was looking intently at his file, apparently too rivetted to wish him good day. Gabriel bowed to Applegate's lowered head and left the room. He nodded to Stevens as he left the station and ventured out into the chill of the street, almost colliding with the waiting Bron.

"Why didn't you wait at the station?" enquired Gabriel. "You must be freezing, standing on this corner. It's a wind tunnel."

Bron began to walk in the direction of the High Street and clearly expected Gabriel to follow him, which he did without thinking about it. "Mind if we have a few words?" he asked, glancing discreetly over his shoulder, but Gabriel suspected that this was for effect. "I'd suggest we return to Kingsway, but I'm not sure my humble abode is quite suitable for visitors at the moment. And it's some way off. Might I treat you to afternoon tea?"

Gabriel had a weakness for tea and cake, which he tried hard to conceal. "If it's private enough for conversation, I'm happy enough to go to Rosie's."

"I'd sooner go to the pub myself," answered Bron. "I'm in great need of a stiff drink."

"Well," ventured Gabriel, "perhaps we should be grateful for the licensing laws."

They turned right when they reached the post office and walked steadily down the High Street. The main street of the town was built on a hill—of which there were many in this part of the world—and they were both forced to slow down as they walked downhill to avoid slipping. They passed several closed pubs, a greengrocer and the Acropolis picture house before turning down a cobbled side road, which until recently had housed the town's air-raid shelter —mercifully never used.

Rosie's tearooms boasted the only powerful splash of colour on the entire road, with a large, bright-red hand-painted sign decorated with teapots and flowers, and red gingham curtains tied back at the windows. As soon as they opened the door and stepped inside, Gabriel was happily caressed by the aroma of Earl Grey. Bron immediately walked towards the most private corner of the tearooms, tucked away from any passerby who might hear through the steamy windows.

"Thank you for joining me, Father," said Bron, removing

his coat. "I hope you won't think it rude of me to ask why you were at the police station? I'm afraid I'm rather at my wits' end about all this."

Bron hardly had the demeanour of a man at his wits' end, but men at that age very rarely did. He was a man who was ageing well, thanks partly to his tendency to look after himself. He had the look of a man who would never have dreamed of leaving the house without being immaculately turned out, his suit carefully pressed, not a single dark hair out of place. Though he had clearly suffered financially because of his estrangement from his father, he had not lost his sense of style, and his effortless charm made him easy to get on with. "Not rude at all, Bron," said Gabriel. "You've every right to ask. I went to see your sister earlier. I hope you don't mind, but I was rather concerned for her."

"Not at all, it was good of you to go to her," said Bron, signalling for the waitress. "How was she?"

"As expected, I suppose, though of course I've no idea what she's normally like. I mean, when she hasn't just had a shock. She was very confused, talking as though Verity were still a baby. Very contrite about what she had done."

"Except you don't think she did it, do you?"

The two men went quiet as a waitress appeared at the table. The management insisted upon the staff at the tea-rooms dressing like Victorian servants, complete with frilly Mrs Mop hats and lace-trimmed pinnies which were looking a little frayed at the edges. This particular waitress, a girl aged no more than eighteen, clearly did not appreciate the look. "What can I get for you gentlemen?" she asked, giving Bron a manufactured smile as though she instinctively knew he would be paying the bill.

"Tea for two, please, Jenny," said Bron. "What would you recommend to take with it?"

"There's a nice Victoria sponge just out of the oven," suggested Jenny without much enthusiasm, "unless you prefer sandwiches."

"Two slices of Victoria sponge would be splendid," said Bron.

Gabriel waited until Jenny had flounced back to the kitchen before turning back to Bron to express an opinion. "She doesn't seem very happy," he said, solicitously. "When I see a young girl so dreary, I always wonder what she must have lost to feel that way."

Bron chuckled. "You're a dear innocent, Father," he said, sitting back in his chair. "The only tragedy poor little Jennifer has ever suffered was her father returning from the war without a scratch. She had the life of Riley during the years he was away, quite out of control. Gallivanting about the place, going off to dances with soldiers when she should have been tucked up at home with her dollies. But her father came home and started laying down the law. Ruined the fun."

Gabriel refused to let his sympathy be quite so easily dislodged. "I sometimes think it must be almost as hard to be reunited with a loved one after a long absence than to live without him. We never really hear that story."

"Look here, Father," Bron cut in, with the beginnings of impatience. "This is going to sound a little forward of me, but I could hardly avoid hearing what you and the inspector were saying. Is it your belief that my sister didn't do it?"

Gabriel could hear Applegate's rebuke hissing in his ears. He liked Bron, but it was only at moments of crisis such as this that Gabriel was aware of how little he ever really knew anyone. Was Bron capable of killing a man? Surely not. But he would say the same of Emma; he would say the same of anyone. Murder was the most unnatural of acts, but a few men and women crossed that line every day. When he had listened to Dimbleby's radio broadcast of the liberation of Belsen, Gabriel had wept like a child, not just for all the innocent lives lost, but because he could not get his head around the idea that human beings could do such terrible things. Boys who had gone to school once, who had sat around the dinner table with their families and played with their friends in the street, had grown up to shoot women and children in cold blood, had thought nothing of herding their fellow human beings into gas chambers.

"You don't think she did it, do you?" repeated Bron, breaking into Gabriel's thoughts.

"Possibly." Gabriel did not like to think that Bron might be milking him for information but doubted he would be convinced by Gabriel's attempts at making himself obscure.

"The awful thing is, Father, it was hardly a surprise when I heard her confess. She hated him; they hadn't spoken for years."

"That's hardly a motive for murder. What about you, Bron? You hardly got on well with your father, did you?"

Bron gave a wry smile, as though acknowledging the trap into which he had lowered himself. "Fair play, Father. You know perfectly well we did not get on famously. You know he cut me off without a penny when I converted—not that there were many pennies, I suspect, once he'd put the money aside for Verity's studies."

"Before you became a Catholic, Bron, were things better

between you?" asked Gabriel. "If Emma hated him, perhaps you hated him too?"

Bron shook his head. "It doesn't work that way. He was a bully; I'll concede that much. No worse than many men his age, but he treated us like little soldiers. Very severe, very demanding. A lot of rules and barked commands."

"It hardly sounds like a happy start to life for either of you, if I may say so."

Bron shrugged. "Water off a duck's back for me, Father. Like most boys, I learnt to keep out of my father's way. When I failed to make a run for it in time, I didn't take it personally."

"But Emma did."

Bron looked gratefully at the approach of Jenny with a tray. He was not the sort of man Gabriel imagined would take much interest in the people who served him, but Bron went out of his way to thank her, fussing unduly over the precise location of the teacups, milk jug and teapot as though mapping out a battle plan.

"If I might ask, Bron," said Gabriel, hesitantly, "did your father have family money?"

Bron took a sip of his tea. "Not a lot, I'm afraid. Much of the family fortune was lost after the Wall Street crash. The bank collapsed. But then, a good many people lost their money back in '29."

"I see."

"He could weather any storm, Father. It's hard to imagine it now, but he was a very successful writer in his day. You might have read his column in the *Times*. His travel books made it onto best-seller lists."

Gabriel swallowed a mouthful of sponge. There was no

way this cake was fresh from the oven; it tasted about three days old. "I'm afraid I may be betraying my ignorance, but I've never read a travel journal in my life. He must have been abroad a great deal."

"Yes, thank God. There were weeks, sometimes months, of blissful respite. And he always came home with plenty of exotic gifts for us. He was nothing if not generous."

"A good quality." Gabriel had a picture forming in his mind of the world in which Bron and Emma had grown up, the cosseted existence of the miserably privileged. Without even knowing it, perhaps, Bron owed so much about himself to his father's professional success; his confidence, his education, his sophisticated tastes, even his well-rounded accent could be traced back to the money his father had invested in a pampered early life of nannies, governesses, outings to galleries and museums, trips to the theatre, the weekly piano lessons. The only cost to them was a perpetually absent father, either thousands of miles away, hiking through the jungle, or locked away in his study, into whose hallowed realm they only ever entered when they were in trouble. Gabriel thought fondly of his own happy childhood and the mad little moments that always came back to cheer him when darkness came. His happiest memories always involved his siblings, all six of them, always up to no good and almost always left happily to their own devices. Gabriel wondered: Had Bron and Emma ever rolled down steep grassy hills for the sheer pleasure of spiralling out of control? Had they ever made dens in the half loft of an old barn or adopted a lame squirrel they had found cowering in a bush? Had there been any spontaneity, any silliness to speak of?

"He was talking about writing another book," Gabriel

heard Bron say with an unmistakable sneer in his voice. "Talked on and on ad nauseam about the idea. Every time I saw him in a social situation, he would be talking very mysteriously about the whole plan."

"Do you know what the book was about?" asked Gabriel.

"Haven't a clue, I'm afraid. I was never very interested in the old man's work anyway—not that I needed to be. He's always been good at attracting attention. I very much doubt there was a new book. I suppose he might have been planning to write about his war experiences, but he's been all sound and fury recently. Not much to show for it."

Gabriel bent forward and poured Bron another cup of tea. Gin would have been more useful for his purposes, but tea would have to do. "If he was writing the book, what would it be about? Humour me for a moment. What do you think he would be writing about?"

Bron ran his fingers through his hair. "Like I said, it would be his war memoirs," he replied, his tone as dismissive as ever. "I daresay anyone with a halfway interesting story must be scribbling away at the moment. Not that there can be very much appetite for such things. We'd all far sooner forget."

Gabriel finally had the sense he might be getting on to something. "Now, that is interesting. A war memoir. So, he was involved in the war in some way. I mean, he was actively involved in the war?"

"Father, he observed. He was a reporter. I don't imagine he ever put himself in any great danger, and I don't imagine he did any great good, but what I do know is that he was desperate to cash in in some way. We were barely talking by the time he came home, so I don't know the details, but I do know that he managed to blag his way into some reporting job with the army. You know, following the brave boys about. I'm afraid he ended up a little out of his depth."

"I see," said Gabriel, trying hard to hide his growing despondency. There was something exhausting about being on the receiving end of so much bitterness; Gabriel almost felt burnt by it. It might have been why he found it a little easier than he expected to say the words, "Of course, dear Bron, you had a motive. If your sister's hatred of your father was motive enough, the same accusation could be placed at your door."

Bron took the accusation without flinching. "I'm afraid you're not comparing like with like, Father. We both had cause to hate him. When a father's only role in a child's life is to punish him when he misbehaves or to hand him little trinkets when he chooses, he's simply not worth loving. But Father didn't want our love—he wanted obedience, and that was what he got. We did as we were told. The difference between poor Emma and me is that I never expected him to be any different. She wanted his attention, she wanted his affection and she could never forgive him for denying it to her. That was why she ended up cowering over a dead body and I did not."

But you have never forgiven him either, Bron, thought Gabriel, as he got up to leave and shook his friend's hand. *You have simply fooled yourself into believing that there was nothing really to forgive.*

7

Gabriel did not sleep desperately well that night. There were so many thoughts crashing around his head after he put the light out that, after he had got up two or three times to stoke the fire, he gave up on sleeping at all and pulled on his dressing gown and slippers, thinking he might feel a little better if he made himself a milky drink.

The cold kitchen only woke him up even more, and after Gabriel had made himself a mug of Ovaltine, he took out Fr Foley's chess set and began to set out the pieces in the hope that it might settle his mind. It was a rather silly exercise in a way, but almost as soon as he had started taking the white pieces out of the box, Gabriel began assembling them as though they were members of the Martin family's ill-fated dinner party. Florence Martin was the queen, of course, which made Horace the king even though he struck Gabriel as one of those insignificant men who slip invisibly through life, preoccupied with their dogs and their horses, much less with their families. The sort of men who never bothered the rest of the world enough to warrant attention.

Then there was Victor's family, Bron and Verity, with Emma hovering at the sidelines. Gabriel made Bron a bishop, which was perhaps a little irreverent; then in the absence of more imaginative pieces, Verity and Emma became rooks. It almost suited them, two women moving in predictable directions, poor Emma with an old hatred she could not stop nurturing, Verity with her obsession with music.

Gabriel was not entirely sure where Paul was supposed to fit into all of this; was he a friend like Horace and Florence? Family perhaps, since Verity desperately wanted him to be, and Victor had behaved not unlike a father-in-law to him when Gabriel had observed them at the party. Gabriel placed a knight next to one of the rooks, laughing to himself that Paul would no doubt like to think of himself as a knight, though without having to deal with all the rules and regulations, the pomp and circumstance, the old-fashioned ideals of chivalry and honour. For that matter, Gabriel could hardly imagine Paul bending his knee before the king or the squire. It was a bad choice, but Gabriel kept it there anyway for ironic effect.

He placed the black king facing downwards in defeat across the middle of the board and began putting the other pieces around him, more or less where Gabriel remembered them at the crime scene: Emma right next to him, Verity a little further off. The flat chessboard did not do justice to the different levels, so Gabriel took a volume of the *Encyclopaedia Britannica* from the bookcase and placed it across the end of the board, placing Bron, Paul, Florence and Horace where he thought they might have been on the upper level. He needed a piece for himself, since he too had been at the scene, even if he could hardly call himself a suspect. There was still a bishop going free and another knight, which presented him with a tricky conundrum. He was sure it would be a sin against humility to make himself a bishop, but he was forbidden to bear arms as well, so a knight was not suitable either.

Gabriel's little game was doing wonders for his sleepiness; he felt himself relaxing as he took the other knight and placed it where he thought he had been standing when Verity spotted her mother down in the ravine. There were weapons in defence of the truth that did not risk the shedding of blood, he told himself. Gabriel was sure he could seek out the truth somehow or other, in the absence of a sword and with Fr Foley's ridiculous old bike as his trusty steed. He needed to speak to Paul; he needed to speak to Florence.

Gabriel wondered as he nodded off in his chair whether it would be wrong to give Molly another task to perform, since those two green threads had shed no light on the situation, other than that they were obviously important. The threads had to have come from somewhere, from someone's clothing. If the clothing could not be found, it had been hidden . . . or perhaps the threads had not come from a piece of clothing at all . . . a blanket maybe, some other object made of cloth . . . Somewhere in the distance, Gabriel heard the clock chiming midnight, but he was too weary to get up and climb the stairs to bed.

"Who were you playing chess with in the middle of the night?" demanded Fr Foley, when he came downstairs early next morning. "Caesar's ghost? Looks like a massacre."

Gabriel was sitting up abruptly in his chair, his heart racing with the shock of waking up in entirely the wrong place. He was not sure how long he had been asleep, but he must have been very deeply asleep for some hours, as his joints felt stiff and sore and the muscles in his neck crunched as he attempted to move his head. On the table in front of him was the chessboard as he had left it, quite literally like the scene of a massacre, with a cluster of white pieces crowded around the horizontal black king. "Maybe they all did it," mused Gabriel, remembering himself. "What time is it?"

"Half past six," said Fr Foley. "I'm off to say Mass."

Gabriel nodded, wondering whether he could risk going back to bed for an hour. He quickly thought the better of it as he heaved himself up the stairs, his knees complaining at every step. By the time he had washed, shaved and dressed, the day would have begun in earnest as it was, without him going back to sleep.

The choice turned out to have been a fortunate one. Gabriel had only just finished getting dressed when there was a knock on the door. Hardly even a knock. The caller rapped on the door repeatedly with the urgency of a man trying to break down the door of a burning building, causing Gabriel to dash downstairs as quickly as he could.

Not a man, after all. Standing in the doorway in an elegant crimson hat and coat stood an extremely harried-looking Florence Martin. "I'm awfully sorry to trouble you so early, Father," she began before he could say good morning, "but I wonder if you might return to the house with me? Something absolutely frightful's happened."

Gabriel suspected he was too sleepy to process the information, but he could think of no polite answer other than to stall for time. "Why don't you come in out of the cold, Mrs Martin?" he suggested, standing aside to let her in. She came in gratefully and began unbuttoning her coat, which gave Gabriel hope that he might have time to find out what was going on before being herded back into Horace's Hatemobile. He was about to assist her in hanging up her coat when he remembered the chess pieces mapping out the murder scene in the sitting room, and he left Florence to deal with her own coat, rushing over to the table to hide his efforts.

"Is everything all right?" called Florence to Gabriel's retreating back. "I'm not interrupting something important, am I? It's just that—"

Gabriel swept his hand across the board, scattering the pieces all over the floor, which would not have mattered if one of the knights had not struck the grate on the way down and lost his noble head. Gabriel picked up the book that had played the part of the upper level of the land and paused awkwardly as Florence stepped into the room. "I promised Fr Foley to clear away the chess set. He can't stand mess," said Gabriel, as naturally as possible. "He'd hate a visitor to come in and find the place in disarray."

"Oh, don't worry about that," said Florence, perching on the edge of an available chair. She watched as Gabriel crouched down and picked up the scattered chess pieces, mulling over the possibility of putting the broken knight back without mentioning anything, in the hope that Fr Foley would fail to notice. "There's been the most awful uproar at home, Father."

"Really?" Gabriel put the chess set to one side and sat opposite Florence. The sight of her seated uncomfortably in his humble sitting room was almost comical. Even in a frantic state, Florence had not deigned to leave her house in anything other than an immaculate state of dress. She wore a mustard-coloured frock which would have looked unsightly on any other woman but which brought out her strong features; her hair was carefully styled, and she had not neglected to put on a string of pearls to complete the effect of barely restrained elegance. "Whatever is the matter, Mrs Martin?"

"The most dreadful thing's happened," gabbled Florence. "I do wish you hadn't left; I'm quite at my wits' end. That awful inspector turned up at the house unannounced late last night. Would you believe it? We were halfway through dinner, and there he was. Apple something."

"Inspector Applegate."

"The very man. It was appalling. It had taken me that long to settle poor Verity after the morning's events, and Bron had returned in a very dark mood. The last thing we needed was this wretched man turning up, declaring that he was going to investigate the murder. *Murder*, Father!"

Gabriel could just imagine Applegate bursting into a tense domestic situation, demonstrating his usual impeccable sense of timing. "Did he definitely say that it was a murder enquiry?"

Florence nodded her head vigorously. "He said there was no doubt in his mind about it. I can't remember all the reasons he gave, something about a bash on the head—I daresay he did bash his head, falling such a long way—I say, Father, are you all right?"

Gabriel squeezed his hand behind his back. "Do carry on," he said, crushing his fingers into a fist. He knew there was worse to come. "He's sure it's murder then."

"Yes, but the worse part of it was that he said he is keeping an open mind as to the killer."

Gabriel put on his most innocent expression. "I shouldn't

read too much into that if I were you, Mrs Martin; he's only doing his job. I'm sure he will be as discreet as possible—"

Florence stood up. "Discreet! There have been policemen crawling about the estate all day as it is! We already know it was Emma! She said as much herself, the poor darling!"

Gabriel got up, unwilling to sit in front of a lady, but he thought it must look as though they were facing one another in a boxing ring. He gestured for her to sit down again, but she ignored him. "Please don't trouble yourself, Mrs Martin. If you would like me to come round later today . . ." He knew he had to avoid raising her suspicions that he had been the one to alert Applegate to Emma's probable innocence, but casuistry had never been a great talent of his.

"Splendid! I hoped you'd agree. I have the car waiting outside."

Florence did not wait for Gabriel's answer, which was strangled somewhere at the back of his throat. She made for the vestibule and began putting on her coat. "Did you mean me to come now?" he asked, his voice quavering. "I shall have to ask Fr Foley . . ."

"We shan't be long," answered Florence breezily, suddenly looking a great deal more relaxed. Gabriel was the one looking harried. "I'm sure you'll have this little puzzle sewn up in a jiffy."

Gabriel snatched his coat and hat from the stand and followed Florence lamely outside. "I'm not entirely sure . . ."

"Excellent, make yourself comfortable."

"You . . . you drive?" he faltered, noting his ludicrous reflection in the shiny black bodywork of the Martin family's motor.

"Ambulances don't drive themselves, Father," Florence replied, a little sharply, seating herself behind the wheel. "I know you're frightfully clever at solving things, Father, and I'd sooner you worked it out than PC Appleface or whoever he is. All you need to do is to prove to him that it was an accident."

Gabriel sat back in his seat, resisting the urge to cross himself, which he was sure Florence would have taken as a sign of distrust. He quickly realised that he had been very wrong to assume the woman couldn't drive. Gabriel had no idea what sort of training ambulance drivers had been given during the war, though he doubted they had been taught such niceties as the three-point turn. Nevertheless, Florence turned out to be an excellent driver, navigating the roads as graciously as she manoeuvred her way around awkward social situations.

Unlike Florence, Gabriel was never going to be the sort of person who navigated social situations with any great skill, and he hesitated to answer. From the safety of a car and without the chauffeur exuding annoyance of the world, the journey to the Martin estate seemed so much shorter than Gabriel remembered. The dank, slippery roads where he had come a cropper on his bike vanished behind them in minutes. "Mrs Martin, you must understand, I can make you no promise about what I will find if I investigate this matter. All I can promise is that I will try to get to the truth. At the moment, I have no idea what happened early yesterday morning."

Florence was silent as she drove slowly between the two leering griffins, and Gabriel could have been forgiven for thinking she might be sulking, but whatever her thoughts were on the matter, she quickly recovered. "I quite under-stand, Father," she said, with good grace. "One should not be afraid of the truth, I'm sure."

"Absolutely."

All very well to say that, thought Gabriel, as the car glided to a halt and he let himself out. *But everyone fears the truth a little, and no one more so than a person with a guilty conscience.* "Mrs Martin," he said, "I wonder if we could go back to the place where it happened. I should like to refresh my memory about the exact location of the body, if I may?"

"Of course," said Florence. "I'll take you directly." Her mood had brightened almost immediately at Gabriel's deter-mination to get down to work, and she led him round the back of the house. "It's quicker this way," she said, when Gabriel hesitated. He had not come this way last time. "One can cut across the croquet lawn; there is a gap between the hedges."

It certainly was a shortcut. From the side of the house, they reached the ravine in only five minutes, but once they were there they seemed very far away from the house. It was a trick of the dense woodland and the ignorance of the visitor. Without knowing about the shortcut, it would take two or three times as long to reach this place from the front door of the house, weaving through those little paths, in and out of trees. "How many people know about that shortcut?" asked Gabriel.

"Oh, virtually everyone," answered Florence, as though the question were completely irrelevant. "Anyone who's ever visited the estate or walked the grounds would have noticed it. One can even see it from the rooms on the upper floor that face this way."

"Would it be possible to see this far from those upper windows?"

"No, no, quite impossible, I suspect. The trees will get in the way, even in winter. One might see the little path between the hedges but nothing more. I'm afraid if you were hoping for an eyewitness, you'd be lucky. There were more than trees to worry about yesterday. One could barely see six inches ahead."

"Indeed," conceded Gabriel. They were standing almost exactly where Gabriel had been standing when Verity had noticed something amiss and hurried off in search of a way down. "Everything about this makes me want to think it was an accident," he said aloud. "It would be the easiest thing in the world for the man to lose his footing and fall. He did not know the area well; he was walking in blank fog; perhaps he was angry. When a man is in a blazing temper, he seldom looks where he is going."

"He might well have been in a temper," Florence confirmed, "not that I saw him before he left, of course. But the man was always in a rage about something. I rather assumed that was why he had gone out for a walk in the first place, to cool his heels before breakfast."

Gabriel made his way down the steep path, which felt a good deal less threatening now that it was becoming familiar. He moved gingerly to the place where they had found the body; it was easy enough to spot, as there were still marks on the ground from where he had fallen, the slightest unsettled soil and dead leaves. Because the ground was so much lower than the rest of the land, it was quite sheltered from the elements, and little had changed in twenty-four hours.

"You really should trust your instincts, Father," said Florence. "That was what we were taught when we joined up. In a desperate situation, with the dead and dying everywhere, one simply has to trust one's instincts. The silly man took a nasty tumble, broke his neck. Poor Emma was wandering around in fog and made herself believe she'd killed him. Simple as that."

"But why would even a disturbed woman believe she had committed a murder she had not committed? Why would anyone believe that about himself simply by seeing the body?" Doubts, when they assailed Gabriel, maddened him like a hair shirt, chafing him every time he moved. "It's such an outrageous thing to think!"

Florence looked at Gabriel in what was almost sadness. "I'm not sure you've ever hated anyone before, have you?" she asked, kindly. "Emma convinced herself that she had killed her father because she wished she had. I'm sure of it. I feel as though I'm speaking ill of the dead by saying it about her, even though she's not dead. I know she can't defend herself, but I'm afraid she was very good at hating."

Gabriel scrutinised Florence as closely as he could without looking as though he were gawping at her. She was an incredibly difficult person to read. He knew Florence was hiding something; she was making quite a mess of trying to pretend otherwise. It was clearly in her best interests for him to be convinced that the death was an accident or Emma's fault, but he was loath to think her a malicious gossip. "It's best to have an honest view of those involved in all this, Mrs Martin. You've known Emma a long time, haven't you?"

"We were at school together, Father; that was where we first met," said Florence fondly. "She hated that too, ran away at least three times before the headmistress lost patience and sent her packing. She ended up having to be educated at home with a governess. Even when we were at school, she was always the girl who bore a grudge. Never forgot anything, any slight, any punishment. She would always find some way to settle the score. Of course, that made her very unpopular."

Gabriel knelt down to look more closely at the place where Victor had fallen, shaking off the suspicion that Florence was waiting for him to take out a magnifying glass. It was certainly true that there was no rocky outcrop either on the ground or anywhere along the steep earth walls that could have caused Victor's head injury, but there was little here he had not seen on the previous day. He heaved himself to his feet with some difficulty, distracted by a sudden glimmer of light a little further along.

Gabriel took two steps towards the thread of light on the ground before bending down again and placing his hand on it. Not light, of course—a thick silver thread, the sort of chain a woman would wear around her neck. He held it between two fingers and pulled, watching as the chain lengthened and finally a pendant shaped like a fleur-de-lis emerged from under a thin layer of soil.

"I say, Father, how clever of you!" chirped Florence. "He must have snatched it from around the killer's neck."

All this tells me, thought Gabriel, turning over the pendant in his hand—the symbol was identical both sides—*is that someone is very, very keen to see an innocent person pay for this*. He had no further time for reflection. An angry voice broke into his thoughts from above, like the sound of an avenging angel calling him to account. "What are you doing down there!" shouted Angel Applegate. Gabriel glanced upwards and saw Applegate glaring down at him, flanked by two constables. "What are you doing crawling all over the crime scene?"

Gabriel held up the pendant by way of atonement. "Finding the evidence you've missed, apparently," he answered, sounding terser than he had intended. "Shall I bring this up to you, or are you coming down?"

He watched as Inspector Applegate and his henchmen walked over to the path and shinnied their way down. "Come away from there, please, Father," commanded Applegate, "well away."

Gabriel raised his hands in mock surrender and backed away from Victor's resting place, closely followed by Florence. "Spare the woman; it was my idea to come down here," said Gabriel. "I'll come quietly."

Applegate gave Gabriel a withering look. "It's not funny, Father. I could have you arrested for tampering with evidence." He turned to Florence. "Mrs Martin, might I suggest that you return to the house? Consider this area out of bounds for the present."

Florence removed herself from the situation more compliantly than Gabriel had expected, leaving him to face Applegate alone. Applegate waited until he was sure Florence was out of earshot before opening his mouth to speak, but Gabriel virtually threw the pendant at him in his haste to hand it over. "It's not evidence, Inspector," said Gabriel, "and you can't possibly have missed it. How on earth would your men have missed something so obvious when they were going over the area yesterday?"

Applegate examined the pendant. "Where did you find this?"

"Very close to where Victor's body was found. It was

obviously planted there afterwards, perhaps quite soon afterwards. But it can't have been there when Victor's body was first discovered, or it would have been found. Someone is absolutely determined to frame Emma."

Applegate nodded in what was quite possibly his first moment of agreement with Gabriel about anything. "If this pendant really does belong to Emma, then it would certainly seem so. Is there anyone who could identify it?"

"Verity or Bron would probably recognise it if it's hers," suggested Gabriel. "Perhaps not Florence Martin."

Applegate raised an eyebrow. "They were friends, weren't they?"

"They know one another well, if that's what you mean," said Gabriel, "but Mrs Martin is a little too keen to implicate her for my liking. In my opinion anyway."

The two men made their way out of the ravine single file, not speaking again until they were on level ground. "I don't suppose we have a murder weapon yet?" asked Gabriel cautiously. "If we're looking at murder."

"No murder weapon and no murderer—for now," said Applegate. "And if his crazy daughter didn't do it, not many leads either. Though the son is an obvious suspect."

"I do hope you're wrong about that, Inspector," said Gabriel, "I do hope so."

"You can hope as much as you like," Applegate retorted. "That won't make him innocent."

"Inspector, Victor Gladstone cut off his son without a penny when he became a Catholic. Bron's not even convinced there was much money."

"Well, we shall see about that. I've a man dealing with the family solicitor as we speak. In my job, the first thing you do is follow the money."

Gabriel could hear the sound of the piano before they had crossed the threshold of the house. He recognised it as the first movement of a Mozart piano concerto being belted out slightly too loud and too fast, the lyrical passages lost in the midst of Verity's grief. "The Martins must have let her practice on the grand piano," he remarked as Applegate pushed open the front door. "I suppose it doesn't matter quite so much now that there are fewer people to disturb."

Florence must have been looking out for them through the window, because she appeared before them within seconds of their arrival through the door, and she could not possibly have heard them over the sound of the piano. "Mrs Martin, I'm afraid I'm going to have to disturb Verity for a moment," said Applegate. "I need to ask a question on a rather important matter."

"Of course. It's the pendant, isn't it?" said Florence, failing to get the hint not to talk about it. "Why don't you come through? I thought it best to let her play in the drawing room where I can keep an eye on her."

Verity certainly needed someone to look after her, thought Gabriel when he saw her at the piano. It was hard to imagine she was the same young woman who had sat so elegantly at the same instrument such a short time before. The shock of the events taking place all around her was clearly taking its toll. Her hair was uncombed, giving her a waiflike, slightly wild look, and her eyes were red and swollen from hours of crying. She was either ignoring Gabriel and the inspector deliberately or was too engrossed in her practice to notice, but she made no acknowledgement of their appearance in the room. Applegate looked at Gabriel for guidance, and Gabriel walked over to where Verity was sitting, placing a hand on her arm. She jumped out of her skin, spinning round to look at him as though she half expected to have to fight him off.

"For pity's sake!" she cried, looking from Gabriel to Applegate in panicked confusion. "You frightened me half to death creeping up on me like that! I thought you were the . . ." She sat back down on the piano stool with her back to the piano, her eyes hot and glistening. "I'm so sorry, Father, I suppose I didn't hear you come in. My nerves are shot to pieces."

"No need to apologise," said Gabriel, pulling up a chair so that he could sit near her. "I shouldn't have crept up on you like that. I'm sure you'd rather not talk about this at the moment, but the inspector needs to ask you a quick question. Then we can leave you in peace."

Verity looked nervously at Inspector Applegate. Gabriel, his differences with Applegate aside, had never thought there was anything particularly intimidating about the inspector's appearance. He was a heavily built man with that steely look of determination one might expect in a man who has fought long and hard to reach the top of his profession, but then Gabriel could not remember how it felt to have dealings with the police for the first time. He was sure he had been overwhelmed by the experience. "Do you recognise this?" asked Applegate, holding the pendant out for Verity to inspect.

Verity nodded, gulping with the effort of trying to answer. "It's my mother's. Why have you got it? Why have you taken it from her?"

"Is it precious then?"

"Only to her," said Verity, her voice quavering with the effort. "She always wears it. She'll be distraught when she can't find it. Why did you take it from her?"

"We didn't take it from her, miss," Applegate assured her, though his tone was relentlessly cold. "It was found near Victor Gladstone's body. Looks as though he grabbed it when he was attacked."

Verity was on her feet again, tears starting to fall down her cheeks. "It was an accident!" she said pleadingly, turning to Gabriel as though seeking out an ally. "Uncle Bron says you don't think she did it."

"Why don't you sit a little more comfortably?" Gabriel suggested, helping her into the high-backed chair he had recently occupied, so that she could lean back. "That's better. Why don't you just catch your breath."

"I can't understand how she could do such a thing!" sobbed Verity. "She was always talking about it, but I never thought she'd do it."

Gabriel noticed Applegate looking up sharply at Verity. "What you mean she talked about it?" asked Gabriel. "People don't usually talk about killing."

"You know what I mean, Father. She'd say, 'I could kill him.' 'If he ever comes anywhere near me, I'll kill him.' People say silly things like that all the time; they don't actually do anything about it."

"Quite," said Gabriel, looking back at Applegate. "Do you have all the information you need for now, Inspector?" he asked.

Applegate nodded. "For the present." He turned to Verity, who was already gravitating back towards the piano. "Young lady, I think it would be better if you stayed here with your friends for the time being. I hope to have this matter cleared up as quickly as possible."

Verity made a brave attempt at a smile. "Flor—Mrs Martin has asked me to stay on. I think Uncle Bron prefers it this

way. Not sure he really wants me getting under his feet."
She seemed to realise how it sounded, because she continued quickly, "Not that he makes me feel unwelcome, you understand. He's been very kind; he's always been very kind. It's just everything's so awful at the moment. He doesn't really know what to say . . ."

Gabriel patted her arm. "Don't worry about anything, Verity. Whatever the truth of the matter, it will come out eventually."

"They won't lock her up, will they?" she asked, appealing to him as though Gabriel had the power to do something about it. All Gabriel could do was smile in a poor attempt at reassurance, when all he could think of was that he needed to leave.

Verity was already back at work by the time Gabriel had left the room, slipping her way uncertainly through the mournful cadences of some slow movement or other. Florence was waiting for him outside, and he wondered whether she had been listening in on their conversation. "I'm not entirely sure I should be encouraging this," she said, peering through a crack in the door at Verity, lost in the world of eighteenth-century Vienna. "I'm not sure it's healthy. She was always like this, even as a child. Never wanted to go out and play with the others, hated to go to school. She only ever seemed happy when she was sitting at the piano."

Gabriel moved away from the door, hoping Florence would follow him, which she did, albeit a little reluctantly. "Well, if she truly wishes to be a concert pianist, she will have to be rather obsessed with the whole thing. Eight hours a day practice and all that. I can't imagine that one could have such a life if one were not completely absorbed in the subject. Who knows, we might be in the presence of greatness."

Florence smiled. "Well, Verity has promised to remember me in her memoirs. Let it be known, it all started here." She glanced back in the direction of Verity's playing. "You might have to prepare her, Father. They won't let her mother stay in the nursing home if they know she killed Victor. And Verity seeing her mother locked up in an asylum will be like losing her a second time."

Someone wants Emma locked up, thought Gabriel glumly, and he could feel a rare stirring of anger within him. *Someone is absolutely determined to have that poor, scared, confused woman locked away in an asylum forever to cover up his own crime.* Gabriel knew better than to share with Florence that the pendant proved precisely the opposite of what had been intended. He knew perfectly well it had not been at the scene of the murder when they had found Victor's body, since he had been one of the first people there after Emma and Verity. And the killer had been too lazy or too stupid to undo the clasp of the chain before dumping it on the ground to make it look as though Victor really had wrenched the pendant from around Emma's neck as he died. There was no way it had been pulled off by a desperate man in his death throes.

8

Gabriel stood at the side of the narrow lane, watching for his promised visitor. As he was being helped on with his coat after speaking to Florence, Gabriel had heard the unmistakable crackle of paper inside his pocket and known on an old instinct not to investigate until he was out of sight of the house. The note, which he suspected Molly had been prevailed upon to put there while Gabriel had been with Verity and the inspector, contained the words, scribbled untidily in pencil: MEET ME IN THE LANE BEHIND THE FOLLY AS SOON AS YOU CAN.

The subterfuge felt childishly melodramatic, but Gabriel had found a reason to leave the house, claiming that he needed to carry out some more investigations elsewhere. He stood now, inspecting the folly from the safety of the sheltered lane. It had been by no means a fib to say that he was investigating; he did need to meet this person, as he could think of no other reason he would be summoned in such a surreptitious way if it were not connected with Victor's murder. He was relieved to have a reason to leave the house all the same.

There was something stifling about it, and it was not just the fraudulent feel of the place he had described to Fr Foley before. In every room, he felt the nagging sense that he was in the presence of evil, and he could not put his finger on what troubled him so much. It was not even the thought that there was a murderer on the loose, as Victor's killer might not be anywhere near the estate by now. Gabriel breathed deeply, taking in the aromas of winter, the bitter-sweet odour of moist soil mingled with the smell of rotting leaves and dank vegetation. The distant folly stood before him like a monument to Victorian pomposity and nostalgia. It was supposed to look like a ruined castle, replete with crumbling stone window frames and tumbled pillars that had never stood straight, a pediment chiselled into brokenness by a skilled sculptor, the remains of a spiral staircase that had only ever had ten broken steps and had always led nowhere. He wondered whether the gardener had deliberately cultivated the weeds twisted around the higgledy-piggledy foundations.

Gabriel heard the crunch of twigs snapping underfoot and turned to see Paul walking towards him, stopping just before he reached the entrance to the folly. He gestured to Gabriel to follow him down the lane. "What on earth are you doing?" hissed Gabriel, when Paul put a finger to his lips to warn Gabriel not to speak too loudly. "Why the cloak-and-dagger behaviour? You might just as easily have found me at the presbytery, and we could have had a private conversation over a cup of tea!"

"I knew you were back at the house. I've been watching the comings and goings," Paul explained. "I saw you being brought in earlier."

"Mr Ashley, the police have determined that Victor's death was indeed murder. Skulking about the estate might give the police the wrong impression."

"Oh, please call me Paul. I can't stand titles," answered Paul, ignoring the warning. "May I call you Gabriel?"

"No, you may not," Gabriel responded, falling into step beside Paul. "I'm sure you'll think me dreadfully bourgeois, but titles have a purpose. In my case, perhaps it is better that you remember I'm a priest."

"If you're expecting me to kiss your hands, you can forget about it," said Paul, quickening his pace. "I don't bow down before anyone."

"I'm not asking you to bow down before me; in fact, I would forbid you to do so. That's really not the point. Anyway, what is it you want?"

"Back to business, that's just the way it should be," said Paul. "Would you mind if we walked to my house? It's not as far as the town, just on the outskirts of Palbury. There's something I need you to see."

"Very well. Might you be able to tell me a little more?"

Paul slowed down and looked round at Gabriel. "You don't think Emma did it, do you?" Paul waited for a response, but Gabriel looked down at his feet, saying nothing. "It's all right, I don't need you to trust me. At least not enough to share information with me. Let me put you out of your misery. You don't think Emma did it; in fact, you are pretty sure she didn't do it, and you are hellbent on proving she didn't. If it helps, I think you might be on to something."

"Oh?" Gabriel looked up cautiously at Paul, aware that the young man was observing him closely in case he betrayed something of use to him. "What makes you say that?"

"Because I don't believe Victor's death has anything to do with his family. I don't think it's got anything to do with the sort of father Victor was. I've no doubt he was a harsh old patriarch in his own home. Let's face it, stern fathers are ten a penny, and most of them don't get bumped off for their pains. Victor was killed because he is a writer. Was."

"I did hear that he was writing the book, or talking about writing one," said Gabriel. "Something about the war. That's all I know."

The path was blocked by a vast muddy puddle, and Gabriel followed Paul on tiptoe around the edge, which was soft and hazardously slippery. The bridleway they were walking along looked as though it had been churned up by many horses' hooves, and they were both forced to slow down as they crossed the uneven ground. In the distance, Gabriel could see a row of cottages which marked out the very edge of Paul's village. "*We* were writing a book," Paul corrected him. "As soon as I found out he was dead, I knew why. Did I mention to you that Victor had gone off with the army during the war as a reporter?"

"Yes, I understood that Victor was thinking of writing his memoirs or something of that nature. I daresay there must be some interest in all that now."

"Not nearly as much interest as there ought to be," said Paul tersely. "Everyone is desperate to get on with their petty little lives and forget any of it ever happened. Shameful when Europe's still in ruins. Victor's story was hardly unique, but it needed to be told."

"I hope this doesn't sound rude," said Gabriel, stifling the nasty feeling that it almost certainly would, "but why were you writing his book with him? Surely he would have preferred to write his book alone? He doesn't strike me as the sort of person who worked with others very easily."

The rough, waterlogged path gave way to a smooth stone road which wound its way past a stretch of uninviting marshland, the boggy, unstable ground pierced through by hardy plants and shrubs. The whole place felt desolate and primitive, like a glimpse into a primaeval world where dinosaurs fought one another to survive. It was hard to imagine that families lived in their little homes such a short distance away, sipping tea and playing cards and going about their mundane daily business.

"Victor witnessed a massacre, Father," said Paul, taking on the subdued tone of an undertaker. "He was fortunate not to be caught up in it himself; the Nazis would certainly have shot him if they had found him. He had wandered off on his own when he saw it. He was very badly affected. I know he must have seemed extremely rude and rather aggressive to you, but he was very shaken by the whole experience. Struggled to sleep and the like."

Gabriel paused for breath. "Was that why he used to go out walking early in the morning? Insomnia?"

"Yes, I suppose so. Though I believe he was always given to rising early. Anyway, he heard about my interest in tracking down Nazis and thought I might be able to help. He was struggling to write the book himself. Typical, really— writer given the perfect story, and he's in too much of a blue funk to do anything about it."

Paul stopped at an extremely rusty garden gate wedged between two tumbledown walls which were slowly being destroyed by ivy. Gabriel had hardly expected Paul to be house-proud or the sort of young man whose garden is his little paradise, but the overgrown garden made the cottage look barely habitable. He waited for Paul to let him pass, but

Paul pushed open the gate and let himself through, leaving Gabriel to follow him, striding up the path to the front door without once looking back.

Gabriel looked up at the tiny cottage with its dirty cream walls in desperate need of whitewashing and its moss-tainted roof. His eyes were drawn immediately in the direction to which Paul was heading in such a hurry. The glass panel in the front door had been broken, and the door had been left partially open. "Oh God, I knew it," said Paul, so calmly that Gabriel wondered if the man was too shocked to take it in. "I knew this would happen."

"Don't go in, Paul," Gabriel warned, touching Paul's arm, but Paul ignored him and went directly to the door, throwing it open. "If you've been burgled, you should go straight to the police. What if there's still someone in there?"

"Then I can have the pleasure of beating him to a pulp, can't I?" answered Paul, without looking round. He stormed into the tiny hallway, planting himself at the bottom of the stairs. "Is anyone there?" he called. "I'm here with the police."

The house was deserted. The interior was in an even more shambolic state than the garden, meaning that, from where they were standing, there was little evidence that there had been any intruder at all. The hall was dimly lit thanks to the few windows being smeared with dirt; a threadbare man's jacket hung over the bottom of the banister; the floorboards were replete with old footprints and accumulated grime, since Paul was unlikely to bother getting down on his hands and knees to scrub the floor and would never dream of employing someone to do such a menial task for him. But nothing was broken or unsettled. Paul moved abruptly towards the door to the left and rushed in, letting out a strangled cry as he did so.

Gabriel followed him into the room and froze. The room was Paul's study, a modestly sized sitting room he had converted for the purposes of work, but the room looked more as though it had been the sight of a small earthquake than a place for peaceful study. This was no mere untidiness, however chronic—the whole room had been searched and ransacked quite systematically. None of the furniture had been overturned apart from the bureau, which had been completely emptied of all its drawers—Gabriel counted four large drawers, and six much-smaller drawers intended to tidy away little bits of stationery, paper clips, cartridges. The drawers had not only been wrenched out of the bureau, they had been overturned, the papers tipped out and rifled through. Filing cabinets, of which there were several up against the wall, had been opened and searched through. The drawers, screwed into the bodywork of the cabinets, could not be pulled free like the drawers in the bureau, but every drawer in every cabinet had been left open to varying degrees.

The floor was strewn with torn pages from the bureau, files hastily ripped open, blue ink slowly soaking into the floorboards where a bottle had been upset during the search. Gabriel looked at the opposite wall and flinched at the large picture of Lenin that Paul had hung there. The intruders had clearly not thought much of it either, as it had been slashed repeatedly and daubed with ink.

Paul made straight for the filing cabinet in the far corner, searching through each and every drawer. "I knew they'd do this!" he exclaimed, turning to Gabriel as though for an explanation. "I knew they'd do this. I should have gone straight to the police with my suspicions."

Gabriel could see sweat gathering at Paul's temples, though the room was bitterly cold. "Who are they, Paul?" demanded Gabriel. "Who are they?"

"I don't know," said Paul, his voice breaking with the effort of keeping his composure. "If I could have given the police a name . . ." To Gabriel's surprise, Paul sat down on the floor surrounded by the detritus of his life and clasped his head in his hands, looking every bit like a little boy who has lost his homework. "It's too late, Father; it's all gone."

"What's gone?"

"The notes!" he shouted, so unexpectedly that Gabriel jumped. Panic had become despair, then anger, in less than a minute. "My notes! Victor's notes! All the groundwork for the book. It's *all gone!*"

Gabriel crouched down in front of Paul. "Paul, think about this. Are you sure it's just the notes for the book that have gone? There's a lot of paper about and a lot of empty drawers."

"Just the notes for the book? *Just!*" yelped Paul, a shade quieter than before. "Look for yourself. Whoever did this knew exactly what he was looking for. The drawers in the filing cabinet where I kept all my notes for the book are empty. Just those drawers."

Gabriel stood up and looked about him, trying to decide where to start in terms of searching for anything. It was all right for Paul—he knew where everything belonged—but all Gabriel could see was carnage everywhere. "They must have tipped out the drawers because it was easier and quicker to search that way," he observed. "The files were torn open and discarded if they were of no interest."

"They wouldn't have been able to tip out those drawers in the filing cabinet anyway." Paul struggled to his feet, using a chair to help himself up. "As soon as I knew Victor was dead, I knew it was because of this. It's far too convenient that a man about to expose a war crime to the world should end up dead."

"Why didn't you tell the police straightaway?" asked Gabriel, though it seemed a little late in the day for recriminations.

"Victor didn't want his family to know about it—the massacre, I mean. I don't know whether he was trying to protect them or whether he just didn't want to be pestered with questions. I suppose he was worried about them finding out, particularly Verity. She's been very sheltered."

"It does seem a rather odd reason to kill a man, if I may say so," said Gabriel, tentatively. "There have been so many atrocities brought to public attention. There've been trials. Why would anyone go so far as to murder a witness to stop yet another massacre being talked about?"

"It might not be so odd if the man responsible for the massacre found out Victor had witnessed it, would it?" snapped Paul, as though Gabriel were an irredeemable idiot. "One war crime looks very much like another, I suppose, unless you're the man looking to hang."

Gabriel would have been very quick to dismiss the idea of a war criminal hiding in rural Wiltshire, waiting to eliminate the only man who could condemn him, but Gabriel knew from experience that such situations were not as farfetched as they sounded. "Look, we'd better alert the police to the break-in. You might have to ask the Martins if you can stay with them for a few days while the police do their work."

"I'm damned if I——"

"Paul, this really isn't the time for pride. You can't possibly stay here. Now, why don't you search through everything again and make absolutely sure that it was only the book notes that were taken?"

Paul nodded wearily and began moving through the room, sifting through the papers and files on the floor, then going through his filing cabinets more carefully this time, checking the labels on all the cardboard folders. "All right, there is something else missing here," he said, staring down at an empty folder. "It must have been taken in error. It was another file Victor asked me to look after. Whoever ransacked this room must have noticed that the file was in the same handwriting or something. It has nothing to do with the book. Horace Martin's going to have a fit of apoplexy."

"What was the file about?"

"Some other investigation of Victor's," Paul explained, "not that he got very far with it. He thought he had something on Horace Martin. He was suspicious about where the Martins were getting their money, but I suppose he couldn't get a juicy-enough story and let it go. He hadn't said anything about it for months." Paul lifted the empty casing of the folder out of the filing cabinet; there was a hole torn out of the end, causing Paul to look back into the drawer for the cause. He pulled out a piece of metal that looked from where Gabriel was standing like a small icon. "Now that is curious," remarked Paul, looking at it closely.

134

"Have you seen it before?" asked Gabriel, extending a hand to take it. Paul gave it to him without hesitation.

"No. I can only assume it was in the Martin file, but I never looked in there."

Gabriel looked up at him in surprise. "Why ever not? Weren't you curious?"

Paul shrugged. "Not particularly. All toffs are crooks; I didn't need to look in Victor's little file to find that out. Anyway, Victor admitted he had nothing on Horace Martin." Paul hesitated, looking back into the cabinet. "I did hear a bit of a clang when Victor put that in the cabinet, but I didn't think much of it. The filing cabinet's made of metal; it goes clang from time to time."

"You mean you never handled the file?"

"No, I told you, it was Victor's. He simply wanted somewhere private to place it. He'd already transferred all his notes on the massacre here, and we were using my study to work in. I suppose he just thought it was a safer place to put it . . ." Paul trailed off. "Unless of course it did have something to do with the massacre," he added, without conviction. "He would have told me. I told him where to put it, and he filed it away himself. I'd barely given it a second thought until I noticed it had gone a moment ago."

Gabriel inspected the metal icon. He had never seen anything quite like it before. It looked a little like a religious artefact of some kind, but the only recognisable symbols were five Hebrew letters lovingly engraved down the middle. "Was Victor Gladstone Jewish?" asked Gabriel.

"No, I'm certain he wasn't," Paul replied, thrown by the unexpected question. "He was quite anti-Semitic, I'm afraid, but many men his age were." Paul appeared to ponder the idea for a moment before shaking his head impatiently. "He was an atheist, Father; he would never have kept a religious symbol. It was a point of principle."

"If it wasn't his, why was it in the file?"

"It might not have been in the file; why should it have been? Horace isn't Jewish either." Paul raised his hands as though calming a situation that was not even aggravated yet. "I assumed it had come out of the file because there was a hole in the file, and that thing was in the bottom of the drawer," he explained, with the growing impatience of a man who wishes he had diverted the line of questioning at the start. "Since I've never seen it before, I assumed it must have been in the file, but I'm not sure. It wouldn't have been at all easy for Victor to transport that thing in the file without it falling out; those cardboard folders are meant for paper."

"And you are sure you haven't seen this before?" asked Gabriel.

"Of course I haven't! How many times do I need to tell you that? I don't even know what it is."

Gabriel put the object in question in his pocket. "Would you mind if I took a closer look at it? If this was left by whoever broke into your house, Paul, it will almost certainly tell us something."

"Be my guest," answered Paul, the familiar tone of scepticism creeping through. "I find it difficult to believe it could have been left by accident by someone who was on the thieve. It's not like a broken cufflink or earring, is it?"

"If it was left behind, it was left for you to find," said Gabriel, making for the door. "There has to be some method in this madness. Could you check the rest of the house to make sure that nothing else has been taken?"

Gabriel stayed where he was whilst Paul dashed through the other rooms and up the stairs, a process that did not take long in a house as small as this. He was back only minutes later, slightly out of breath. "Nothing," he confirmed. "You know, I could stay in the house. No other rooms have been touched; I suspected that when the hall was all right. I can board up that broken window until I can call a glazier in."

Gabriel frowned. "I really wouldn't stay in this isolated place alone, Paul. For your own safety. If you've had intruders in once, you can't be sure they won't come back. Even if the police don't want you to leave—"

"This is my home," answered Paul icily. "I'm not being chased out by thugs. Whoever robbed me may well have killed Victor. Somehow or other I'm going to get this book written. I've no idea how with all those notes gone, but I'll write it even if I have to do it from my memories of talking with him. I can't let it die with him."

"Were there any other witnesses?" asked Gabriel. "Anyone else you could talk to?"

"Of course there weren't!" exclaimed Paul. "It was a crime. There were never supposed to be any witnesses! If those Nazi scum had found Victor at the time, they would have shot him on the spot."

Gabriel walked out of the front door with a heavy heart. He felt certain he should not leave Paul on his own, but he knew that Paul would only become short-tempered if Gabriel continued to press the subject. "It's not for me to tell you what to do, old chap," he said, "and I think you must write this book. But please be careful. If it was worth killing for once, it's worth killing for again."

Paul gave Gabriel a thin smile. "Half this town think I'm a dirty little coward," he said calmly, "too chicken to fight. I have a heart condition; I was never called up. And I can prove I'm not a coward."

9

Gabriel was not sure why Bron had been so shy about taking him to his home when they had had their first proper conversation. True, it was the wrong end of town in relation to the Martin estate, but it was the affluent end. Kingsway was one of the oldest residential streets in the town, consisting of a crescent-shaped row of Georgian dwellings overlooking a green space with a small ornamental lake. To anyone with an interest in architecture, it was undeniably a carbon copy of the much larger and richer Royal Crescent in Bath, and as a result, it felt rather incongruous at the edge of a poor market town like this. Gabriel had never had reason to set foot in this hallowed world before. The inhabitants of Kingsway were far too sophisticated to invite a Roman priest to darken their doors, and even Bron, when he had been taking instruction, had always insisted on visiting Gabriel at the presbytery.

That was it, of course, thought Gabriel sadly, as he climbed the five steps to Bron's front door. *He didn't keep me away from his home because he was ashamed of the home; he didn't want his neighbours to see him with a man in funny clothes.* Gabriel was not sure of the kind of welcome to expect under the circumstances, but he gave the doorbell a hearty jangle all the same. He heard a steady patter of footsteps approaching the door before it was opened slowly by a large woman who Gabriel suspected was almost old enough to be his mother. She was plainly dressed, wearing a large, square apron, and though her clothing was not as antiquated and formal as that of the domestic staff the Martins employed, the woman was recognisably a housekeeper. "Good morning, sir," she greeted him politely. "How may I help you?"

Gabriel was about to explain himself when he heard movement behind the guardian to Bron's abode, and Bron himself appeared. "It's all right, Mrs Whitcomb, I'll take care of my visitor."

Mrs Whitcomb nodded politely, throwing Gabriel a suspicious glance as she went about her business, as though she thought Bron had made a terrible mistake in trusting him. "Should I lay out a place for lunch, sir?" she asked Bron from the top of the back stairs.

"Well, yes, I suppose you ought," he answered. "Thank you."

Gabriel felt himself blushing at the faux pas of inadvertently inviting himself to lunch. He had lost track of the time as usual. "I don't want to impose," he began, uncertain as to whether it was even polite to take his coat off. He did not want to seem as though he were making himself too comfortable. "I shan't be a moment. Please don't let me take you away from your lunch."

"Don't be silly, Father," replied Bron, more amiably. "I wouldn't hear of it. In any case, it will be good to have some company after a morning of dealing with my father's paperwork. Let me take your coat."

When Gabriel was ready, Bron showed him into a cosy

drawing room where a fire burned brightly in the grate. It was immaculately clean thanks to Mrs Whitcomb's diligence, and the walls looked newly painted, giving the room a bright, warm feel that was much needed after the cold street. "Do take a seat near the fire," said Bron. "Mrs Whitcomb will summon us for lunch in a moment."

"I'm so sorry to interrupt you," said Gabriel, seating himself in a snug beige armchair. "I'd forgotten how many practicalities there are to deal with after a death. It seems unfair somehow. One is in the worst possible state to deal with it all, but it comes anyway."

"I know how heartless this must sound," answered Bron, sitting down himself with an air of weariness about him, "but it's mostly just a frightful bore. The problem with a sudden death is that my father had not put any of his affairs in order. It almost seems a bit ludicrous—his solicitor expecting me to deal with everything, I mean—when I know I shan't get a penny for my pains. I almost feel as though I'm intruding."

"I quite understand."

"And then there's a wretched murder enquiry going on all around us." Bron gave Gabriel a wry smile. "I assume that's why you've come to see me, Father? Not come to wipe away my tears and give me spiritual direction in my hour of darkness?"

"I'm quite happy to give you my counsel if you wish, Bron," Gabriel answered, "but you're quite right, of course." He took the amulet from his pocket and held it out to Bron. The metal gleamed bewitchingly in the firelight. "Do you recognise this at all?"

Bron looked up at Gabriel in confusion. "Ought I to recognise it?"

"I was wondering whether it belonged to your father, but you've obviously never seen it before."

"I'm afraid not, old man. Anyway, wouldn't it belong to a woman? It looks like a piece of jewellery."

"I think it's an amulet of some kind. It's not something I recognise. I think it's very old and possibly more valuable than it looks. Jewish by the looks of things, if the Hebrew markings are anything to go by."

Bron laughed, giving Gabriel's amulet a dismissive wave of the hand. "My father was definitely not Jewish, Father. He was a narcissistic atheist. I daresay that like most children, he attended Sunday school, though not with any great enthusiasm. I can't see how an object like that could have belonged to him. I don't think it would even have interested him."

"I take it he was born and raised Protestant then?" said Gabriel. "Even if he fell away as a man."

Bron's look of feigned confusion returned. "Whatever he was taught as a child, it can't have run very deep. He was quite fond of Christian art and architecture; he saw Christianity as a relic of a past age we all ought to have grown out of by now. Something to be remembered fairly fondly but always to be thought of in the past tense." He looked at the amulet as Gabriel carefully put it away. "Where did you find it, anyway? Not another ornament found suspiciously near the murder scene?"

"Might he have bought it perhaps?" Gabriel persisted. "Or brought it back from his recent travels?"

"I very much doubt it; all he brought back from his travels was bad memories as far as I can see. Made him even more unbearable than he had been before." Bron stared into the fire in what would have been sulkiness in a younger man. "I'm dreadfully sorry, Father; he deserved more kindness from me than I gave him when he returned. I never wanted him to go. It seemed such madness for a man of his years to go gallivanting about war-torn Europe with danger everywhere. I knew travelling with the army wouldn't be good enough for him. It was only a matter of time before he was going to get bored and go off on his own without any protection whatsoever. He could be incredibly arrogant, so sure of himself."

"Paul told me that your father witnessed a massacre, but he didn't want his family to know the details."

Bron leaned back in his chair and gave a long, bitter laugh. "Father, Paul Ashley is the most self-important little prig in the northern hemisphere if he told you that!" He looked away from the fire and leaned closer to Gabriel, who was reddening again, and not from the heat of the fire. It was dawning on him that he had been taken for a ride, and not for the first time. "Paul likes to imagine that he was uniquely important to my father. That he was the man he trusted beyond anyone else. He's a useless journalist, Father. Real Nazi hunters do not live in little tumbledown cottages in the back of beyond. They're working undercover in the cities, stripping away false identities, trailing suspects. Paul Ashley is a dreamer, and that's all he is. My father talked incessantly about what happened, long before Paul ingratiated himself into my father's confidence."

Gabriel looked calmly at Bron. There was so much anger there, so much hurt and resentment again, that Gabriel hardly knew where to start. There was undoubtedly some truth in what Bron said about Paul, but Gabriel was more inclined to put Paul's self-importance down to youthful idealism and the desperation to be of significance to the world. All people wanted to believe that they were important and had some unique role in the ongoing war for justice and truth. "What did he tell you, Bron? It might be important."

"I very much doubt it, Father."

"It was important to him." Gabriel tried another tack. "I know you said before that you were hardly talking by the time your father returned from the war, but that's not entirely what you are suggesting."

Bron shook his head, aware that he had contradicted himself. "I told you, he talked incessantly to begin with, to anyone who would listen. So yes, he did tell me about that."

"And?"

"It certainly changed him. He was still angry and domineering when he returned, but the old confidence had gone. There was none of that devil-may-care approach to life I remembered from him when I was child. He should never have gone!"

"Don't think about that now, Bron," said Gabriel softly. "Just try to remember what he said."

Bron shifted position so that Gabriel was no longer anywhere near his line of sight. "He spent the last days of the war in Germany," said Bron, sounding as though he were giving evidence in the witness box. "He said it really was hell on earth. The whole country was in ruins. Desperate people everywhere; homeless, hungry little children running around barefoot. Women and girls who'd been . . . who had been . . . you know. Violated. He said he walked through a park and found an entire family hanging from the trees.

144

It looked as though the father had hanged the mother and their three children, then hanged himself."

Gabriel crossed himself silently, closing his eyes to avoid the need to look at Bron. There had been so many atrocity stories that the world was in danger of becoming weary of them, but Gabriel felt the same stabbing pain in the heart every single time he heard of some new horror. The pain was becoming more familiar, but the expected numbness of time never seemed to happen to him.

"In the final months before the Russians and then the British and Americans arrived, it was an open secret in Germany that the war was over. There were hundreds of suicides, and the Nazis no doubt had to resort to more and more brutal methods to keep people in check. My father said he saw a group of very young men being marched away by a group of soldiers. Hitler was recruiting boys as young as fifteen into the German army by then, and those who tried to desert were shot on sight. My father thought that these boys must have tried to run away and been rounded up. He hid himself away and watched as they were marched into the ruins of an old warehouse. The Germans were forcing them to their knees in groups of ten and shooting them in the back of the head while the others watched."

Gabriel got up and stood at Bron's side. "Forgive me," said Gabriel. "I hadn't realised you had been so badly affected by it. I'm sorry."

Bron shook his head vigorously, though Gabriel noticed the unmistakable glistening of tears escaping his eyes, a second before he brushed them away. "Perhaps it explains why my father was so awful when he got back. No one knew what to say to him," said Bron. He had had to move again to avoid Gabriel, and his voice took on the thin, expressionless timbre of a person disengaging from his own topic of conversation. "My father said as he watched those young men being killed that there was one particular victim who haunted him. It was always his face he remembered in his nightmares. My father said the boy was incredibly small for his age, and he was calling his mother. The others were too shocked to put up much resistance, but he fought like a wildcat, sobbing and calling for his mother to come and save him. In the end, they tied his hands behind his back and shot him as he struggled on the floor. He said it was that sight that made him desperate to bring the perpetrators to justice. He said he wanted to see them hang for the sake of that poor boy's mother, whoever she was."

Bron sat in silence with his head in his hands, wheezing and gasping with the effects of holding himself together. Gabriel heard the door being softly opened behind them and realised that Mrs Whitcomb was watching them both in alarm. Gabriel turned to her and put a finger to his lips. She nodded and walked silently out of the room. "I'm sorry, Bron. It must have been very hard for you all."

"Father, he tried to end his own life. When I was still living at home, I found him in the bath with his wrists cut. I had to call an ambulance. When he was found dead, my first thought was that he'd committed suicide."

"Bron, I have to ask you this. Is it your belief that he was killed because he was writing a book about the massacre he witnessed? If he was the only witness to that atrocity, someone must have had an interest in silencing him."

Bron shook his head wearily. "Why should anyone have wanted to kill him over that? There were so many massacres, so many violent deaths. Half of Europe seems to have met a violent end. And it wasn't as if my father's war history was a secret. Perhaps Paul really believes that, but everyone knew he'd witnessed a massacre."

"Everyone?"

"It was the only way he could bear it, I suppose," Bron retorted, a little tersely. "He talked incessantly on the subject when he returned home. I've heard that story so many times, I feel as though I saw it with my own eyes! He talked and talked; no one in our vicinity could possibly have failed to know. Then suddenly, he stopped talking about it. He went completely the other way. He wouldn't speak of it anymore; he wouldn't answer any questions. Perhaps that was the shock hitting him at last. I don't know."

Gabriel stepped back as Bron got to his feet. "Perhaps I really am barking up the wrong tree here," said Gabriel, following Bron out of the room. Bron had glanced at the clock and realised it was lunchtime; the shift from one room to the next would provide a useful distraction to both of them. "It just seems too much of a coincidence that a man like that would die and all the notes of his books be stolen or destroyed soon after."

Bron looked at him in disbelief. "Who said my father's notes had been destroyed? The police didn't have the decency to tell me anything about that!"

Gabriel winced at the thought of yet another mistake he had made. There was no going back: "The police will only just have found out," Gabriel explained, jolted by the sudden cool of the hall after the warmth of the drawing room. The dining room door directly opposite was open, and Gabriel could see a table draped in a white damask cloth, neatly laid out with a generous lunch by Mrs Whitcomb, who stood waiting patiently for them. "Oh dear, perhaps it isn't important after all. I'm afraid Paul returned home to find that some thug had been in and ransacked his study. All the notes were being held there for safekeeping."

Bron strode past Gabriel into the dining room and sat down without waiting for his guest to sit. Gabriel sat down uncomfortably opposite him, feeling his appetite waning with every passing second. "A fat lot of good Paul Ashley was at keeping things safe, by the sound of things! Those notes are irreplaceable!"

"Paul did say that Victor had spoken to him at great length about the events, and he thought he could probably still write the book. I can't help thinking that if the two of you were to get together—" A single, forbidding glare from Bron made it abundantly obvious to Gabriel that the two men would never get together for anything.

"I'm sorry, Father," said Bron, pouring Gabriel a drink, "but short of finding Dr Mengele working at the nursing home, I think it singularly unlikely that my father's misadventures have anything to do with the matter. Murder always comes down to love or money. There was no love in my father's life and sadly, very little money either."

Gabriel smiled appreciatively at Mrs Whitcomb as she served him a bowl of soup. He had had some extremely awkward meals in his life, but this luncheon promised to be one of the worst.

It was just after three that Gabriel arrived back at the presbytery, in time to find Fr Foley playing patience at the kitchen table as his afternoon tea brewed. "Afternoon," greeted Fr Foley, without looking up from his cards. "Good of you to drop in. Could you smell the tea and cake all the way from the crime scene?"

"I'm sorry," said Gabriel, sitting down opposite him. "You would not believe what's been going on. Mrs Martin insisted on taking me back to the house. Then Paul Ashley had a break-in. I had to ask Bron Gladstone a few questions, and I'm not sure he'll ever speak to me again now. Then I had to send a telegram—"

"It's all right, son," Fr Foley said, cutting him off, "I don't need an inventory. Have you ever considered the morality of cheating at patience?"

Gabriel smiled, knowing he was forgiven. "It's always seemed pretty pointless to me, given that one plays the game against oneself. But then, I suppose, in the end any cheating is cheating against oneself. Which makes all cheating point-less."

"Thank you for your contribution," answered Fr Foley, throwing down his remaining six cards. "Do you have time for a cuppa before you vanish into thin air again?"

"I won't, thanks. Bron did at least give me a good lunch, even if we ate in virtual silence."

"I think this is a plot," commented Fr Foley, pouring a small quantity of milk into his mug. "Carry on like this and you'll be so unpopular with absolutely everyone, you'll have to return to your abbey to avoid a lynch mob."

"I hope no one actually wants to string me up from the nearest tree," said Gabriel, picking up the deck of cards for want of anything better to do. "I've always wondered why detectives are never murdered in crime stories. I mean, if you think about it, the killer is trying to cover his tracks, so why not go after the person who is trying to track him down? You never hear of anyone trying to knife Hercule

Poirot in a dark alley. No one dropped cyanide into Sherlock Holmes' afternoon tea."

Fr Foley hesitated to pick up his own tea. "Thank you for that. Case going badly, is it?"

"I'm not getting very far, if that's what you mean." Gabriel had begun to shuffle the cards, sorting them into their suits, starting with the aces. He knew it would madden Fr Foley, who was terrible at shuffling cards and would keep getting a predictable hand for the next twenty games he played. "I cannot seem to get the measure of the man. The dead man, I mean."

"I've barely heard a good word said about him, for what it's worth," said Fr Foley. "Always troubles me when people speak ill of the dead. If a man can't win some sympathy when he snuffs it, something must have gone wrong."

"That's the thing," lamented Gabriel, busying himself searching for the three of hearts. "The only person who seems to care he's dead is a young man who had something to gain from his friendship with him. If Paul Ashley could have got his name on the dust jacket of a book alongside a formerly well-known writer, it would have done his career the world of good. Now it's unlikely the book will ever be written, even though Paul claims he can still do it. But what he's feeling can hardly be described as grief. The only one who cried was his granddaughter, and I'm fairly sure her tears were for her mother, not him."

The men sank into silence, Fr Foley watching Gabriel working his way systematically through the deck of cards. "I would say, 'What you sow you reap,' but that sounds a little harsh under the circumstances. Nobody deserves to be killed like that."

"Have you ever broken a belt?"

Fr Foley had become quite used to Gabriel's random questions during the time Gabriel had been living with him, and he didn't miss a beat. "Unless you count my father's through overuse, but I'm not sure that's what you mean."

"That's not at all what I mean."

"I suppose I've had a few wear out in my time. The odd buckle breaking on me. Dare I ask why?"

Gabriel got up and picked up his knapsack, which he had left carelessly by the door. The broken belt was coiled up under his folded pyjamas, like a toothless old snake in a charmer's basket. He held it up in front of Fr Foley. "What does that look like to you?" he asked.

"Where did it come from?" asked Fr Foley, glancing impassively at the exhibit. "I assume you didn't remove it from the corpse."

"Molly found it in his room. The leather's not worn; it was obviously cut. It just seems like an odd way to remove a belt when one could just as easily unbuckle it."

Fr Foley shrugged. "You're making rather a meal of this, if you don't mind my saying."

"It's odd, and it was in the dead man's possession," answered Gabriel. "Of course I'm making a meal out of it."

Fr Foley reached out to take it and examined it more closely, though Gabriel suspected that he was merely going through the motions of looking at the thing to appear interested. "You know what this reminds me of?" said Fr Foley finally. "It looks like something a doctor or nurse would do." He drew an invisible line up the side of his body. "You know, when some poor soul's suffered a horrible accident, they just cut through his clothing to reach the injury."

Gabriel pondered the possibility as he put the belt away. It was a plausible suggestion. In fact, it was the only halfway plausible suggestion Gabriel could think of, the alternative being that he was chasing the wrong scent as usual. He shook his head impatiently. "I am swimming through a shoal of red herrings," he added. "Of course, the thought has occurred to me that some complete stranger might have killed him. Applegate must also be considering the possibility. He was alone in misty woodland. Private land, of course, but anyone could have slipped in undetected."

Fr Foley busied himself putting the cards away. "I suppose it's a question of whether anyone actually would. It's not like a man being mugged on a London street after dark. Or someone falling foul of a pickpocket. Those sorts of crimes happen in cities and large towns. No one would have been skulking about that quiet land waiting for some hapless individual to walk past." The playing cards neatly stowed away in their carved wooden box, Fr Foley returned his full attention to Gabriel. "Was he robbed?"

"Not at the site, certainly." Gabriel sat down gingerly opposite Fr Foley. "You're not going to like this, but I wonder if I might be excused for a couple of days?"

"Days?" echoed Fr Foley. "What are you up to?"

"It may be nothing, but you see, I have to find out. I need to return to the abbey to ask Abbot Ambrose something. But then I may need to go on to London. I've an old chum in town whose a——"

"Why would anyone want to go to London?" Fr Foley paused. "I'd forgotten—of course, you were a Londoner, weren't you?"

Gabriel nodded. "I know it's a long way to go, but I need

some information or I'm never going to get to the bottom of all this. And I've a friend at the Albion Museum who might be able to help me."

Fr Foley was clearly itching to tell Gabriel to forget about the whole thing, but he knew that the man would be impossible to live with for weeks if he were prevented from following this particular trail. He was a bloodhound in search of meat. "Leave me your diary so that nothing gets forgotten," he sighed. "Come back as quickly as possible. I need you back before Sunday."

Gabriel was on his feet and running out of the room to the stairs before Fr Foley could say anything else. He hurried up to his room, snatched up a clean set of underwear and hurried back downstairs, discreetly tucking his undies into the knapsack he had not yet unpacked from his last adventure. He hovered sheepishly in the doorway of the kitchen. "I don't suppose you could lend me the train fare, could you?" he asked quietly.

Fr Foley stood up, walked wordlessly over to the petty cash tin he kept on the windowsill and handed it to him. "Come back in one piece, and we'll say no more about it," he said, patting Gabriel affectionately on the shoulder. "I don't like what you said about killers turning on the detective. Fortunate you're so bad at it, really."

10

It was already dark by the time Gabriel set off, the nights drawing in as early as four in the afternoon at that time of year. Gabriel's bicycle had no lights, a detail he had failed to consider until he was speeding down the road with no way to warn any oncoming driver of his precarious presence. He had no problems after the first helter-skelter stretch of blind bends and heart-stoppingly steep downward cambers on the way out of town. Like many ancient towns, it was built on a hill and all roads out spiralled downwards, but after that, Gabriel reached the old Roman road across Salisbury Plain and his way became smoother, wider and—mercifully—flatter.

Gabriel kept as close to the edge of the road as possible, fearing that a motorcar might creep up behind him and fail to catch sight of him in the headlights before hitting him, but the road was eerily quiet. It was only when he was forced to stop to catch his breath that Gabriel remembered: it had been market day yesterday, and the road would have teemed with traffic of all kinds. The day after was like the day after a feast day at the abbey: quiet, lazy and a little mournful. The Plain was in the hands of the armed forces, but beyond it, isolated farms were dotted about—mostly dairy, but there were two piggeries Gabriel knew of—all desperately trying to keep their heads above water. There was an old saying that a farmer's belt had notches all the way around, but Gabriel wondered how many of those families would go to bed hungry tonight.

Gabriel got going again, taking his time getting back into his stride. He felt the first raindrops touching his face as he neared Stonehenge, nodding to that glorious pagan monument to heaven knew what as he picked up his pace. It was another three miles to the abbey, and he was desperate to get there without looking like a drowned rat.

As it turned out, the rain was nothing more than a light drizzle, but it was surprising how quickly Gabriel found himself getting wet, cycling through a thin mist of raindrops. First, the damp coated his hair and clothes; then it began to seep steadily through the fibres of his coat and down his neck, chilling him to the bone. Within a mile, he was shaking his head constantly to keep the tiny raindrops out of his eyes. When he crossed the hamlet of Little Coombe, Gabriel dismounted the bicycle and walked through the narrow, uphill lanes, across a bridge beneath which the river was already swollen and fast flowing, threatening to flood the nearby cricket pitch.

The streets were almost deserted already, the five hundred or so inhabitants of the hamlet sensibly indoors. Gabriel could see chinks of light between partially closed curtains and the odd tattered trail of red, white and blue bunting still hanging from the occasional house, relics of the impromptu street party held to mark the marriage of Princess Elizabeth late the previous year. Gabriel felt himself lingering as the road levelled off again and the houses melted away, leaving him surrounded by pitch darkness as far as the eye could see. It was the worst penance of winter, those long, long hours of darkness, when the sun set so early; teatime felt like a midnight feast. He cycled off, through the darkness and drizzle, thinking fondly of the welcome he would receive from his brothers before the hour was out.

"Good heavens, man, you look like a drowned rat!" exclaimed Abbot Ambrose when Gabriel stepped through the door into the great man's study. "What were you thinking of, walking all this way?"

"I didn't walk, Father Abbot," said Gabriel, bracing himself to stifle his shivers. Now that his pulse had slowed down, he felt cold again. "I cycled here. It's almost easier in the dark; I had the road to myself."

Abbot Ambrose gestured for Gabriel to sit down and looked across at Father Dominic, the infirmarian, who had accompanied his old friend into the room. "I think Dom Gabriel might be in need of a change of clothes," said Ambrose. "I wonder if you could see to it, please. I think he's about the same size as you."

Dominic smiled. Gabriel was indeed about the same height as he, though thanks to a limp from childhood polio, Dominic appeared to be several inches shorter. He was also at least ten years older and blamed the encroachment of age for his widening girth and rapidly greying hair. "Is that all, Father Abbot?"

"I daresay you're hungry after your trek?"

"Well . . ." Gabriel had been brought up never to impose

and certainly never to admit to hunger, which might place the host under an obligation to feed him, but he was too afraid to lie to Abbot Ambrose. He was starving.

"Perhaps you could also go down to the kitchen and find a little something for Gabriel to eat," Ambrose instructed Dominic, before turning his attention back to Gabriel. "I presume you will not attempt to make the same journey back this evening?"

"Actually, I need to get to London," Gabriel explained, then realised that the two men were glancing at him in confusion. "It's quite urgent. I came here only because I needed—"

"You'll be going nowhere tonight," ordered Ambrose. "Wherever you think you're going, you may set off in the morning."

Dominic shuffled back towards the door and left, leaving Gabriel with that uncomfortable feeling he remembered from his days at the abbey of having lost a guardian angel somehow. He folded his arms and looked back at Ambrose's egg-like head, wondering if it would be impertinent to talk first. He was spared the bother by Ambrose. "What are you up to, Dom Gabriel? I assume Fr Foley knows you're here?"

"Oh yes," Gabriel assured him, "and he knows about my plan to go to London. I shouldn't have troubled you at all, Father Abbot, but I'm afraid something rather awful has happened, and I wanted to ask your advice."

Ambrose's expression softened immediately. It was not the first time Gabriel had got himself into a scrape, and Ambrose knew from experience that it was generally not Gabriel's fault. "What troubles you?"

Gabriel felt himself relaxing. "Have you heard about the

murder of Victor Gladstone?" Ambrose shook his head. "An elderly man was found dead in the grounds of the house where I was a guest. I shan't bore you with the details, but I've been doing a little digging around. This object was found among his files and papers. I wondered if you knew what it was."

Gabriel took out the amulet he had wrapped in a clean handkerchief and had concealed about his person, placing it gingerly on the desk between them. He unfolded the handkerchief like a magician about to amaze everyone. Ambrose looked steadily at it, then put on his reading glasses and picked up the amulet to look at it more closely. "Where did you say you got this?"

"Victor Gladstone was a writer. He left some files with a friend for safekeeping. The papers were stolen—at least that's what we think happened—but that amulet seems to have slipped through the file where it was concealed. We found it at the bottom of one of the drawers of the filing cabinet. It's obviously Jewish, but Victor's son said his father was certainly not Jewish himself and had no connection with that faith."

Ambrose's face was thunderous as he turned the amulet over, then over again before placing it back on the handkerchief. "I'm afraid I've no idea what it is," he admitted. "I'm not an expert in such things, but it's obviously stolen." Gabriel sat up with a start. "It's a simple enough deduction. If a man who was not a Catholic and was known to be entirely uninterested in the Catholic faith happened to have a valuable relic of one of the saints in his possession, you might deduce the same thing."

"He might have bought it," ventured Gabriel. "He spent

the latter years of the war on the Continent. There must have been many poor people, displaced people selling everything they had."

Ambrose sighed. The sight of the amulet was unsettling him far more than Gabriel had thought possible. He seemed unwilling to look at it, let alone touch it again, and Gabriel found himself covering it up, though he made no effort to remove it from the desk. "There was also a great deal of Jewish art stolen before and during the war. Homes and synagogues looted all over the place. There is still a very murky underworld that deals in such objects, but I would want nothing to do with any man caught up in such a trade. Who knows what happened to the poor soul who owned that amulet? Even if this man you speak of bought this object, he must have known he was buying stolen goods, quite possibly taken from around the neck of a dead body."

Gabriel flinched. "I thought you said these things were looted?"

"They were, Gabriel. But you've no idea how terrible it was. You remember once when you asked me about the concentration camps and what I'd seen?"

Gabriel nodded, stifling the memory of being hurled out of this very room by Abbot Ambrose in the worst rage Gabriel had ever witnessed. "I remember."

"Good," answered Ambrose. "When families arrived in those places, they were stripped of all their belongings, even their clothes, even the hair on their heads. I've no idea what happened to the piles of spectacles and old suitcases and shoes, but anything valuable would have been sifted through and taken away. If this man bought this artefact, I find it very difficult to believe that he would not have realised it was stolen. It was such a dirty business. Anyone involved in a trade like this was caught up in murder as much as they were caught up in theft."

Gabriel felt his eyes filling with tears, and he told himself it was exhaustion making him irrational, but he had an overactive imagination at the best of times and Ambrose's words conjured up a thousand horrible images. He imagined a synagogue (such as he could, never having entered one) torn apart by a mob, windows smashed, furnishings overturned and broken up; flames. No, he would not think of burning buildings. He squeezed his eyes tight shut, but he could see the amulet around the neck of a young woman, kneeling against the grave she had been forced to dig. He has heard of such outrages, too many to count, but because most of the news reports he knew about had come to him via the wireless, the images of death and misery in his mind always involved people he loved. He would see his own brothers and sisters lying dead in a mass grave, his mother being harassed and spat upon by a thug in uniform, Giovanna trapped in a burning building . . .

"Gabriel!" The voice almost shouted at him from far away.

"Forgive me, Father Abbot. I'm afraid I'm a little tired."

"Is this why you wish to travel to London?" asked Ambrose gently, noting Gabriel's changed countenance. "To get someone to look at this artefact?"

"Yes, Father Abbot. I have an old friend from school who knows about things like this. Even if this has nothing to do with Victor Gladstone's murder, I couldn't bear to keep it in my possession any longer. There must be some way to get it back to its rightful owners, assuming they're still alive."

"I'm not sure that's an assumption you can make, my son.

But you are quite right, of course. Whomever that amulet belonged to, it's unlikely it belonged to this man Gladstone; but it certainly does not belong to you." Ambrose hesitated, looking fixedly at the covered amulet. "What happened to the Jews cries out to heaven for vengeance." If he was slipping into one of those dark moods Gabriel recognised from days past, Ambrose snapped himself out of it. "Do you have the means to get yourself to London?"

"Yes, Father Abbot. I have enough for the train fare."

"Where will you stay?"

Gabriel struggled to answer. In all honesty, he had hardly thought that far. "I suppose I thought I should come back the same day."

"It's a long way to go for one day, Gabriel," Ambrose warned. "It's a long time since you've lived in London. Where did you say your friend worked?"

"Not far from the cathedral, Father Abbot. I shall need to find my way to Victoria."

"Then I shall send word to Clergy House, asking them to take care of you for one night."

"Thank you, Father Abbot," said Gabriel, barely containing his excitement. He had never stayed at Clergy House before, but it was right next to Westminster Cathedral, a place he had visited every day during his old life, living and working in the Big Smoke. He would be staying right in the heart of Catholic London.

"And I want you to take someone with you," added Ambrose, dampening Gabriel's spirits immediately.

"I assure you, Father Abbot, it won't be necessary," said Gabriel. "I grew up in London; the streets are very familiar to me."

Ambrose smiled kindly. "I'm not worried about your getting lost, Gabriel; I'm not even concerned that you'll get yourself into mischief. I should prefer you to have a companion. There's something about this matter that makes me uneasy. Take Brother Gerard with you."

Gabriel nodded, scooping up the amulet as though it were a family heirloom and putting it away out of sight. "I should like that," he said, for what it was worth. If he was to have any companion on his trip to London, he was glad it was mad little Brother Gerard, who would stop him taking himself too seriously. And young Gerard did not belong to the London life Gabriel had left behind.

"Penny for your thoughts, lad?" chirped Gerard, breaking Gabriel out of his gloomy meditation. He had been sitting alone in the refectory, enjoying the excellent supper Fr Dominic had rustled up for him: a large bowl of oxtail soup with a round of the abbey's own crusty bread, followed by a generous slice of Woolton pie, the vegetables dripping with flavoursome gravy. As a culinary act of defiance towards ongoing austerity, the cook had slipped in a layer of lardons between the vegetables and the potato pastry, a happy taste of good times to come. "Wakey wakey, Gabbers!" chimed in Gerard, when Gabriel failed to respond. "They starving you at Saint Paddy's or what?"

"I wasn't thinking about the food," said Gabriel, "though Fr Foley's housekeeper must be the only woman in England who'll miss rationing. There'll be no more excuses for her cooking."

"Glad to be home?"

Gabriel nodded, though his predictably poor timing had

left him feeling like a bit of an imposter. It felt unnatural to be seated in the corner of an empty room built to feed at least forty men. "They're a good sort at Saint Patrick's, you know. I mustn't complain. Did Percy snuff it to provide these crispy lardons?"

Gerard laughed. At not quite twenty years of age, Brother Gerard looked a great deal younger, his face still fresh and ruddy from his childhood on a farm and his hair unkempt because he had yet to work out the point of combing it. He no doubt would when Abbot Ambrose threatened to shear it off. "Percy kicked the bucket donkey's years ago! That's Percy's son and heir you're eating. Took Maccabee to the knackers before Christmas."

"That really is in appallingly bad taste," said Gabriel, helping himself to another mouthful all the same. "The name, I mean."

"I'm to take my vows at Corpus Christi," declared Gerard, filling Gabriel's glass. "Do you think you'll be back by then?"

"Congratulations, Gerry, that's wonderful news!"

Gerard beamed. "Assuming I don't foul up between now and then." He watched Gabriel finishing off his meal. "Thanks for the trip to London, by the way. I've never been." Gabriel smiled. Yes, Gerard was the best possible companion for a journey he was quietly dreading. Gabriel had not seen London since before the war, and part of him wanted to stay away so that his memories would not be destroyed by the sight of what the great city had become. "Will you have time to show me the sights?" Gerard chimed into Gabriel's thoughts. "I've always wanted to see the . . ."

Gabriel was prepared to go anywhere the overexcited boy

wanted—time permitting—if they could only stay away from anywhere important to Gabriel. He touched the pocket where the amulet was safely hidden to remind himself of why he was taking this journey into the past and offered a word of thanks for small mercies. For a few short hours, he was home. He would pray with his brothers, and he would rest his head in a quiet place of refuge from the world. Tomorrow and its uncertainties could wait.

Gabriel slept soundly and dreamlessly, leaving him feeling pleasingly refreshed as he slung his knapsack over his shoulder and went to find Gerard. Gabriel's better spirits, however, were nothing compared with Gerard's uncontainable excitement. As they walked down to the village's only bus stop, Gabriel felt as though he were taking an energetic young terrier for a walk, except that this terrier not only kept skipping ahead, compelling Gabriel to move rather faster than was his wont, but he had the power of speech and talked incessantly for the entire forty minutes they were walking and waiting for the bus.

Gerard paused momentarily when the bus arrived to clamber aboard and settle himself into the backseat. At that early hour, it was virtually empty, with only the driver, the conductor and one other passenger, an elderly man with his cap pressed down over his face to avoid having to talk to anyone. "You know, we really didn't need to sit quite so far back," protested Gabriel, hoping the backseat would not bring on his travel sickness. "There's plenty of space."

"Aww, didn't you always rush to the back of the school bus? Me and me mates—"

"I didn't go to school by bus," answered Gabriel, bracing

himself as the bus lurched in the direction of the railway station. It was a three-mile bus ride to the railway station in the next village, but it took Gerard into new territory, and that was all that mattered.

"I forgot, you were a posh boy, weren't you? Locked you in all term."

"Shades of the prison house begin to close upon the growing boy."

"Eh?"

"Nothing. A long train journey with a trunk at the beginning of term, another train journey at the end."

"Why's that house an octagon?" asked Gerard, jabbing a finger at the old tollhouse they were passing. It was, in fact, hexagonal in structure, though Gabriel had no idea why, and he suspected it would be a bit like living in a lighthouse, the interior made up of several large, awkwardly shaped rooms stacked around a spiral staircase. "Imagine trying to put furniture in it! You'd have to get a carpenter in—"

"I thought Lancashire folk were supposed to be men of few words?" suggested Gabriel, abandoning his rule of never interrupting, simply to get a word in.

"Yeah, Dad were like that," put in Gerard immediately, apparently unaware of the veiled criticism. "Don't remember him having anything much to say for himself. Though I suppose he must've said 'I do' on his wedding day. That was the one thing Ma couldn't say for him . . ."

The overexcited terrier showed no sign of tiring as they boarded a train for Paddington Station. They scrambled along the corridor and found an empty carriage, heaving their bags onto the overhead luggage racks. "Don't worry about anyone else trying to come in," said Gerard, sliding the door shut. "The other passengers would rather cling onto the train roof than sit with the likes of us."

"I fear you may be right," said Gabriel, settling himself into his seat; he removed his hat and placed it next to him on the seat, just in case anyone else decided to come in and sit with them. There were three types of Englishman a priest encountered in such a situation: a small minority of Catholics who were blissfully unfazed by clerical dress; those who found any hint of popery so overwhelmingly disgusting or intimidating that they would not go within a radius of a hundred yards of a priest unless they had a gun to their heads; and those whose knowledge of Catholicism had never grown further than some vague sense that Roman Catholics burned people and tortured scientists, who made it their mission in life to pick fights with any man in a collar in the hope of enlightening him.

There appeared to be none of the first and third varieties on the train today, and Gabriel could not judge whether the second was in evidence. He sat back and gazed out of the window, letting Gerard's cheerful prattling wash over him like a friendly wave. It was not misty outside; it was only the light film of condensation gathering across the window that gave such an impression. Dawn had broken at least half an hour ago, but the sky was so overcast that the outside world seemed trapped in a perpetual twilight. Gabriel had not travelled on this railway line since he had first entered the monastery as a postulant, and he found the experience of taking that fateful journey in reverse as unsettling as he had expected. He had had only his army knapsack with him then, and something had compelled him to wear the suit he had been given when he had been demobbed after just six months of active service. He had been called up in 1918, giving him just enough of an opportunity to say that he had served in the war, but he had known plenty of young men who had joined up late in the day who had still not lived to see the armistice.

"Well?"

Gabriel looked at his companion in confusion and realised that Gerard had stopped talking. He had stopped talking because he had asked a question and was awaiting an answer. Gabriel shifted uncomfortably in his seat. "Sorry?"

"Why didn't you join the community in London?" asked Gerard.

"Why didn't you join the community in Yorkshire?" asked Gabriel, batting off the question. "I'm assuming it wasn't beneath your Lancashire dignity to cross the Pennines. London belonged to the life I was called to leave behind."

Gabriel felt that yawning sensation in his chest that he remembered from those terrible days, the grief that was almost fear. He took out his beads as a signal to Gerard that he needed him to stop, but he did intend to pray. Gerard realised his mistake and gave Gabriel an apologetic smile. "It's all right, mate," he said, in a more subdued manner than came naturally to him. "Why don't we pray together?"

Gabriel nodded reluctantly, but he continued to stare fixedly out of the window to focus his mind on the world outside. It was only because everything looked so dead that it was affecting his mood, making him melancholy when he might almost have been excited by the thought of returning to London. A little excitement at least, the smallest murmur of pleasure might have been there at the thought of meeting an old friend for the first time in so many years. That was surely worth getting excited about. But Gabriel felt the gloom of a desolate winter morning enveloping him, and he held a small wooden cross in one hand, determined to offer it all up.

11

Gabriel was not sure how long he slept, but he woke up to find himself slumped into the corner of the carriage, with the mother of all backaches and Gerard jumping up and down, calling, "Wake up! Wake up! Paddington Station!"

Gerard was already throwing down their bags from the overhead luggage rack and putting on his hat and coat. He was so desperate to get outside that he managed to get the buttons of his coat in the wrong holes, and Gabriel had to stand up and help him get himself together. "Do you have your ticket?" he asked solicitously, heaving on his own coat.

"I have both of them," said Gerard triumphantly, holding up Gabriel's ticket. "You dropped yours on the floor when you dozed off."

Gabriel staggered wearily after Gerard as he scampered down the corridor to the train door. "I really would calm down if I were you," said Gabriel, watching in alarm as Gerard came within a whisker of falling into the gap between the train and the platform edge. "People have been through the Blitz, they've lost their homes and their families. Bear in mind that this is a city that has suffered before you go jumping about like a jack-in-the-box."

"We weren't allowed to play with them as kids," said Gerard, missing the point entirely. "Dad said they were blasphemous . . ." The rest of Gerard's chatter was lost in the noise of the busy station platform. Gabriel stood stock-still, unable to move and unable to speak. He was surrounded by the sights and sounds of a city that had nurtured him and been his playground once. He glanced up at the vaulted Victorian station roof, beneath which hundreds of men and women were hurrying on their journeys. The air swirled with the clouds of steam and ash belched out by those vast round-bellied engines.

Gabriel felt humbled to be standing in the middle of this monument to the Industrial Revolution—humbled and a little uneasy. It was a long time since he had been in the middle of a crowd, and the noise overwhelmed him. He was aware of every raised voice, every whining child, the thunder of boots, the call of the street traders, the coughs and sneezes, even the tiny scraping noises of matches being struck and pipes and cigarettes being lit. He noticed Gerard some way ahead, turning around to see where Gabriel had gone and attempting uselessly to move back towards him. Gabriel shook his head to wake himself up and moved towards his friend before they could be separated by the crowd.

"I don't know why you are being so mournful," said Gerard. "We are going to go on one of those big red buses, aren't we?"

"I was rather thinking we might take the Underground," suggested Gabriel, plaintively, but he could sense mutiny coming. He knew Gerard was desperate to get on a bus so that he could get a better view of London, and there was not a great deal to see through the window of a tube train.

"All right, all right." He thought he remembered where the bus terminus was and led Gerard out of the station.

Gerard had been right that Gabriel's suggestion to calm down had been uncalled for. For a city that had endured one of the most savage bombing campaigns of the war, it seemed to have a cheerful atmosphere everywhere they went. There was the same joie de vivre he remembered from long ago, the same understated sense of thousands of ordinary men and women getting on with life. Everywhere they looked, there were reminders of the war's destruction, but it was as though the inhabitants of London had made some wordless decision to behave as though nothing had happened. As the bus lurched towards Victoria, they passed magnificent buildings reduced to rubble, some of them being used as playgrounds by children with nowhere else to go; there were dapper young men weaving through the traffic on bicycles, flower sellers plying their trade just as he had remembered, and the occasional elderly man wearing a top hat and polished walking cane, striding elegantly down the street as though the last forty years had not yet come to pass.

"Is that the Thames?" asked Gerard, pointing at the magnificent stretch of water they were passing. "D'ya reckon we'll have time to go on a riverboat—"

Gabriel stood up and rang the bell. "Next stop's ours," he said. "Watch your step as we get out."

> TWENTY *bridges from Tower to Kew —*
> *Wanted to know what the River knew . . .*

Gabriel thought better of quoting Kipling at Gerard, and they walked towards the Albion Museum with Gerard offering a running commentary at every step. Gabriel was never as irritated by the compulsively talkative as he felt he ought to be; the inability of a chatterbox to engage in an actual conversation worked in favour of a man like Gabriel, who had a great deal on his mind and needed time to collect his thoughts. Whilst Gerard talked, Gabriel could think.

Except that Gerard was no longer talking. Like the persistent low rumble of water pipes, Gerard's chatter was only ever noticeable when it stopped abruptly and silence fell. Gabriel looked around for whatever it was that had rendered Gerard speechless and smiled at the sight before them. They had turned the corner into Presentation Road, a long, tree-lined road steeped in the grandeur of the past. Massive, ornate buildings towered over them on both sides, some bearing the scars of the Blitz: chipped and crumbling masonry, scorch marks, cracks and pockmarks across stone façades. There were empty spaces where buildings had once stood. The rubble had been cleared away, but the work of rebuilding had yet to commence. Gabriel's smile faded. "Every time I see a damaged building," he said, "I find myself wondering who died in there."

Gerard gave Gabriel a sympathetic look. "I don't think many of these buildings were ever lived in," he consoled him. "They would have been empty at night. And there were thousands of air-raid shelters . . ."

"Thousands dead, though. *Tens of thousands*. All those poor families in the East End."

They stopped at the foot of a short flight of stone steps leading to the imposing entrance of the Albion Museum. Gerard skipped up the steps ahead of Gabriel, turning around to encourage him inside. "Come along, Brother. We're here. Your friend'll be waiting."

Gabriel reddened, entering the museum behind Gerard. "I'm not sure about that," Gabriel whispered. He was not sure why everyone always whispered in a museum, but there was something about those pristine stone floors and immense vaulted ceilings that inspired reverential silence, even if it was just that the environment magnified the slightest sound. He busied himself studying a headless statue on display near the door, suddenly noticing that it was female and gloriously naked. He turned his back, blushing ever deeper. "I sent him a telegram saying I was coming up to town."

The uncomfortable truth of the situation was dawning on Gerard. "So you didn't wait for a reply then?"

"Not exactly, no."

"So, you can't even be sure he received the telegram."

Gabriel looked around for assistance and noticed a middle-aged woman regarding them in quiet astonishment from behind a desk. He was quite used to being looked at as though he had just metamorphosed from a giant bat, and he gave the attendant a friendly smile. "May I help you, sir?" she put in before he could speak. "The Roman gallery is open today if you care to have a look."

If the reference was intended as an obscure insult, it was lost on Gabriel. "I haven't come to visit the museum," he explained. "I was hoping to meet with Mr Ellsmore."

A frown flickered across the woman's thin face. "Mr Ellsmore is a very busy man, sir. Our archivists do not meet with members of the public."

Gabriel felt as though she were shepherding him towards the tradesmen's entrance. "Oh, we're old friends," he explained, hopefully. "I'm sure he'll see me."

If her last expression had been a frown, she looked now

as if she was trying hard to suppress a yawn. "I'm sorry, sir, do you have an appointment?"

"In a manner of speaking," Gabriel began. "Perhaps it would be easier if you were to give him a message from me? I'm only in town today, you see."

The woman looked impassively down at her desk, helping herself to a piece of paper and a pencil. There was a time Gabriel could have given her his calling card, but the days of such vanities had vanished into the smog at around the last time he and Alan Ellsmore had met. "Whom shall I say wishes to see Mr Ellsmore?" she asked, tersely, looking up at him for an answer only to put her pencil down abruptly.

Gabriel looked over his shoulder, following her gaze. He heard the uneven squeak of old shoes against stone a moment before his eyes focused on a bearded figure who looked strangely familiar. A man of middling height walked stiffly in Gabriel's direction, his face crowded by a pair of steel-rimmed spectacles, an unruly mop of greying brown hair and a beard that would not have disgraced the face of a Franciscan. Alan Ellsmore was dressed so completely as Gabriel had imagined an archivist ought to style himself that Gabriel was not sure whether the effect was deliberate or whether poor Alan had spent so long seated in the bowels of his museum, poring over artefacts and manuscripts, that he had one day found himself dressed in slightly frayed trousers, a shirt and tie badly in need of a trip to the laundrette and a hand-knitted jumper darned so many times he could not be entirely sure what the colour of the original wool had been.

"Eminence!" Alan called, his face breaking into a broad grin. "Well, well, well! If it isn't the great man himself."

Alan and Gabriel shook hands warmly. Gabriel had wondered what it would be like to meet his old school friend again after so many years, but the sincere show of affection was tremendous after the journey back to London and all its connections with the past. "It's good to see you again, Nell."

Gerard, unwilling to be forgotten, bounced up beside them. "Eminence? Nell? Don't they have proper names at public school?"

Gabriel smiled, grateful for Gerard's presence to dissipate the emotions they were both feeling. "This is Brother Gerard," said Gabriel, waiting while the two men shook hands. "He's keeping me company in case I get into any mischief."

"Well," said Alan, turning back to look at Gabriel. "I told the boy at the door to come and let me know immediately if a priest turned up, and he came running to me out of breath, thoroughly overexcited, saying that there were two clerics advancing on the museum. I think he expected double the tip."

"Not a priest yet," said Gerard, quietly.

Alan led them into a small side room, the walls lined with glass cases containing small, ancient artefacts: coins dug up by some lucky farmer years before, random pieces of jewellery, bracelets, a ring; broken pots, combs, objects for which there was still no known use; the fragments of an ancient civilisation modern man could view only in tiny, disconnected shards. Gabriel felt uncomfortably like an impostor, crashing into another man's place of work without invitation. "Nell, it's awfully decent of you to see us like this. I know you must be dreadfully busy."

"Dreadfully busy," echoed Alan without irony. "We're still completing the process of gathering in our treasures from their hiding places."

"I do hope you didn't lose very much," asked Gabriel solicitously. The concern was genuine. As a lover of history, Gabriel hated to think of how much had been lost irrevocably during the bombing raids: old buildings, books, artworks . . . People's lives, people's families. That was the problem: in a world mourning the loss of millions of lives, it felt heartless to feel sorry for the loss of material objects. But he felt it all the same.

"Anything of value was packed up and stored away in safe places," Alan explained. "Mercifully nothing was lost, but as you can imagine, the process of bringing everything back, sorting, cataloguing—well, we're almost there, but it's taken us this long."

"I can imagine it's a labour of love," said Gabriel, then immediately wondered whether he had sounded patronising.

Alan laughed. Gabriel remembered him as a compulsive giggler, the sort of boy who was constantly being thrown out of class for laughing at an entirely inappropriate moment. "Well, it's no way to make one's fortune. When you told me you were entering a monastery, I rather imagined you sitting at a desk all day copying manuscripts." He patted Gabriel on the shoulder, sensing his anxiety at blundering in on him out of the blue. "No need to look so worried, old friend. I'm not too busy to be curious. I'm dying to know what was so urgent that you should come all the way to London to talk to me about it."

"I hope it won't be an anticlimax."

Alan ignored him. "I shall be stopping for lunch at one.

Why don't you and your friend take a walk around the museum, and we can meet for a bite of lunch at that little eatery opposite?"

Gabriel and Alan shook hands again, and Alan walked away to the cavernous cellars of the museum where he did his work.

Gerard was a little too happy to make himself scarce when Gabriel suggested that he might not be very interested in sitting through a lengthy conversation about an old amulet. Fr Foley had given Gabriel more than was required for the train fare, appreciating that trips to London were expensive, and he handed Gerard some spending money with the instruction to enjoy himself for a few hours and meet him at the cathedral at six o'clock sharp. Gabriel felt a little as though he were giving his annoying little brother pocket money for sweeties to get him out of the way, but Gerard trotted off enthusiastically, giving him a cheery wave as he went.

With Gerard out of the way, Gabriel took a final walk around the atrium of the museum before making his way across the road to the Château d'Or where Alan had suggested they meet for lunch. Gabriel had never been blessed with a strong sense of irony, but the interior of the restaurant left him suppressing a wry chuckle as he glanced around for the quietest place to sit and settled on a table for two in a far corner, close enough to the kitchen door to mean that any conversation was likely to be blocked out by the sound of food being prepared and waiters talking animatedly.

For starters, the restaurant clearly had absolutely no connection with France, but there was something about a French name associated with food which made an establishment immediately feel chic and sophisticated, the sort of place where caviar and foie gras would be served. He did not recognise the language the staff were using to talk to one another, as well as to some of the other diners, but a Polish flag was pinned up against one wall and had been lovingly decorated into what almost looked like a shrine. Gabriel glanced down at the menu, which was smeared with grease from handling by many hungry fingers, and he noticed quickly that he did not recognise a single dish on the menu.

It was with some relief, therefore, that Gabriel saw Alan walking through the door, conversing easily in Polish with the waiter, before looking round and spying his friend waving discreetly from the corner. "Where did you learn Polish?" asked Gabriel, admiringly. "You've no connection with Poland, have you?"

"Not exactly, old chap," Alan said, sitting opposite Gabriel. He did not bother looking at the menu; Gabriel suspected that he came here every day. "I've always had a fascination with languages, as you know. When this little place opened six months ago, I was curious. It's very convenient, nice and close to the museum. Since almost all the customers are Polish, I asked the waiters to teach me the language. Once a week, that charming young lady laying the table over there gives me a lesson."

Gabriel glanced at the beautiful young woman, a good ten years Alan's junior, who was working with undue care. She looked up briefly, made eye contact with Alan and smiled cheekily before disappearing back into the kitchen. Gabriel was no expert, but he had his suspicions about Alan's sudden interest in the Polish language. Having said that, claiming to have a fascination with languages was the understatement of the decade coming from Alan, who had left school speaking five languages fluently and seemed to have an almost super-human ability to absorb information. "I'm afraid I shall need your help with the menu," said Gabriel, sheepishly. "English and Italian food are about all I know."

"You'll love the food here," Alan reassured him with the same easy chuckle. "I placed my order when I walked through the door, and I asked them to bring the same to you. The dumplings are a bit of a speciality here."

"They sound delicious. I'm fond of dumplings."

"You were not so fond of them at school," laughed Alan, leaning back in his seat. "But then, these ones are actually cooked." He looked across the table at Gabriel, his face becoming more serious. "It's good to see you again, old friend. I've often wondered how you got on, hoped you'd be all right."

Gabriel found himself avoiding Alan's concerned gaze. "I suppose it must have looked as though I were running away. Escaping from everything. It wasn't quite like that, you know. I thought very hard about it before I entered, and you know, they don't let men take vows immediately or anything. There are years of waiting and studying."

"I'm sure. I'm sure you knew what you were doing. It was just, I always wondered—"

"I'm perfectly happy," Gabriel broke in. "Truly. I would not have it any other way now."

Alan hesitated as though standing at the edge of a mine-field, wondering the best way to tiptoe across. "You don't miss the old life? Even a little bit?"

"I miss people, if that's what you mean." Gabriel could feel his hands trembling under the table. Part of him wanted desperately to change the subject, but Alan was one of his few links with the past, and he was one of the only people with whom Gabriel could have such a conversation if he was ever going to have it. "The anniversary is coming up, of course. I always find it a little hard at this time of year. Nicoletta would be twenty now."

The awkward silence became a deathly pall, broken only by Alan's Polish teacher laying out glasses before them filled with something Gabriel did not recognise. She exchanged a few words with Alan. Gabriel watched in silence as Alan slipped his hand around hers, caressing her fingers lovingly, but it did not occur to either of them that the gesture of affection was visible. A moment later, she scurried away. Alan found his voice again. "I'm so sorry; it was so cruel. I'll never forget—"

"Don't," said Gabriel hastily, cutting Alan off before he said anything Gabriel could not bear to hear. Time was never a healer, not really; it simply dulled the pain. Sitting with a man he had met for the first time in a dusty common room at the age of seven, Gabriel realised that he was as unwilling to talk about it all as he had been in the days after the tragedy had occurred. Even with this man. "Faith helps, and my new life has been a cause of great solace to me," said Gabriel quietly. "There are so many broken hearts, Nell. Half the country seems to be grieving someone. Look at the Poles sitting around us. How many of them lost their families? How many of them witnessed death? If they've lost nothing else, they've lost their homeland. I think it makes it easier for me to minister to those souls."

Gabriel felt bile rising in his throat. Grief so like fear again. He reached into his pocket to take out the amulet and handed it to Alan as though he were handing him the Holy Grail. Alan looked quizzically at him before unwrapping the handkerchief as though he half expected it to be a trick of some sort. "So this is what you hiked away to London for, is it?" he asked, but to Gabriel's relief, Alan appeared transfixed by the object before him. He picked it up gingerly in one hand, looking at it intently, before turning it round to take a look at the other side. Finally, he looked back at Gabriel, but his face had hardened in a manner Gabriel had never witnessed before. "How the devil did you get hold of this?" he asked coldly. "Do you understand what it is?"

"I know only that it's Jewish," said Gabriel, falteringly. "That was why I assumed it would be important."

"But where'd you get it?" asked Alan. "How did you come to possess such a thing?"

Gabriel felt an unexpected attack of nerves. His friend's characteristic bonhomie had distilled into the manner of an interrogator remarkably quickly at the sight of that amulet. "I'm investigating a murder," Gabriel began, but he saw Alan's eyes rolling to heaven and suspected he would have burst out laughing if the mood of the conversation had not darkened so seriously. "No, I really am. I know how mad it sounds to you, but that's exactly how I came about it."

"I think we'd better take this from the top," said Alan. His voice was calmer and softer now, but he continued to look searchingly at Gabriel in a manner that made Gabriel want desperately to look away. The only break in the tension was Alan's lady friend appearing with steaming plates of food, forcing Alan to take his attention away from Gabriel, scoop up the amulet safely out of the way and smile at Beata before she disappeared again. "It's all right," Alan continued when they could no longer be heard. "Please don't imagine I'm accusing you of anything, but I'm not sure you understand what you've got yourself into. That's why I think it would be better if you told me what was going on."

Gabriel swallowed, but his mouth still felt dry. "I know how it's going to sound, but I was at a dinner party, and an elderly man was found dead in the grounds of the house the following morning. I've been trying to find out who did it . . ."

"I see. Go on. Who is this man—was this man?"

Gabriel gave Alan the best summary he could of everything that had happened: Victor's death, the confession of Emma, his complicated family life, the massacre he had witnessed and wanted to write about, Paul's study being ransacked, those notes being stolen along with another file and the discovery of the amulet at the bottom of the filing cabinet drawer. "That's the gist of it, really," said Gabriel, morosely. It made even less sense when he talked about the case to an outsider. "I had assumed that someone was trying to silence Victor Gladstone because he was the only witness to a war crime. The discovery of the amulet confuses things a little. Victor Gladstone was definitely not Jewish himself, so I assumed—well, I can only assume that he picked it up during his travels. Perhaps he found it in the possession of one of the victims and kept it as evidence."

Alan shook his head. "I very much doubt it. If this had been in the possession of a man murdered by the Nazis, they would have stolen it from the body themselves, not left it around the dead man's neck for someone else to take. You have no idea how much Jewish art was stolen by the Nazis before and during the war. Not just Jewish art—Europe was pillaged. It's a disgrace, a crime on a scale you cannot possibly understand unless you work in this field."

"I know about stolen Jewish artefacts; my abbot thought it was stolen. That was why he gave me leave to come here. He said what happened to the Jews cries out for vengeance. Justice, anyway. If there is any way I can restore this to its rightful owner . . ."

Alan shook his head sadly. "You know you will never do that; the rightful owner is almost certainly long dead. What troubles me about this amulet is that it is extremely valuable. It's well over a thousand years old, virtually priceless. It's the sort of object a man like me might handle once or twice in his entire life. That is how rare it is. It's not the sort of object a person would come across by accident. When it was stolen, my guess is that it went directly into the hands of some high-ranking Nazi who would have passed it on only to someone he trusted."

Gabriel's queasiness was coming back to get him again. He leaned against the table, his food untouched and now quite unappealing. "But Victor Gladstone was trying to expose a Nazi war crime!" Gabriel began, but he was struggling to get his thoughts in order. "Whatever else he was, I don't believe he was a Nazi. And . . . and . . . well, in any case, if he really had been given that amulet as a gift, is it likely he would have placed it in the care of his Marxist friend? It would've been too risky. What . . . what if he'd realised what it was? He was a shrewd man, if he was nothing else. I can't believe he would have taken such a risk. Wait—"

Gabriel was suddenly aware of Alan shaking his arm in an increasingly desperate attempt to get his attention. Gabriel glanced blankly at him, the fog slowly starting to clear. "What on earth's the matter, man?" asked Alan anxiously. "You're as white as a sheet. For goodness' sake, eat something!"

Paul would not have realised the significance of the amulet if Paul did not know it was there, thought Gabriel, helping himself to a mouthful of food simply to avoid the need to speak. *If Victor had hidden that amulet away in his file on the Martin family, Paul would have been none the wiser.* Gabriel swallowed hard. "Victor was not the war criminal; he took it from someone who was."

"Do you know who?" asked Alan. "Or can you at least guess?"

"I can think of only one person who could have come into possession of such an item," said Gabriel listlessly. He stared blankly at Alan. "Is treason still a hanging offence?"

Alan shook his head. "Only in time of war, I believe. Why?" But he did not need Gabriel to answer. "Listen, old chap. It hardly matters. If this man—Gladstone—took possession of this amulet to expose its owner as a Nazi traitor, he would be worth killing. It wouldn't matter if the guilty party would be spared a death sentence. Exposure like that would ruin a man."

Gabriel rose to his feet. "I have to get home, Nell. I shall have to act quickly, or they'll cover their tracks."

Alan motioned for Gabriel to sit down. "Don't go rushing off. You have to think about what you're going to do. Now, I'm loath to let you take this amulet away. It's very precious, and it would be a tragedy if it were lost again. Might I suggest—"

"I shall need it to bait the owner," said Gabriel. "I'll need to confront him with the evidence."

"This is a job for the police," warned Alan, wrapping up the amulet, but Gabriel was so distracted, he could barely focus his attention on what his friend was saying. "I'm not sure you appreciate what a dangerous world you've blundered into. Let me hold on to the amulet. You go to the police and tell them what you know."

Gabriel held out his hand for the amulet, which Alan had wrapped neatly for him. "Please. I need to confront him myself. If it really is so dangerous, it can hardly be safe for you to get caught up in all this. I shouldn't have involved you if it had occurred to me . . ."

"You may have been followed."

Gabriel glanced around him, taking in the reassuring sight of happy people chatting and laughing over plates of dumplings and pancakes and juicy sausages. Even with his elevated pulse, Gabriel could see nothing untoward around him, but he guessed that spies hardly announced themselves. "If there's any risk of that, you must give it back to me. I won't have you caught up in this. It's not fair."

"I don't mind."

Gabriel held out his hand again. Alan held the package, clearly weighing up in his mind whether he had the right to refuse to give it back to Gabriel, before handing it over with the utmost reluctance. "I'll take care of it, I swear. I'll take the next train out of town; I'll go directly to Inspector Applegate, and we can seek out the killer together."

Alan nodded, apparently reassured. "Good man. I'll be a great deal easier in my mind if I know you're working with the police on this." Alan looked around for Beata. "Do you want me to get a message to your companion?"

Gabriel's hand went to his forehead. "I'd almost forgotten poor Gerard. No, no, it's fine. I'll meet him as planned, and we can catch the train together."

Alan shook his head. "No, you won't. You will go directly to Paddington, and you will get yourself out of London. I'll meet your friend and tell him to follow you tomorrow."

"It seems a bit beastly just abandoning him like that," Gabriel protested. "He's never been to London before."

Alan stood up. "Under the circumstances, Eminence, I don't think the usual social niceties apply. Now leave me to settle up here, and go. Send me a telegram when this matter is settled. You'll need my help with that artefact again."

Gabriel shook Alan's hand and left without further word.

The amulet felt as heavy as a lump of iron ore in his pocket as Gabriel hurried through the darkening London streets. It was not long past two o'clock, but the sky was leaden, threatening an imminent downpour, and the stifling atmosphere had caused the smog to linger with greater intensity than usual. It might have been Gabriel's imagination, but he was sure he had walked through cheerier, brighter streets with Gerard earlier that day, though that might have been simply a reflection of Gerard's enthusiasm.

Gabriel needed Gerard's high spirits to help him hold his nerve if nothing else. He needed a young man to watch his back, thought Gabriel, turning off the main road into a residential side street. It was a quiet time of day. The children would be back at school by now, the men and a few of the women out at work. Those who remained would be safely ensconced in their homes, cleaning and preparing meals for the daily family reunion at the end of the afternoon. As he walked further along, the smooth, solid stone pavement crumbled away into a mass of cracks and large, jagged fragments, and he had to tread more carefully to avoid falling.

On either side of him, there were no longer houses, at least not houses in which anyone could attempt to live. The buildings had not been reduced to rubble like other neighbourhoods across the great city, but the houses had been sufficiently badly damaged as to be rendered derelict. Roofs were caved in, glass panes smashed in their window frames, walls partially collapsed to reveal sad, wrecked emptiness within. The occupants of these houses who had survived had no doubt taken away what belongings they could salvage, and scavengers had done the rest in spite of the harshest penalties for looting, but Gabriel could still see the odd stick of broken furniture; the remains of a dining table or a mouldy, filthy armchair; the ragged remains of a set of curtains a young housewife must have made and hung there so proudly years before.

There was something about the burn marks he could still make out across the shells of the buildings that unnerved Gabriel terribly. It was not just the sense of disorientation that came from walking straight from a busy, thriving thoroughfare into an apparent wilderness that caused him to break into a sweat. There was something so inhuman about houses burning. To be buried in rubble could hardly be so terrible a death, knocked into instant oblivion by tons of brick and wood and roof slate. But to burnd . . .

Gabriel had to get out of this accursed place. He was not

just anxious now, he was being overwhelmed with panic. In a minute, he would be completely helpless. Gabriel turned around, making a split-second decision to retrace his steps out of this neighbourhood. He would find his way to the nearest Underground station and take the Tube to Paddington. Then he could get on the train and leave. Leave London, leave this mausoleum to his worst memories.

He was not going anywhere. Gabriel had no recollection of what happened in the few seconds that followed other than that he found himself collapsed on the ground, paralysed with what he took to be fear and completely unable to draw breath. He was so stunned that for a moment he thought he had simply fainted in distress, his body unable to cope with the surge of unwelcome emotions that had ripped through him out of nowhere. He could feel the pain, half remembered from childhood, of grazes on his knees and hands from falling onto rough ground, but there was a thudding pain in the small of his back which told him that he had been struck from behind, powerfully enough to be winded and thrown forwards.

There was no time to think any further. A pair of hands grabbed his arms and hurled him over onto his back. Gabriel found himself staring up at a man swathed in black from head to foot, his hat pressed down low over his face and a scarf wound carefully around his mouth to make it impossible for anyone to get a good look at his face. With the reflex of an old soldier, Gabriel glanced at the man's gloved hands and noted that his assailant was unarmed. He must have thrown a piece of debris at Gabriel from a short distance away to avoid Gabriel noticing the man creeping up on him, though Gabriel had been so distracted he might well have missed a hostile force bearing down on him.

Gabriel found his voice with great difficulty. "I'm a priest," he said, more calmly than he felt. "I've no money to steal. Please——" He was stopped by the man's fists coming down against his cheekbone, so heavily and painfully that Gabriel knew the man was armed after all. He felt the knotted metal links of a knuckle-duster under the man's glove a second before blood filled his mouth.

"I'm not after any money," said the man, removing his gloves. Those would be the only words he said or the only ones Gabriel remembered afterwards, but memory could be as merciful as it was sadistic, and Gabriel's only clear memory of the hideous minutes that followed was of his own panic that the stolen object in his possession was about to be stolen again, and this time it was entirely his fault. In the punch-drunk delirium before he lost consciousness, he saw Alan Ellsmore telling him that the amulet should be left in his care, he heard Abbot Ambrose—the eternal, unyielding voice of conscience—warning him, always warning him against his every mad escapade . . . and he saw Victor Gladstone gloating over a terrified woman, swinging the amulet before her eyes like a demonic hypnotist.

12

Gabriel could still taste blood in his mouth when he woke up. He could hear dull murmuring voices very close to him, but for a time he found it impossible to move or speak. In his confusion, Gabriel thought he was on a battlefield again, lying curled up in a crater in no-man's-land, about to bring his ignominiously short military career to a humiliating end. He could feel the sodden earth crumbling beneath his hands and the acrid taste of cordite at the back of his throat as the last residues of the explosion hovered in the dank air. There were voices, the hushed sounds of stretcher bearers trying to decide the best way to reach him. His ribs throbbed with pain every time he drew breath, causing him to breathe too shallowly and risk losing consciousness again. Through a film of smoke, he could see two male figures standing over him who he instinctively knew meant him no harm.

"Help me," he whispered. "I'm wounded, help . . ."

"You certainly are, old man," came a voice Gabriel did not recognise, but he had not expected to. He blinked in surprise at the sight of a man who looked far too old to be anywhere near a theatre of war, dressed in civvies, bareheaded, with a stethoscope slung casually around his neck. "You've nothing to fear; you are quite safe," said the man, in an almost coaxing tone. "Keep nice and still, there's a good chap."

The rest of the room came into focus very slowly. Gabriel was lying in bed, tucked in securely by layers of thick, soft blankets, his head and shoulders propped up by several plump pillows. He did not recognise the room at all and feared he ought to somehow, but there was no detail of it that made any sense. His eyes rested on an olive wood crucifix displayed discreetly on the otherwise plain wall directly opposite him, and he felt himself relaxing momentarily at the sight of the one recognisable detail in the whole room.

Another face came into focus. It was Alan Ellsmore, looking solicitously down at him with something very like regret on his face. Gabriel's stomach lurched. "The amulet!" He tried to shout, but his throat was dry. "It's gone, isn't it?"

The doctor placed a hand on Gabriel's shoulder as he struggled to move. "You stay where you are, please. No sudden moves."

"But I've been robbed!" wailed Gabriel, attempting to search his pockets, but even in his state of confusion, Gabriel knew he was on a fool's errand. He was practically tied to the bed and could not have moved if he'd wanted to. As to his clothes, he appeared to have been relieved of them while he was senseless and was now dressed in a pair of ill-fitting pyjamas.

"I'm afraid so, old man," said the doctor. "You've been mugged. Some women found you in the street, out for the count. They summoned the police, and when the police realised how far from home you were, they searched your pockets and found Ellsmore's card."

"The amulet . . . ," Gabriel whimpered, but a whimper

was the best he could manage. It was so painful to breathe, and speech required too much breath to be worth the trouble.

"I'm afraid I did a rather shabby thing," said Alan ruefully, seating himself at Gabriel's bedside. "I suppose it might be just as well, but I shouldn't have done it anyway. I'm afraid I didn't quite trust you with the amulet. I could see how important it was; I've known men do desperate things to recover items like this. It occurred to me when I was asking you to let me look after the amulet for you, that if you had indeed been followed, it would be better if I held on to it but made it look as if I had given it back to you. I slipped it away when you were distracted and wrapped your handkerchief around a couple of pennies, hoping you wouldn't notice the difference in weight."

"You have it?"

"Yes, I have it."

Gabriel closed his eyes, letting a cool wave of relief wash over him. "Gerard . . ."

"Don't worry about him. I sent someone to find him at the cathedral and invited him to come here. He's downstairs, settling his nerves over a mug of Horlicks. It's mostly Horlicks."

Relief and exhaustion were sweeping over Gabriel in equal measure. "I'm sorry," he said, closing his eyes. "I'm sorry about all this bother."

Alan laughed lightly. "No bother at all, old chap. Now, it's getting late, and you need to get some rest. It could have been worse, but you have been quite badly beaten up. The doctor's going to give you something to see you through the night."

Gabriel was too shattered to ask anything else and attempted to return Alan's smile as his Good Samaritan left the room. He remembered Alan as the sort of boy who had always been in the background of school life, quietly getting on with things, wordlessly anticipating and dealing with every minor crisis. Gabriel watched as the doctor prepared a hypodermic needle and gingerly rolled up his patient's sleeve, since Gabriel did not seem up to the task himself. As unconsciousness claimed him again, Gabriel offered up a prayer of thanks for friends and kindness in a desolate world.

It was late the following morning that Gabriel was awoken by a soft knock on the door and Alan walked in cautiously, carrying a tray of breakfast. Gabriel was thrown once again by the unfamiliarity of the room; for a moment he wondered what on earth Alan Ellsmore was doing at the presbytery, before his mind began to clear and he remembered where he was. "Good morning," said Alan, but his cheerful tone did nothing to distract Gabriel from the anxiety written all over his face. "How are you feeling?"

Gabriel felt a horrible sensation across his own face which reminded him of the morning after a trip to the dentist. The whole of his jaw throbbed with pain, and when he felt along the inside of his mouth with his tongue, he could feel ragged patches and the beginnings of ulcers. There were other, lesser rumblings of pain whenever he breathed. "What on earth happened?" he asked lamely. "Why am I in your house, Nell?"

Alan set down the tray on the bedside table and helped Gabriel to sit up, a process that was harder than either man had anticipated. Gabriel was not just in pain—he felt stiff as a board and had to work his way up into a sitting position inch by eye-watering inch until he was finally sitting up in bed with his pillow offering much-needed back support. "You were mugged," said Alan, avoiding the temptation to beat about the bush. "You were brought here. The doctor took a look at you, and you've had a good sleep. I have the amulet."

Gabriel accepted a cup of tea gratefully, staring down into the cup as he gathered his thoughts. "A couple of thugs wanted the amulet, but you'd kept it for me. I think I can remember everything now."

Alan handed Gabriel a plate of toast. "Brother Gerard was able to ring your abbot late last night. As you can imagine, he was very worried and wants you to return to the abbey as soon as you are fit enough to travel."

Gabriel swallowed hard. He was hungry after the shock of the previous evening, but the pieces of toast in his injured mouth were as harsh and unpalatable as sandpaper. "I'll take a train this morning," declared Gabriel. "I have to find the man Victor Gladstone was about to expose, or I shan't be safe even in the abbey."

Alan topped up Gabriel's cup. "I'm not sure you should attempt a train journey today, old chap. The doctor was none too happy that you weren't in hospital, but I thought the police would be less inclined to pester you if you were here. I thought you'd rather not talk to the police."

"Quite," affirmed Gabriel, taking a sip of the milky tea. It felt beautifully soothing, and he slowly drained the cup. If he had nothing else to sustain him for the rest of his short life, let him always have plenty of tea. "I'm not sure the Metropolitan police could help anyhow. I'll let the inspector know as soon as I am absolutely certain who was behind this, and he can make an arrest. Heaven knows, I cooperate with him seldom enough."

"Rest another day before you travel," said Alan, seating himself in the armchair near the bed. "Give yourself some time to recover."

"I have no time," Gabriel insisted. As the last effects of the sleeping draught evaporated, Gabriel became more and more aware of the urgency of the situation. He had only ever meant to be away for twenty-four hours at the most. He ought to be back on a train already, chugging through the Wiltshire countryside. "Nell, I can't do this to you. It's not your job to nurse me; I know you should be at work by now. In any case, whoever robbed me will have discovered fairly quickly that he failed to gain possession of the amulet. It's only a matter of time before I'm traced here."

"If you think I'm afraid of Nazi thugs . . . ," Alan began, but Gabriel shook his head. "You mustn't worry, I told a little white lie this morning and said I was unwell. I've not taken a single day off work since I first took up that position. And I'm damned if anyone is going to break in here and rob you a second time."

Gabriel placed the cup and plate back on the tray and eased himself very slowly out of bed. He noticed that he felt a great deal better standing up; it was bending and stretching that posed more of a problem. "Where's Gerard?"

"He's having a cup of tea in my kitchen," said Alan. "He was up at the crack of dawn, so I suggested that he take a little walk before breakfast. I hope you'll forgive me for saying this, Eminence, but I'm not normally up with the lark. I found his enthusiasm a little too much."

Gabriel laughed, only to regret it immediately; he hugged his aching torso. "Surely not? You should see what he's like when he's overexcited."

Alan smiled, moving towards the door. "Why don't I let you get yourself ready? I'll be downstairs if you need me."

Gabriel watched Alan's retreating figure and the sight of the door closing slowly with a prolonged creak. It occurred to him that Alan had always lived alone, the archetypal bachelor, apart from his years of war work. He must be finding the sudden intrusion of unexpected visitors quite difficult. All that extra noise, the need to make conversation. Gabriel had not given much thought to what life must be like for his friend, but if it was nothing else, it was quiet. Alan woke up to an empty house, ate his breakfast alone and travelled to work, probably without speaking to another soul before he arrived at the museum. Even there, his was a quiet profession, with little need for chatter and the inanities of small talk. Gabriel hoped that Alan's friendship with his lovely Polish-language teacher would blossom in the months to come. He would make a good husband; God willing, even a father. It was not quite too late for him.

When Gabriel had found his way downstairs, Alan and Gerard were poring over a train timetable together. "Cor, would you look at your face!" Gerard blurted out, pointing at Gabriel in case the man had not noticed that half his face was swollen and purple. Gabriel had had enough of a shock when he had glimpsed himself in the shaving mirror. "You look like you've been in a boxing match."

"And lost," answered Gabriel wryly, sitting down at the table. *Thank you for your sympathy*, he thought, irked with himself that he had expected Gerard to smother him with kindness and concern. He had been friends with Gerard long enough to know that his teasing was a safety valve to dispel emotions with which he was incapable of dealing.

"I've been looking up train times for you," said Alan. "I can't help thinking it would be better if you went home through Salisbury. That way, you could take a train from Waterloo rather than Paddington. If someone really is watching you, they'll be waiting at Paddington. It will give you a clear run home, and you'll be well out of harm's way by the time anyone notices you've left London."

Gabriel nodded. "Good. That'll give me enough time to meet the people I need to speak to and alert the police."

Alan pushed the train timetable towards Gabriel and indicated the time of departure. "You'll need to get a move on to catch the train, but it's not too far from here once you're on the tube. If I were you, I'd get this whole situation tidied up as quickly as you can and get yourself back to your monastery. These people are evil. They stole from condemned men."

"Well, you're scintillating company," commented Gerard, breaking into Gabriel's thoughts. Gabriel had been staring through the murky window at the fields and trees whizzing past them, but it had been a long time since he had been aware of what he was looking at. His mind was many miles away. "Do you realise you've been staring into space for half an hour?" asked Gerard. "I've smoked two cigarettes, and you haven't even complained yet. I lit up only to try to get your attention."

"Sorry," murmured Gabriel, rubbing his eyes. The act of touching his face brought with it a painful reminder of the previous day, and he shuddered. "I'm rather sorry I got you caught up in all this. I didn't expect it to be a particularly pleasant journey, but I never expected it would end this way."

"Don't be silly, Gabbers, you didn't ask to get bashed about." He reached into his bag and pulled out a round of sandwiches wrapped in greaseproof paper. He opened it up and offered one to Gabriel, but Gabriel shook his head. "Come on, you need to eat something. I'm worried about you."

Gabriel looked away awkwardly. "Don't be. For the first time since Victor Gladstone's death, I feel as though I'm actually getting somewhere. I knew Alan would be able to help."

"Got the killer's name written down, have you?" asked Gerard, in the manner of a ham horror villain.

"Not quite." Gabriel cleared his throat. "Gerry, would you be able to find your way back to the abbey without me? I need to go to see someone, and he may not be quite so open with me if I have company. No offence or anything."

"I'm not supposed to leave your side," said Gerard through a mouthful of corned beef sandwich. "We're supposed to return to the abbey together. Abbot Ambrose wants to see you."

"I know. I will come back, but I have to clear this up first. Today, in fact. If I don't, the culprits may well cover their tracks, and I'll never be able to get to the bottom of this."

"Who are the culprits?"

"I can't tell you that at the moment, I'm afraid," said Gabriel. "There's just one detail I have to confirm. That's why I need to speak to Gladstone's son."

Gabriel stared out of the window again. In the distance

he could see the outskirts of a Bronze Age fort, the name of which escaped him for a moment; the southwest was marked out by dozens of ancient monuments. The marks of civilisations past were etched into the land, offering the tiniest whisper of a memory that a great civilisation had lived there once before slipping away into the mists of time. It was like Alan Ellsmore's work, the gathering together of tiny fragments from thousands of years ago, that desperate attempt to piece together the daily lives of people who had lived and thrived only to be completely blotted out from the face of the earth.

"Have you ever wondered what would happen, Gerard," said Gabriel, "if Hiroshima happened again? Happened here, I mean. Do you ever find yourself wondering about that?"

Gerard looked down at the remains of the sandwich before shaking his head. "No," was his emphatic reply. "Why would the Americans want to drop a bomb on the West Country? D'ya think there might be Russian spies hiding out in Salisbury or something?"

"What about when everyone has one? Not just our allies —our enemies. What will happen then?"

Gerard suppressed a giggle. "Why would any country drop the bomb on Wiltshire?"

"London then." Gabriel looked intently at Gerard. "Before the war, I took all of this for granted. Everything. The towns and the universities and the millions of people going about their business, each of them with his own history, his own plans for the future. Then the war came."

"There have been a few wars before," Gerard suggested, but he spoke with the halfhearted manner of a man who knows he is wasting his time.

"But not a war like that. Millions dead, many we will never even account for. We will never know their names. And then the Americans dropped a bomb more destructive than anything the world has ever seen or ever will see."

"If it hadn't been them, it would've been—"

"Gerard, don't you ever stop and think how easily civilisation, our own civilisation, could melt away into history leaving little or nothing behind? Hundreds of years in the future, there might be men like Alan Ellsmore trying to piece together what we were all like and having precious little understanding of what we stood for. The whole of civilisation as we know it might be remembered from a few torn books, from the broken shards of a set of teacups. No one will know the difference between an essay by Cardinal Newman and an old lady's shopping list because no one will recognise the language anymore."

Gerard rolled his eyes, practically thrusting a sandwich into Gabriel's hands. "Eat your lunch and shurrup, you morbid old git! Listening to you makes me lose the will to live."

Gabriel laughed in spite of himself. "Pardon me for breathing," he said, biting into the sandwich, which was already a little damp and had lost its flavour, assuming it had ever had any. Whilst Gabriel ate, Gerard embarked upon a lengthy account of his own modest adventures in London whilst his companion had been confined to bed. Someone had enjoyed his brief sojourn in the Big Smoke, anyhow.

Gabriel walked with his hat pulled down low over his face and his eyes turned downwards, all the way to Bron's house. There was something about a man with a bruised face that seemed to elicit consternation rather than sympathy, as though everyone who saw him assumed that he had picked a fight with a bigger man rather than been the victim of a crime. Bron's neighbourhood was too genteel for a man in his condition, but he moved as quickly as he was able, ignoring his many aches and pains until he came to the door of Bron's splendid little home.

Bron was clearly in the house, as Gabriel could hear the sound of two raised voices before he had even mounted the steps to ring the doorbell. Bron had a most unwelcome visitor, and Gabriel would ordinarily have had the common sense to turn around and walk away rather than step directly into the hurricane of a blazing row, but he did not have time to postpone the meeting. He was about to ring the bell, wondering whether anyone would in fact hear him, when he noticed the front door was unlocked. He pushed it open, stepping into the hall in time to hear Paul Ashley's voice shouting, "I never asked for his filthy money, Bron! I don't want it; I won't take it!"

"Don't be ridiculous! Don't tell me for a moment you had no idea my father intended to give you his money. Verity had nothing to do with it, did she? You were just using her to get close to a rich man."

"I had no idea he was so rich! Neither did you, evidently."

Gabriel drew in as deep a breath as he could manage under the circumstances and pushed open the drawing room door. Bron and Paul turned to look at him before hastily stepping apart from one another. Gabriel doubted that the argument would have come to blows, but they had been standing far too close to one another for comfort. "You might have had the decency to knock, Father!" protested Bron before recoiling in shock. "What the devil's happened to your face?"

Gabriel took a step back, shaking his head. "Nothing to worry about. I'm afraid I found London a little less friendly than I remembered."

"But what happened?" Bron persisted. "You look as though you've been in a pub brawl!"

"An attempted mugging, nothing more," Gabriel explained. He wondered whether he was feeling just a little too relieved that Bron was so taken aback. If it was an act, it was a very good one, and Bron had never struck Gabriel as the sort of man who had a talent for playacting. If he was genuinely surprised at the state Gabriel was in, he had no prior knowledge of the attack. Paul, on the other hand, had not reacted at all and had moved himself further back into the room, positively trying to stay away from the conversation. Gabriel considered, though, that Paul might simply be relieved that Gabriel had interrupted an argument he was losing, giving Paul time to catch his breath and reconsider his position.

"You have my sympathies," Bron replied, throwing a scathing glance in the direction of Paul. "I've been the victim of a robbery myself. This disciple of Marx here has taken my inheritance."

"I did no such thing; you knew perfectly well you'd been disinherited," answered Paul, standing where he was. "I never asked your old man for a penny. I despise money! The accumulation of wealth goes against everything I believe."

"For a man who believes that money is the curse of the world," Bron retorted, "you seem to be rather good at getting your hands on it."

Paul turned to Gabriel as though he expected him to

mediate. "I never asked Victor for a penny. All I asked for was the means to assist him in writing his book. But he had agreed to give me that anyway."

"So, you did ask him for a few pennies then," said Bron. "There's a good living to be made out of this Nazi hunting lark, isn't there?"

Gabriel held up his hands as though attempting the calming of the storm. "Bron, did your father leave all his money to Paul? Were there no other legacies?"

"He left a substantial sum in trust for Verity's musical training," said Bron, "but he set that money aside for her years ago. When she was ten years old, Verity was selected to perform at a children's festival in London. When he heard her play, he was convinced that she was a musician in the making, and he promised to help her. The money was put in trust for Verity's use when she turned twenty-one. The rest of his fortune, every single dirty penny of it, goes to Paul."

"I don't want his dirty money!" exclaimed Paul, the temperature in the room accelerating again. "I'm happy to give it to you. I never asked for it; I don't want it. If you can bring yourself to leave me enough to help me write your father's book, I would be grateful. But I'll write the book whether or not you grant me the funds."

Bron's face had taken on a deep red tincture, and Gabriel could feel the second wave of the battle approaching. He interjected as quickly as he could. "Bron, it seems to me that Paul is attempting to patch things up with you. Perhaps you should listen to him? Surely there was hardly any money anyway? I understood that your late father had not done very well in recent years. I don't imagine there's enough money here worth fighting about." *Or killing for,*

Gabriel thought, but he did occasionally remember to keep his mouth shut.

Bron looked at Gabriel guardedly. Gabriel suspected that Bron would normally trust him without question, but his decision to defend Paul had made Bron wary. "Father, we are talking about a fortune. I've no idea how my father made his money, but he died a very wealthy man. I dread to think where he got it from, unless there were a few unexpected royalties cheques over the years." He looked at Gabriel as though gauging his reaction, only to dash forward and grab Gabriel's arm, moving him swiftly into a chair. "Look here, Father, I'm not sure you should be up and about in the state you're in. You've obviously taken a nasty bash to your head. Can you hear me?"

Gabriel looked morosely at Bron. It was true that he felt a little lightheaded, and Bron had probably noticed him swaying slightly, but there was a great deal more weighing him down than the memory of being mugged. "Bron, I'm very sorry to have to ask you this, but is there any chance that your father may have made his money on the black market?"

"Don't be ridiculous!" came the answer, and it was Paul, not Bron, who was speaking. "Victor Gladstone was not the most principled of men, but a war profiteer he certainly was not. Did he look like a spiv to you?"

"I wasn't thinking of that sort of black market," answered Gabriel shakily. If Paul was offended by the idea that Victor Gladstone may have traded in black market petrol coupons or pork sausages, he would go straight for Gabriel's jugular when he heard what was coming. "I mean stolen art. There was an awful lot of it circulating, if one knew where to look. Victor had contacts; he was a cultured man. He might easily have—"

Paul was towering over Gabriel in an instant. "Have you taken leave of your senses? Victor Gladstone trading in Nazi loot? If you weren't so old—"

Bron stepped between Paul and Gabriel as though asserting his proper place in the pecking order. "Father, you've a right to ask, I suppose, but that's quite impossible. My father was many things. He could be very greedy. But he would never have got his hands dirty like that, not at the expense of innocent people. Remember what he saw."

Gabriel nodded. "I understand."

Yes, Gabriel understood. He understood the extraordinary way in which family loyalties could compel a man like Bron to defend his father's honour against the most horrific of slurs, even though his father had cared so little for him. Gabriel did not imagine for a moment that Victor Gladstone had bequeathed his fortune to Paul for any generous reason —a sense of deep-rooted paternalistic affection, the belief that Paul and Verity would wish to marry one day and would need material help setting themselves up. He had given that money to Paul out of sheer spite, dealing his son a humiliating blow after death not only by cutting him off without a penny but by ensuring that Bron was forced to watch another man enjoy the spoils.

Gabriel reluctantly accepted Bron's offer of a lift home, only because he knew he would never be able to walk all the way and because he knew Fr Foley would be terribly worried if he did not return soon. He tried to listen to Bron's lengthy justification of an anger that hardly needed justifying, but Gabriel's mind was on Victor Gladstone, who had died a violent, unprovided-for death with so much on his conscience.

13

Gabriel braced himself for Fr Foley's reaction before stepping into the presbytery, half tempted to keep his hat and scarf on to avoid the conversation altogether. No such ruse was going to work, as Fr Foley had clearly been waiting for Gabriel's return and knew all about his misadventure. "I don't think you want to return to the abbey after all," was the first thing Fr Foley said, when he glanced up from the table where he was seated and noted Gabriel's arrival with some sort of bodyguard he appeared to have acquired. "I think you're trying to give me another heart attack so that you can stay here and take over my parish. It won't work, son."

Gabriel swallowed the words "I'm awfully sorry" on the grounds that it sounded too pathetic by far and tried a distraction technique instead. "Have you met Auberon Gladstone?" asked Gabriel, as though he were introducing two friends at a cocktail party. "He kindly gave me a lift."

"Of course I've met Bron," Fr Foley retorted, not to be batted off course. "Hundreds of times." He looked back at Gabriel, his expression softening. "Are you all right, son? You don't look too chipper."

"I'm quite well; please don't worry," said Gabriel, knowing perfectly well Fr Foley must have done little else since the previous day. "It could have been worse."

"It could also have been a good deal better. Your abbot sent me a telegram so that I wouldn't wonder why you hadn't returned. I suppose I might have guessed trouble would find you."

"That was good of him," said Gabriel, but his eyes rested on an envelope set to one side on the table with his name and address written on it in clumsy, untidy writing. "What's that?" Gabriel asked, not wanting to snatch it up without Fr Foley's permission, even if it was his letter.

Fr Foley glanced where Gabriel was pointing and smiled. "Sorry, I'd completely forgotten. That letter arrived for you while you were away. Looks like it came from a child."

Gabriel picked up the letter, noting the local postmark before opening it. "I wasn't expecting a letter."

"Abbot Ambrose wants you back at the abbey, Gabriel," said Fr Foley, "at least until this business is over. He's worried about you." Fr Foley glanced at Bron. "Forgive me for keeping you standing like that. Would you like to sit down? I'll put the kettle on."

Gabriel shook his head before Bron could answer. "I'm not sure we'll be able to stay. I need to go to the Martins' house. Molly has written to me, asking me to come as soon as possible."

"What's happened?" asked Bron. "Not ready to confess, is she? Sorry." He looked down to avoid Gabriel's indignant look. "Sorry, that really was in poor taste. I suppose I just wish someone would confess."

"You may continue to dream of that possibility," answered Gabriel. "Life would be a good deal easier if everyone simply owned up—or dare I say it, avoided the temptation to kill one another in the first place."

"I'm not sure you're in a fit state to go anywhere," Fr Foley put in, "especially the site of a murder. This is a matter for the police, Gabriel."

"She's frightened," said Gabriel. "If she trusted the police, she would have gone to the police." He could see Fr Foley about to speak again and added quickly, "It's all right, I shall get the police involved myself. I owe it to Applegate to tell him what I know."

"What do you know?" It was Bron this time. Gabriel looked from one expectant face to the other. "Would you like me to take you to the Martins'?" suggested Bron. "I should like to see how Verity is getting on, and this would give me a reason to be there. If you want me to take a message to Inspector Applegate, I could do that on the way back."

Gabriel shook his head. "By the time you get back to town, it will be too late. Applegate may have gone home. If you could just wait a moment . . ."

Gabriel moved over to the table. He had not removed his hat and coat because he had known since he arrived that he would have to leave almost immediately, and he was suddenly sweltering. "Father, may I cadge a piece of paper and an envelope from you?"

Fr Foley went over to his bureau and took out the requested materials from one of the drawers. Gabriel smiled, realising that Fr Foley was using the kitchen table to work only because the bureau was too much of a mess to be used. The room was slowly being buried in paperwork. "Do you have your pen with you?" asked Fr Foley, indicating the bottle of india ink near his place at the table. "Help yourself."

Gabriel sat down and took out his fountain pen. The

sense that there were two men looking quizzically at him made him clumsy, and he struggled with the mundane task of inking his pen and scribbling a note to Applegate that contained only two sentences. He was so distracted that he failed to notice the blotter directly in front of him until Fr Foley thrust it in his face. He was almost relieved that Fr Foley took the notepaper from him and folded it himself, deftly placing it in the envelope before handing it back to him. Gabriel sealed it and scrawled Applegate's name untidily across the front.

Bron was at his side. "Are you sure you don't want me to deliver that for you?" he asked.

Gabriel looked at Fr Foley. "Is there any way you could dash over to the police station?" he asked.

"It's a while since I have been able to dash anywhere," answered Fr Foley wryly, but he took the envelope from Gabriel. "It's all right, I'll pop next door and ask Mrs Foster to send Doris round with it."

Gabriel nodded. Doris was an athletic twelve-year-old whose physical fitness was outdone only by her exhausting enthusiasm for life. She would race over to the police station quicker than Fr Foley could make his way the twenty steps back home. He turned back to Bron. "We'd better go."

Gabriel told himself that he only felt overcome by queasiness as they stepped out into the courtyard because he had left his coat on and the icy temperature outdoors came as so much more of a shock. He tried and failed to resist the temptation to look back over his shoulder as they walked towards Bron's motor, desperate for some reassurance that Fr Foley really meant to take his note round to Doris immediately. There was no sign of Fr Foley emerging from the presbytery when he looked back for the third time. "You'll turn into a pillar of salt," commented Bron, opening the car door for him when Gabriel was too distracted looking back at the presbytery to get into the car himself.

"Only if Saint Patrick's can be likened to Sodom and Gomorrah," Gabriel responded, getting into the car. He looked again back at the presbytery and saw Fr Foley, true to his word, ambling out of the door in the direction of Mrs Foster's house. "What if Doris isn't in?" asked Gabriel anxiously. "I wonder if Fr Foley will have the presence of mind to—"

"Of course he will, Father," Bron reassured him, in the tone of a schoolmaster trying to placate a neurotic child, but Gabriel was used to being spoken to like that. "If it's really so urgent, we could have driven round to the police station and dropped it off ourselves and then gone on to the Martin estate. It would have been only a short detour."

"No, no," said Gabriel emphatically, "it's important that we don't arrive at the same time as the police."

Bron looked guardedly at Gabriel. "What the devil are you up to?"

"I'm not exactly up to anything. Well, I suppose I am up to something. It's just that it would be easier for the person concerned to confess to me before he or she confesses to the police."

"Unless the person concerned does a runner before the police can arrive," suggested Bron. "I'm really not sure you've any business . . . I mean, are you saying that you know who killed my father?"

"That's not exactly what I said," clarified Gabriel, "but somebody is going to be arrested this evening, and it's going to be rather ghastly, I'm afraid. You see, I think your father was very good at stumbling upon situations accidentally. I kept thinking about that when Paul was talking to me about the massacre. Of course, there was so much killing during the war. I suppose, if one were travelling with the army, one might stumble upon a situation like that. Even so, it was unfortunate."

"Unfortunate?" exclaimed Bron. "That's one way of putting it! You do realise, don't you, that my father never recovered? You must know by now without any shadow of a doubt that I did not get along with my father. In fact, I think it's fair to say that we fell out with one another when I was about seven years old. I'd be a rank hypocrite if I pretended to be the grieving son. Even in death, he's found a way to hurt me. But no one deserves to witness what he saw."

"Please forgive me," Gabriel put in, genuinely mortified at how he had sounded. "Of course, I don't mean that the massacre was unfortunate or that your father's pain was unfortunate. I'm sure he must truly have suffered. All I meant was that the Nazis were very good at concealing their crimes. They murdered millions of people—*millions* —and they were so good at hiding their crimes that there are still people who don't believe the Nazis did anything wrong. That's what I meant when I said it was unfortunate. To have been in exactly the wrong place at the wrong time. I didn't get the impression that your father was on the trail of a war criminal or anything like that. He just happened to be in a deserted place at precisely the moment the Nazis chose to commit that outrage."

"I understand, Father," said Bron, more calmly. "I suppose I just get so sick of the way everyone is trying to pretend that nothing happened. I wanted my father to expose that crime to the world, even if it meant getting that weasel Paul involved."

"He mayn't be a weasel, Bron."

"He's a weasel. If a man like Paul cared so much about bringing down the Nazis, he should have been prepared to risk his own life resisting them. He just sat there. Got himself a cosy desk job while young men were dying on the beaches of Normandy trying to liberate Europe. I'm sorry, I'm not making any sense."

"Bron," said Gabriel, quietly, "it's not unreasonable that you should feel such a sense of conflict. Witnessing a massacre does not make a man a saint, any more than suffering does. But I would caution to be a little careful about Paul. There were many men with invisible illnesses who were unable to fight during the war, who were labelled cowards."

"Father, Paul Ashley has made a huge song and dance about the fact that he refused to fight on a point of principle. The principle that he didn't want to get killed, presumably."

How absurd, thought Gabriel, fidgeting in his seat, *that a man such as Paul should have been so consumed by pride that he claimed to be a conscientious objector to hide his infirmity, even at the risk that other men would think him a coward. How humiliating pride is!* "Bron, I know I've asked you this before, but can you tell me again what you remember your father telling you? I'm sure there's something here I'm missing."

"I can't see that there's any need for me to pore over those details again," said Bron tersely, gripping the steering wheel as though he were strangling it. "As I said before, I'm sure, when he got back from the war he talked to anyone who

215

would listen. Then suddenly, he stopped. It was as though a great big blank wall came down and he couldn't speak of it again. I think shock sometimes happens that way. That was why he got Paul involved. He couldn't cope with reliving it all on his own, but he needed the company of someone who didn't know him very well. Some men open up more easily to relative strangers."

Gabriel tried to steady his mind by looking out the window. Nothing normally settled his thoughts more quickly than a glimpse at the passing countryside, but it was already dark and he might have been looking at a series of underexposed photographs, all blurs and smudges of black with the odd patch of light here and there in all the wrong places. "You said the victims were young boys; that was the detail that haunted your father."

Gabriel noticed Bron clenching the steering wheel ever tighter. "Look, Father, there was nothing he said that was out of the ordinary. That's the sad fact of the matter. There were many massacres, and this one appears to have followed a familiar pattern. He said he became separated from the men he was with and found himself in a deserted village. There was a sudden downpour of rain. He ducked into the nearest empty building, an old warehouse of some kind, he thought, and decided to wait there until the storm passed. As he was looking out through the window, he saw uniformed men marching a ragtag group of boys in the direction of the warehouse. He hid behind some old crates and watched from his hiding place as they were brought inside."

"He must have been petrified," said Gabriel, by way of a prompt, as Bron had sunk into silence. Gabriel could see Victor Gladstone in his mind's eye, not as the rude, overbearing elderly man he had encountered at that fateful dinner party, but as a terrified soul, lost and alone, cowering in the darkness of a death chamber. Petrified. Literally unable to move, scared for those hapless strangers who had been singled out for murder, perhaps for no other reason than that they happened to be—like Victor—in the wrong place at the wrong time. And petrified for himself and the certain death that would come to him if he were discovered.

"The rest you know," said Bron, breaking into Gabriel's dark thoughts. "They were all shot, the struggling boy first because they probably had to kill him before he sent the others into a blind panic. Afterwards, the executioners went round making absolutely sure no one survived, and they went out, laughing and chattering. My father couldn't understand what they were saying, of course, but he knew they were very, very pleased with themselves."

A nasty thought came over Gabriel. He could well understand why the image of a young boy calling for his mother would have haunted a witness, even a witness as apparently hard-hearted as Victor Gladstone. But a particularly unsavoury detail of that death was troubling Gabriel, and he could not find a way to frame the question that did not sound obsessive. "Bron, you know when you told me before that your father had said that a boy had his hands tied behind his back because he was struggling so much? Did he say what they used?"

Bron took his eyes off the road just long enough to throw Gabriel an exasperated glance. "Why on earth would he have told me that? A bit of string? An old cloth? Why would it matter?"

"Would they have used a belt?" he asked, stoically ignoring Bron's indignation. He anticipated the response that was coming to him. "I know it's a small detail, but—"

"It's a ludicrous detail, Father. Some poor kid who's never hurt anyone, dies crying for his mother and you want to know how they tied him up? Who cares?"

Gabriel sank back in his seat as Bron drove a little too aggressively between those stone pillars, the two griffin sentries reminding them, as ever, that they were most unwelcome. The way Bron put it, Gabriel's hunch did sound odd, but his response seemed to confirm that Bron knew nothing of significance about the belt and had never seen it. Now that Gabriel considered it, it would be a horribly macabre souvenir to remove from a body, hardly of use as evidence. An identity card taken from the dead boy's pocket or a dog tag from around a soldier's neck was one thing—a man might take such an item with the hope of tracing the dead person's family or ensuring that his death was not forgotten. Gabriel tried to think of a more positive reason Victor might have cut the boy's hands free. He could not quite imagine Victor acting so tenderly, but if he had been as badly affected by witnessing the boy's murder as Bron suggested, he might have been overwhelmed by a desire to help him in some way, even if the gesture was futile. Untying the boy's hands and moving his body into a more dignified position might have been the only act of kindness Victor could have thought to do for him.

"I don't suppose I'm allowed to know why this is all so urgent?" asked Bron as he parked the car. "Is this to do with something you discovered in London? I can't imagine there'd be—"

"I'm here to warn Florence Martin, and I'm here to warn Molly," said Gabriel, opening the door. "I'm afraid they've both been extremely indiscreet, and they are both about to be punished for it. Molly put far more into that letter than she needed to, without guessing that it might be read by a third party before I saw it."

Gabriel made a dash for the front door, not waiting to see if Bron had followed him. Gabriel was hardly a past master in the art of subterfuge and could scarcely have hidden his tracks if he had wanted to; Florence clearly heard the car screeching to a halt outside the house and watched Gabriel hurrying to the door from the comfort of the parlour window. Before Gabriel could reach for the doorbell, Florence threw open the door, glaring at him like a thing possessed. "I don't know how you have the cheek to come back here!" shrieked Florence. The thirty-seconds-or-so warning had given her time to work herself up into a lather of indignation, and she stood before Gabriel like a high-class Medusa, hissing serpents carefully pinned away from her enraged, petrifying eyes. "You put her up to it, didn't you? You sent that stupid little girl spying on me!"

Gabriel cleared his throat, not that he could hope to compete with Florence Martin's volume. "That's most unfair, if I may say so, Mrs Martin. If the letter Molly sent me suggested—"

The enraged Medusa's face took on a look of bewilderment. "How can you possibly know what the little wretch put in that letter? I caught her writing it this afternoon and tore it up in front of her eyes. Five minutes before I sacked her."

Gabriel's own confusion was tempered by the news Florence had been good enough to share with him. "You've sacked Molly? Oh, but it wasn't the poor girl's fault!" Florence Martin's bewildered face had returned to its default position again, and Gabriel felt the ground sliding from beneath his feet. Molly must have been so desperate to get a response from him that she had attempted to write a second letter, and she had paid for it with the loss of her position. "Mrs Martin, where is she now? Did she say where she was going?"

"She's here, Father," answered Florence coldly. "I've given her until the end of the month."

Gabriel felt relief flowing over him. There was always some small shred of humanity somewhere, even with people as self-serving as the Martins. "It's awfully decent of you not to turn her out. At least she'll have time to find somewhere to go."

"I couldn't possibly let her go any sooner, Father," Florence retorted. "It will take me until the end of the month to find a replacement, and I can't afford to be a pair of hands short."

Gabriel felt his spirits sinking into the abyss. "I see," he said glumly. "Might I have a word with her?"

Florence's painted lips slipped effortlessly into a smirk. "I don't think so, Father. Now, I think you'd better leave. I should rather not hear from you again, if it's all the same to you."

"Mrs Martin," said Gabriel, reaching forward to try to stop her from closing the door in his face, "I think it would be better if you trusted me. You can't possibly hide your ill-gotten gains before the police arrive."

Florence hesitated, the door partially concealing her from view. "The police?"

"Mrs Martin, I'm afraid you are about to be arrested for dealing in stolen property. And for the murder of the man who was blackmailing you."

Florence threw the door open with the full force of her strength. "How dare you use that word to me! I didn't do it!" It was no good; the indignant tone sounded forced. "Father, do you honestly think me capable of killing a man, even a parasite like Victor Gladstone?"

"You had motive," said Gabriel steadily. "The court will not believe that you were too ladylike to bash a man over the head. And he was blackmailing you, wasn't he?"

Florence stood helplessly in the doorway, the light behind her throwing her whole figure into shadow. She looked blankly at Gabriel for a few short seconds, as though trying to determine how much he really knew; then the burden of a miserable secret crushed her, and she covered her face with one hand. "Yes," she choked. "He was bleeding me dry." She stepped to one side to let Gabriel in, and he followed her into the warmth of the house. He could hear the faltering steps of Bron bringing up the rear.

"Shall I wait in the car?" whispered Bron. "I'd rather not pry."

"You shall do no such thing," Florence replied, without turning to look at him. "Verity is practising, as you can probably hear. I suggest you go up and keep her company. I'll send Molly up with tea in a little while."

They could indeed hear the piano playing, but it was such a permanent part of the noise of the house that neither Gabriel nor Bron had registered its presence. Bron smiled at Florence and went on his way.

"Where is your husband?" asked Gabriel as they walked together into the drawing room. "It would be better if he joined us."

"He's not been well these past few days," said Florence, helping Gabriel off with his coat. "It's Trevelyan's night

221

off," she added, before Gabriel could ask why there were no servants about. "Horace has barely left his room since yesterday."

Gabriel waited while Florence settled herself by the fire before joining her. He couldn't help looking round the room and thinking how well they had resisted the temptation to display some of the pieces that must have slipped through their hands over the years. The room was richly furnished, but the paintings and figurines so tastefully dotted about the room were unexceptional works collected over generations —from the prizes acquired by young men coming home from their Grand Tour to the small, commissioned pieces intended to support struggling artists who had long since slipped into obscurity. "Mrs Martin, your husband can't hide away from the world forever. When the police arrive, he will have questions of his own to answer. I know you did not work alone."

"I will not have him shamed for any of this," said Florence, and her eyes were shiny with tears. "It was my idea from the start. He had friends. We used to spend our summers in Germany when we were newly married. Some of his friends became very influential. There was almost more need after the war had ended. Some of these men got themselves into terrible trouble; they were terrified of falling into the hands of the Communists. They were selling everything they had."

Gabriel could see the images of one of the few newsreels he had seen, flashing before him again. He saw those mounds of skeletal corpses, those emaciated, listless children in striped uniforms, staring into the camera from behind barbed wire fencing; he saw one particular image that had implanted itself so deeply in his mind that he knew it would never leave him—a little boy no more than six or seven years old, huddled up next to the body of a woman who was clearly his mother, stroking her hair as he waited for her to wake up. He had heard a rumour that the cameraman who had captured that terrible moment had taken his own life shortly afterwards. Gabriel struggled to swallow, his mouth was so dry; but he could sense Florence watching him closely, noting his change of expression. "Mrs Martin, those men you speak of were criminals. They had innocent blood on their hands. How can you live with yourself? You know that you funded the escape plans of men who were running from justice!"

"But what sort of justice would the Communists have given them?" Florence demanded, desperately seeking some common ground between them. "The Soviets have committed their own atrocities! What did they do to the women of Germany? Just because nobody here cares about Germans getting killed, it doesn't mean it hasn't happened!"

Gabriel reached into his pocket and carefully took out the amulet, cradling it in his hands so that she could get a good look at it, whilst making it clear that she did not have any business touching it. "Which man in terrible trouble gave you this?" he asked, watching for her response as she looked at the amulet, but she was giving nothing away. "It was obviously someone important."

If Gabriel had expected a confession of guilt, he was greeted instead by a look of confusion from Florence. "Why would anyone try to trade a thing like that?" she asked, gesturing for him to put it away. "I only ever dealt with valuable works, things that would raise a lot of money very quickly. This cannot be worth much; it's just an old pendant."

"It's mine, Father," came a rumbling voice from the doorway, startling them both. Neither of them had heard Horace approaching the room or had any idea how long he had been standing there, listening to them. "At least it was mine before that snake in the grass stole it from me. I still don't know how he found out about it."

"It was never yours to begin with," said Gabriel coldly. He was almost more angered by the man's indignation on his own behalf than the magnitude of the crime in which he had embroiled himself. "Though the evil man who entrusted this precious object to you is now dead, is he not?"

Horace nodded wearily. "I believe he was killed trying to escape from Berlin. Nothing could help him in that hellhole." He looked at Gabriel, noticing the frown creeping across his face. "Father, if you imagine I was smuggling goodies for Heinrich Himmler, I did no such thing. The man who entrusted me with that amulet had no great power."

"He had the power of life and death over a good many innocents, I suspect," answered Gabriel, "and that is the most formidable power a man can ever be granted."

Horace sat down heavily, staring ahead into the fire to avoid having to look at his wife to his right or Gabriel to his left. Gabriel suspected that Horace was fully aware of the despicable nature of his crime but was too implacably proud ever to admit to being in the wrong. "It's a piece of metal, Father," he said, quietly. "A very ancient, very valuable piece of metal, but nothing more. I didn't kill anyone; I didn't hurt anyone."

Gabriel looked at Horace's rugged profile, which would have been handsome before the years had etched themselves into Horace Martin's flesh and before overindulgence in a time of hunger had caused hundreds of tiny capillaries to burst across his cheekbones, leaving behind a pattern of little red spiders. Horace was yet another pathetic link in a chain, one of those invisible little men who aid and abet evil, who profit from it and make themselves comfortable on the back of the cruelty and murder of others, who never take a stand, never express the smallest reservation about the corruption all around them—men without whose greed, selfishness and moral equivocation, the bloodiest atrocities on the planet could never occur.

"Have you any idea what fate befell the family who owned this amulet?" asked Gabriel, his voice trembling with anger he was sure Horace would mistake for weakness. "Or any of the little treasures you have guided through the criminal underworld, for that matter?"

Horace rose to his feet, his hypertensive face flushing even deeper than usual. "If they were killed, it had nothing to do with me. I didn't kill them; their deaths mean nothing to me."

Gabriel jumped up as though jolted by a bolt of electricity. The two men stood inches apart, the fire throwing their bodies into relief as though they were two souls battling at the gates of hell. "Would you say that if they had been your own people?" shouted Gabriel, causing Horace to brace himself as though he expected the priest to take a swing at him. "Would you be so sanguine about it all if your own family, your own children, had been shot dead by death squads?"

"Plenty of our own people did die, Father," answered Horace, "or perhaps you failed to notice, tucked away in your monastery?"

Florence was at Gabriel's side. "Father, this is my fault," she said, desperately. "It was my idea from the start."

"Florence, be quiet!" ordered Horace. "I'm perfectly capable of answering for my own mistakes."

"This is not your mistake!" Florence persisted, but Horace grabbed her by the arm and began propelling her swiftly out of the room. "I think you should check on Verity. I can't hear the piano."

"Mr Martin," said Gabriel. "I would like to speak with your wife alone."

Horace stopped in his tracks, glaring at Gabriel. "This is no business of yours! Our affairs are no business of anyone's!"

"Tell that to the police," said Gabriel, turning to Florence to gauge her feelings, but she was looking at him in undisguised horror. "Would you like your husband to stay, or shall we speak alone?"

Florence moistened her lips, avoiding her husband's deathly glare. "I should like to speak with you alone," she said in a rush of hushed words. Horace growled indignantly, but he said nothing. "Please, darling," she said to her husband, still not looking at him. "We may not have much time. He may be able to help us."

"Don't tell him anything!" Horace commanded her. "He has no business what—"

"*Please.*"

Horace hesitated, waiting for either Florence or Gabriel to have a change of heart, but they both stood in silence, waiting for him to leave. In the distance, they could hear Verity at the piano again after a short break, the complex melodies providing a strange sense of normality to the situation. "Very well," said Horace gracelessly, and he left.

Florence collapsed into a chair almost immediately. "It really is my fault; I wasn't just trying to save him," said Florence breathlessly. "It was almost all my work, but I know the police won't believe it. They'll be happy to think that my husband was the brains behind it all and I was his witless assistant."

Gabriel sat opposite her. It was the first time he had noticed the toll the whole case was taking on her. Florence was attempting to maintain standards, but he could not help noticing how haggard she looked under that thin film of makeup and how hard she was finding it to keep still. She was a woman who had been brought up to sit upright, ankles crossed, hands folded in her lap, but she sat before him with her shoulders hunched, wringing her hands like a schoolgirl awaiting a reprimand.

"I'm sorry about what happened to you in London," Florence said with what sounded like a considerable effort. "I'll take responsibility for everything else, but sending those men after you was not my idea. I would never have let anyone hurt a priest. Especially you."

"Thank you," said Gabriel, though in his clearer moments it would not have occurred to him to be grateful to a person for not having him beaten up. "Was that your husband?"

"He paid some men—please don't tell him I told you this! He'll never forgive me for sneaking on him. They were only supposed to take back the amulet; he didn't tell them to hurt you."

Gabriel sighed. "Madam, you can hardly hire criminals

to do your dirty work, then expect them to behave themselves," he commented, but Florence was drawing out a handkerchief from her pocket, sending out a cloud of jasmine. It was an unusually exotic scent for a woman like her, but it was the least of his misjudgements about Florence Martin's personal habits. "Why did you do it? You're a good woman, Mrs Martin; how on earth did you get yourself involved in such a dirty trade? If your husband has no compassion for all those murdered Jews, surely you feel something?"

Florence burst into tears, which was either a very good or a very bad sign. Gabriel had no sense that he was being manipulated; he suspected that Florence was genuinely remorseful, and not just because of the prospect of a criminal charge. She had persisted in her activities by convincing herself repeatedly that she was doing nothing wrong or by avoiding thinking about it at all. The mildest possible brush with the truth and the paper-thin wall she had constructed around her conscience had come tumbling down in a moment.

"Father, I tried so hard not to think about where all those beautiful things were coming from," sobbed Florence. "My family had worked in the antiques trade; that was why they gave me my name. I grew up surrounded by paintings and statuettes and tapestries. Beautiful things everywhere. Harmless things."

"You know this was different," said Gabriel. "You have always known."

"It was so tempting!" Florence responded. "You've no idea, you've no idea how tempting it was. I couldn't bear to lose our home. We needed money, lots and lots of money to pay the death duties after my father passed away. Even during the war, we realised how precarious our position was. We avoided the house being requisitioned only because we agreed to take in evacuees. Vermin, Horace called them."

Gabriel looked around the room. He had never thought a great deal about the origins of the house other than that it was old, if not nearly as old as it pretended to be, but the significance of the estate's history jumped out at him in a blur of telltale signs. He stood up to get a better look around him. "This was your family's estate, Mrs Martin, not your husband's."

"Yes," said Florence, standing up to avoid Gabriel having to look down at her when he spoke. She walked past him to the large bay window and looked out at the imposing entrance to the estate and the path down which all visitors travelled. "I was born and brought up here, Father. My great-grandfather built the house. My whole life is bound up with this place; I have never lived anywhere else. I'm not sure I could live anywhere else now."

Gabriel followed Florence's gaze along the empty path. He could just imagine Florence as a child, sitting in this bay window with the curtains converting the little space into a convenient hidey-hole. He thought of her watching the world going by, the tradesmen early in the morning—the butcher's boy on his bicycle, the postman, the milkman with his pony, the greengrocer—all hurrying down the path before quickly slipping round to the back entrance; then the elegant visitors of the evening, done up to the nines, wholly uninterested in a little girl hiding from her nanny and the tiresome rituals of bedtime. "So, this is what it was all about," mused Gabriel, "hanging on to the family home."

"I'm not greedy, Father; I didn't want to make money for the sake of it," Florence persisted, stepping a little closer to him than he liked. He turned to face her, taking a step back as he did so. "I'm sorry, Father, but you must understand. We needed money to pay what we owed in taxes and to convert those outbuildings. The rent from that clinic is what keeps us afloat."

"How did Victor Gladstone find out what you were doing?" asked Gabriel. He was not standing by the window out of whimsy—he expected the police to turn up at any moment, and once Applegate had blundered into the house, Florence was unlikely ever to speak to him again. "This is important. How did he find out?"

"How should I know?" snapped Florence, bristling at the very mention of Victor's name. "He had a nasty, suspicious mind. I suppose he noticed that we were rather flusher with cash than most families in our position, and he couldn't resist interfering. I've no idea how he got hold of that pendant of yours, though; I'd never seen it before you showed it to me."

"I suspect Horace never intended to sell that amulet," answered Gabriel, "or at least not for many years. It's too rare and too obviously a stolen Jewish artefact. But Victor was blackmailing you both, wasn't he?"

"He called it a business agreement," said Florence bitterly. "He took ten percent in return for keeping his mouth shut."

Gabriel could hear the rumble of a car driving along the path outside. "Mrs Martin, we don't have long. I need to ask you this. Did you kill Victor Gladstone?"

"Of course I didn't, for pity's—"

"Did your husband?"

Florence gaped at him. "Of course not."

"Can you give him an alibi?"

"I . . . well, I don't know where . . . he wouldn't have done that!"

Gabriel looked back at the path and saw Inspector Applegate clambering out of the car, along with two constables. "A court will say that if he could hire a couple of thugs to beat and rob a man, he's perfectly capable of killing or ordering the killing of a man who was taking his money."

Florence rushed to the window, but the thunder of fists on the door warned her that she was out of time. "Help me!" she cried. "I did not kill him!"

"The police will say that you invited Victor Gladstone to your home with only one intention," said Gabriel calmly. "Why did you invite a man to your home when he was hurting you so much? You can see how it will look."

There was the sound of the door opening and Horace's raised voice. "We didn't invite that louse to our party; he invited himself!" exclaimed Florence. "He turned up to gloat over us and frighten us! I was on edge all evening, terrified he'd say something!" The door handle rattled behind them. "I'm glad he's dead, Father," she whispered. "Whoever did it deserves a medal around his neck, not a noose, but I didn't kill him."

Applegate was standing in the doorway in his coat and hat. Behind him, Gabriel could see the two constables and, a little further into the hall, three others. Applegate stepped nonchalantly aside to allow the constables in, followed by a protesting Horace, a subdued Bron, and Verity, who was predictably on the verge of tears. Gabriel had not noticed that the piano had stopped, but he supposed that if he no longer noticed the sound, he would not have noticed the silence. "Well, well, well," said Applegate, in the sardonic tone Gabriel had come to expect every time the inspector spoke to him. "Why am I not surprised to see you here?"

You know exactly why, thought Gabriel uncomfortably, praying Applegate would not give away that he had been the person to tip him off. "I thought you might give me brownie points for keeping out of your way for most of this investigation," suggested Gabriel, hoping to lighten the atmosphere a little. It had never been his gift to put anyone at ease, and he could see immediately that Applegate was not in the mood for a friendly exchange.

"A pity you didn't think to keep out of the killer's way, by the look of things," Applegate retorted, pointing at Gabriel's bruised face in a manner that simply looked rude. "I heard about your mishap. Maybe you'll think twice next time about trying to do the police's work for us." Applegate turned his back on Gabriel and looked steadily at Horace Martin. He gestured to one of the constables, who produced a set of handcuffs. "Horace Martin, I'm arresting you on suspicion of trading in stolen goods and for the murder of Victor Gladstone. You have the right to remain silent; anything you do or say may be taken down and used in evidence against you."

Horace glared at Applegate, but he knew better than to prevent the constable from cuffing his hands; an added charge of resisting arrest would do him no good. "I shall need to telephone my solicitor before I speak with you," he said, with admirable calm. "Now, might we leave with as little ceremony as possible?"

"If you drape your coat over your shoulders," Applegate suggested, "the handcuffs should not be visible. Not that there are many people to see." He turned to Florence. "I'm afraid you're going to have to come to the station with me too, Mrs Martin," said Applegate, in a noticeably warmer, almost apologetic tone. "I'm arresting you as an accessory to murder. You have the right to remain silent—"

"I'll do no such thing!" shouted Florence, shrinking away from the constable and clutching her hands behind her back. "Neither of us had anything to do with Victor Gladstone's death. You're making a terrible mistake!"

"Mrs Martin, I think you'd better go with them," said Gabriel, but he felt the queasiness in the pit of his stomach as yet another plan backfired. His message to Applegate had never said that the Martins were murderers. "With any luck, you'll be home in the morning."

"But she's innocent!" came a timorous voice from the background. Verity was being held by her uncle Bron, but there were tears streaming down her face, and she was struggling to free herself from him so that she could go to Florence. "Inspector, this can't be right! These are good people; Florence wouldn't hurt a fly. Neither of them would."

Verity's tearful concern seemed to rally Florence, and she stood up straight, holding out her hands to the constable in what was almost defiance. "Let's get this over with, shall we?" she said to him, curtly, then turned to Verity and Bron. "Is there any way the two of you could stay on here until we return? I hope it will not be very long before this unpleasant business is cleared up, but I can't bear the idea of the house being unsupervised in our absence."

Bron nodded, letting go of Verity so that he could pat

Florence's arm. "Don't worry about anything," he said soothingly. "We'll stay as long as we need to. You needn't concern yourself with anything here."

Florence nodded appreciatively. "Thank you, Bron. I knew I could rely on you."

Gabriel stood guiltily in the shadows as Horace and Florence were led out of the house and into the threatening darkness. The queasiness had been replaced by a fluttering in his chest, that half-guilty, half-anxious feeling of having boarded the wrong train and having no way to disembark. Gabriel looked back at Bron and Verity. Verity had calmed herself down and was wiping away her tears in a handkerchief; Bron was looking at him almost sheepishly, which gave Gabriel hope that neither of them had worked out his involvement in this whole sorry affair.

"If you need to get home, I'm sure I could drive you back," said Bron, "but I'm loathe to leave Verity here, even for an hour."

"There's no need, Bron," said Gabriel, a little too quickly. "I'll put a call through to the presbytery and tell Fr Foley I'll be home tomorrow. He won't miss me if I'm back in good time. You're right; I don't think Verity should stay here on her own."

"I won't be on my own," said Verity, with forced brightness. She was speaking with the tone of a girl attempting to sound more confident than she really was. "I can sit in the kitchen and chat to Molly while you're out. It'll help pass the time. She's feeling a little out of sorts herself, I think."

"You will do no such thing," said Bron sternly. "Sitting in the kitchen gossiping with servants. You ought to know better than that at your age."

"Oh Uncle, don't be so old-fashioned," said Verity, but it was abundantly clear that Bron had no intention of leaving her in the house without his supervision.

"Please don't inconvenience yourself on my behalf," Gabriel put in, desperate to avoid the two of them having a domestic quarrel in front of him. "I shall call for Molly now and ask her to make up two more guest rooms. It shan't take a moment if I help her."

"Father!" protested Bron when Gabriel walked towards the door, indicating that he was going to go down to the kitchen to talk to Molly rather than ring for her.

"You needn't concern yourself with my position," said Gabriel over his shoulder. "I am a servant myself. I shall be quite at home helping Molly carry the linens."

14

Gabriel hurried down to the kitchen door and knocked softly before entering. The scene before him could easily have been mistaken for one of domestic serenity. Cook stood near the oven, idly stirring a pot that was giving off a cloud of enticing aromas—cinnamon, nutmeg, autumn fruit. In a chair by the stove, Molly sat next to a pile of darning, staring down at the man's sock she was repairing. It was only when Gabriel closed the door behind him a little too loudly that the tension in the room became palpable; Cook looked up with a start and Molly jumped out of her skin, dropping her work at her feet.

"What happened to you, Father?" demanded Molly, getting up and hurrying over to him. "Who did that?"

"It's nothing, Molly; please don't concern yourself."

"Is that what all that noise upstairs was about? Is that why the police came?"

"No," replied Gabriel. "Mr and Mrs Martin have been arrested. But I think you knew they would be."

Molly threw a mortified glance at Cook, who was glowering at her. "I saw the bobbies coming in, so I made meself scarce. Didn't seem right to gawp."

Cook took the pot off the heat, shaking her head in irritation as the steam condensed on her skin. Her fleshy face was so deeply lined that it was impossible to imagine that she had ever been young, whilst her voice, on the rare occasions when she saw fit to speak, sounded too loud and too full-bodied to have come from such a weathered vessel. "And what are we supposed to do? Nobody ever tells us nothing!"

"There's nothing to worry about for the present," said Gabriel, as calmly as he could, though he knew that these women had every reason to worry. He had no idea what punishment the Martins would face if they were convicted of dealing in stolen goods, but he suspected that a clever lawyer could help them both wriggle out of that particular charge. If either of them were to be convicted of murder, however, the repercussions would be huge, and not just for whichever of them went to the gallows. Molly's fate had already been decided, but where would Cook go? She was a woman in her sixties who had probably first arrived at the estate when she was no more than fourteen, a wide-eyed girl joining a small downstairs community of maids, footmen and gardeners. The community had shrunk, the men lost to wars, the women to the economic squeeze faced by these old households and the prospect of better employment in the towns and cities. But Cook had never had to leave, had never known any other life than the quiet, secluded world of the Martin estate.

"Nothing to worry about?" echoed Cook. She had the indignant tone of a woman whose personal fiefdom has been invaded by a male interloper, and Gabriel doubted she would relax until he had admitted defeat and fled the room. "Nothing for *you* to worry about, no doubt. What about us?"

Gabriel cleared his throat. The aches and pains of his assault had had the effect of making him tire easily, and he would have loved to have been invited to sit down, but the two women were too preoccupied by the news to note his discomfort. "I doubt Mr and Mrs Martin will be kept in custody for long. They will be interviewed by the police, then Mrs Martin will be free to return home and Mr Martin will be formally charged. That is what I imagine will happen." He noted the look of intense panic on Molly's face and endeavoured to distract her before Cook noticed. "Molly dear, Miss Verity is staying for the time being, and Mr Gladstone, and I have also agreed to stay whilst Mr and Mrs Martin are away . . ." Gabriel groaned inwardly, thinking he had made it sound as though the Martins had gone to the seaside for a few days. "I'll only be staying the night, but . . ."

"I'll make up your rooms directly," said Molly, noting Gabriel's warning glance before scampering back to her place by the stove to clear away her things. "Why don't you make yourself at home in the drawing room? I shan't be a minute."

"I wonder if I might use the telephone?" he asked. "I need to put a call through to the presbytery, or Fr Foley will be wondering where I've got to."

"Of course," she said. "Straight up the stairs. It's behind the curtain, next to the coat stand."

Gabriel nodded before making his way back to the hall and finding the telephone. The telephone had been built snugly into a little compartment hidden behind a thick curtain, designed both to conceal a vulgar modern contraption and to offer a modicum of privacy to the caller. That was one thing that puzzled Gabriel about the scene of this crime. The house did not offer a great deal of privacy. For all its artfully created alcoves and compartments, it was a nosy parker's dream. There was something about the echoing acoustic that made it difficult to have a private conversation anywhere—Gabriel had overheard Bron and Victor because they were outside his room at the time, but he suspected he would have heard them from the foot of the stairs in the absence of any solid internal walls to block out the sound. The sound of Verity playing the piano could be heard all over the house, albeit quietly, even when she was playing in that room in the far corner of the building that had been specifically intended to contain the racket of noisy children.

Only the cover of thick fog could have concealed this murder, and even then, Gabriel could not get it out of his head that someone would have witnessed the killer if he had left the house. Was that the only reason he thought that Horace must be innocent? Could Gabriel really believe that he had slipped out of the house entirely unnoticed, when there were more people than usual in the house, and the servants busy taking care of their needs? More food to prepare and ferry about, more fires to light, more breakfast trays to carry from the kitchen to the upstairs bedrooms . . . or perhaps it merely confirmed that Florence had indeed been an accomplice. If the killer had been resident at the house on the morning of the murder, an accomplice would surely have been essential.

Gabriel was still musing over this possibility as he replaced the receiver, his ear smarting from the strength of Fr Foley's near-exasperated feelings on his latest vanishing act. He peered out through the narrow gap of the curtain and watched as Molly emerged into the hall and began to climb the main stairs. Gabriel pushed back the curtain and followed her, letting her get a short distance ahead of him before he called her softly. Even with a distance and with Gabriel's subdued tones, Molly still jumped like a scalded cat and very nearly lost her balance. "For pity's sake, Father!" she yelped, grasping the banister. "Whatever were you creeping up on me for?"

"I wasn't creeping up on you, I promise," said Gabriel, climbing the stairs until he stood at her side. "I was going to offer to help you prepare the rooms."

"I . . . I wouldn't dream . . . I wouldn't dream of it, Father," Molly managed to reply, but the suggestion had thrown her. "I can . . . well, I can manage."

Gabriel walked with her onto the landing and down the corridor, stopping only when Molly paused by a cupboard door, carefully painted to blend in with the rest of the wall. She hesitated as though embarrassed to reveal its contents, before gingerly opening the door to a deep cupboard with shelves heaving with sheets, towels, pillowcases and blankets. Molly was nothing if not orderly, and every single item was crisp, spotlessly clean and perfectly folded into neat piles that would not have disgraced a military establishment. Only the items at the very bottom of the cupboard were slightly ruckled from being laid on the uneven base of the compartment, a detail which Gabriel suspected must irk a person as particular as Molly. "Let me carry the bedclothes," said Gabriel, holding out his arms to take them.

Molly gave an uncomfortable smile and took out the necessary items for two guests before closing the door with evident relief. "I'm sorry, but Madam doesn't like guests to see things like that. She'd . . . well, not that I suppose it matters much anymore."

"I hardly imagined the house was cleaned by magic," said Gabriel, following her into the room he had inhabited the night before the murder. He put the linens down on the table to keep the bed clear. "Molly, I'm so sorry for your trouble. Mrs Martin told me she'd dismissed you. Have you anywhere . . ."

"Not yet, but I'll think of something," said Molly, taking a sheet from the pile and spreading it out over the mattress. "I'm sorry I'm so nervy, Father. I'm afraid I've a lot on my mind."

"Molly, if you need a reference to find yourself another position," Gabriel began, "I could get you some work at the presbytery, and then . . ."

"That won't be necessary, Father. I was going to hand in my notice before my marriage, but I needed to save a little more."

Gabriel sat down in the easy chair, watching Molly's back as she stooped forward to tuck in the corners of the sheet. "Molly, why are you really so nervous? This isn't just the loss of your position, is it? You were frightened when you saw the police coming into the house."

"Of course I were frightened!" exclaimed Molly, turning round to face him. "Sure, the police here hate Paddies!"

Gabriel shifted position, forcing himself not to look away. "Molly, I'm sorry I sent you snooping for me. I should never have asked you—"

"I was only looking for some old clothes," she retorted,

sounding almost irritated by the conversation. "And all I found for you was an old broken belt. There are worse things to lose sleep over."

"Such as?"

Molly looked at him, her eyes glistening. "You know, don't you?"

"That Victor Gladstone paid you a rather more substantial sum to go snooping for him?" said Gabriel. "That you were the one to discover those pretty things carefully hidden about the house? That you were the one to tell him about the shadowy figures who turned up at the house from time to time?"

Molly sat on the edge of the bed before she could fall, trembling from head to foot. She nodded miserably. "Yes."

"And was it you who took the amulet from wherever Mr Martin was hiding it and handed it over to Victor Gladstone?"

Molly looked up at him in horror. "Oh no, I never stole nothing! I would never have done that!"

"Do you know how he got hold of it then?" asked Gabriel.

"I . . . I let Mr Gladstone into the master's study, that's all," said Molly, "one day when there was no one else about."

"Did you see him take it then?"

Molly shook her head. "No, Father. But that evening there was a terrible rumpus in the house. Lots of shouting and the master in a foul temper, so I guessed something had been taken. I worked out what was missing only when I heard them arguing about it upstairs."

Gabriel counted to ten silently before attempting a response. It was extraordinary to him that such a lie was so easy for a person to maintain. *I didn't kill anyone; I only handled their stolen property. I didn't steal anything; I only helped another person to steal it, did nothing to stop him and told no one what had happened.* It was the most insidious of lies, repeated thousands upon thousands of times over the past decade. *I am not responsible for the actions I allow and encourage and from which I profit.*

"Is this my fault?" asked Molly in a small voice. "Is that why they've been arrested?"

"Molly, the Martins are being called to account for their greed," said Gabriel carefully. "That is not your fault. But the police believe that they also killed Victor Gladstone, and I do not believe they did so. Not alone, anyway."

"Mrs Martin wouldn't do a thing like that," said Molly softly. "It weren't a woman's crime."

Gabriel raised an eyebrow. "What makes you say that?"

Molly shrugged as though she regretted giving her opinion. "I don't know, I suppose if a lady killed someone, she'd poison him or something. I can't imagine her thumping a man that size."

Gabriel drew his chair a little closer to her. "Molly, tell me honestly, did you see or hear anything on the morning of the murder? Anything at all?"

Molly closed her eyes, shaking her head aggressively. "Nothing, Father."

"Are you sure?" He knew Molly was lying, and not just because she had shown herself to be unreliable. "Molly, if there's anything you know that might help find out who killed Victor Gladstone, you really must tell me. It might not be safe . . ."

"I've told you everything I know."

Gabriel tried a more direct approach. "Molly, do you know who did it?"

But Molly was on her feet again. "Father, how could I possibly have seen anything?"

"You were up and about long before the guests. Verity was locked up in that practice room, lost in some concerto or other, and even she said she thought she saw her grandfather leave the house. You must have seen something."

Molly stretched out her hands in exasperation. "Father, I was in the kitchen. I'm not supposed to wander about the house unless I've something to do. Have you any idea how noisy the kitchen gets?"

"What about when you took up the breakfast trays?"

"I took Mr Gladstone's first," said Molly. "I ought to have taken Mrs Martin's first since she's the oldest lady, but Mr Gladstone seemed rather cross. I thought I should serve him first."

"And?"

"He'd already gone. I told the police all this when they asked me."

Gabriel gave Molly a reassuring smile to indicate that the interview was over and got up to pass her a pillowcase. "If you happen to remember anything, you will tell me, won't you?"

Molly nodded without looking at him. "Course I will."

"Even if it doesn't seem important to you."

But Molly had nothing left to say to him. Soon after, Gabriel made his excuses and went back to the drawing room, where Bron was attempting to interest Verity in a game of whist.

Gabriel slept as badly as could be expected that night. He was getting a little sick of finding himself in a strange bed, wearing another man's pyjamas, and Horace's pyjamas were so large about the girth as to be barely decent when Gabriel put them on. Through the stilly watches of the night, Gabriel was troubled by the ache of bruises and the recurring memory of the moment a metal-clad hand had struck his face. He found himself replaying the moment he had stepped into that side road with its unfathomable sense of menace; he saw himself making an about-turn and leaving immediately for the busy thoroughfare he had so recently left. He imagined it not happening at all . . .

At the sound of a distant clock chiming four, Gabriel sat up in bed and turned on the bedside light. He was clearly not meant to sleep, and the pragmatist in him told him that it was better to be wakeful and productive than to toss and turn uselessly whilst the hours trickled slowly away. It would help considerably if he had a notepad and pencil at his disposal so that he could put his thoughts into some sort of order. Now that Gabriel thought about it, it would help if he had any of his personal possessions with him.

He filled the sink, ignoring the freezing-cold temperature of the water—it was too early for the water to have had time to heat up—and he shaved with as much care as he could muster at that hour of the morning. He felt an irksome discomfort at using another person's shaving brushes and razor blade, but being in a strange house was never more unpleasant than during a sleepless night. Back at the presbytery, he would hardly have felt like an imposter, venturing downstairs to make a cup of tea, whereas here, he found himself haltingly whispering the words of his morning prayers as though he might disturb others simply by being up and about.

There was a sense of finality about getting dressed, an

abandonment of nighttime rest, but by the time he had got himself ready he felt wide awake and well prepared to face the day. Gabriel turned off the bedside light and stepped out into the corridor, hesitating as his eyes struggled to adjust to the darkness. The window at the end of the corridor closest to him was not covered by curtain or blind, and it was a clear night, but even with the mild slivers of moonlight to guide him, Gabriel was forced to creep along tracing his fingers against the wall, unable to shake off the sense of being a burglar.

It was ridiculous to feel a sense of guilt, Gabriel rebuked himself; this was a house of thieves, enriched by theft, and the Martin family's latest journey into the mire of blood money was probably not the first time this great family had made itself wealthy on the suffering of others. He knew he had no business feeling guilty that he happened to be wakeful whilst the rest of the household slept—what was left of the household—when he was the invited guest of a woman who was currently lying in a police cell, no doubt even more wakeful than he was. Gabriel reached the linen cupboard and prised open the door as quietly as possible, shuddering at the slow strangled creak of the hinges. He had not been able to get the thought out of his mind that there was something under those slightly ruffled bedsheets other than a rough shelf. It was not just the fact that the piles had looked unsettled, it was that Molly had seemed unsettled. He could not quite accept that it was merely social embarrassment that had made Molly so unwilling to let him look inside.

Gabriel looked quickly down the corridor to ensure he was not being watched before sliding his hand under the bottommost sheets to see what he could find. Nothing. Only the bare, unpolished base of the cupboard. Furthermore, he suspected but could not confirm in the poor light that the bedsheets were now perfectly aligned and in good order. Either he had imagined that something was amiss in his desperation to discover some devastating clue, or the clue had been moved before he could reach it. And if it had been moved, it could have been moved only by Molly.

Gabriel closed the door softly, his mouth dry with embarrassment and nerves. He decided to go down to the kitchen and make himself a hot drink, which had been his original plan. He could sit by the stove with a milky drink and work things out. That was all that was really missing: time and space to think things through. Gabriel told himself as he descended the stairs into the eerie shadows of the hallway, that all the clues were there already. They had been there right from the start.

It was only when his feet touched the stone floor at the bottom of the stairs that Gabriel realised why he was suddenly feeling more relaxed. The change had happened almost imperceptibly as he had walked down the stairs: the slowing of his pulse, the deepening of his breathing, the loss of that uneasy sense of being a lonely figure creeping about a vast, sleeping house. He could hear the piano playing softly from the north wing. Verity had been unable to sleep either, troubled by the arrest of her friends, and had instinctively gone to the one place where she could seek solace. As Gabriel walked towards the sound, he was aware that she was playing a very different work to the passionate, angry concertos he had come to associate with her. Aptly, she was playing a nocturne by Debussy, one of Gabriel's favourites.

It was the sort of piece Gabriel associated with his past life, when he had been a regular guest at London musical soirées and Giovanna had taken her turn to delight everyone with some *aria* or *lied* she had practised for weeks but still managed to perform as though she were singing it effortlessly for the first time.

He could not bring himself to interrupt Verity's performance and bring to an end that brief, delicious reverie into the past. He stood outside the door to her practice room, willing the last note not to die away too soon, hesitating to knock even when it did. Sensing that Verity might be frightened by the sudden appearance of an unexpected person, Gabriel said quietly, "Verity, it's me," before fully opening the door and stepping inside.

Verity was sitting at the piano, stroking the keys as though communing with a beloved pet. She was wearing a thick crimson dressing gown over her nightdress, and her hair was uncombed. She turned slowly to face him, and Gabriel saw that her face was still moist with tears. "Did I wake you?" she asked, with the apologetic tone of a musician who has frequently impinged upon the solitude of others.

"Not at all," promised Gabriel. "I heard you only when I came down the stairs. I'm afraid I couldn't sleep either."

"My mother loved Debussy," said Verity, turning back to the piano. "I always play it when I miss her."

Gabriel would have quite liked to offer her some comfort, but he felt uneasy about being alone with a young woman in the middle of the night. "Verity, this isn't good for you," he said anxiously. "You need to rest."

"The doctor gave me something to help me sleep," said Verity, her hands still brushing the ivory keys. "Paul doesn't like me to take the sleeping powders. He says it's not natural; I shouldn't let the doctor control me."

Gabriel resisted the urge to roll his eyes. "It sounds to me as though the doctor's trying his best to look after you," he said. "Come along to the kitchen now. It's cold in here and you need tea. Every conversation ought to be had over a pot of tea."

Verity gave a half smile and got up from the piano, closing the lid with the utmost care before following Gabriel out of the practice room and into the kitchen. She switched on the light, revealing the impeccably tidy kitchen, every surface scrubbed, not a pan or so much as a teaspoon out of place. Gabriel looked around for the necessary apparatus to make a pot of tea. The kettle was easy enough to spot, but he had no idea where the teapot was tucked away and would probably have to turn the place upside down to find the tea caddy.

Verity gave a low giggle, sensing Gabriel's restrained panic. "Sit down, Father," she said. "I'll make the tea."

Gabriel was being served again, and all because of his incompetence. "Why don't I boil the kettle?" he suggested, taking the kettle over to the sink while Verity took a teapot out of the cupboard and reached up to bring the tea caddy down from a high shelf on the dresser. Gabriel was quietly impressed by how at home Verity clearly felt; she was a member of the household, as comfortable moving about the kitchen here as she would her own home. In so far as she had a home. Bron had no doubt done everything in his power to welcome her and care for her, but it could hardly have been an easy existence for a growing girl. Here, there was space and female company, women to mother her and advise her. Or at least there had been.

"Verity, I'm so sorry about what's happened to the Martins," said Gabriel awkwardly, "if that's what's kept you awake—"

The whistle of the kettle boiling made Verity flinch. Gabriel went to remove it from the hob, but Verity got there first, filling the teapot with boiling water in what was almost impatience. "I can't believe they'd do anything so horrid, Father," she said, concentrating intently on the task of putting the lid on the teapot. "They're good people. Flor —Mrs Martin has been so kind to me. I can't believe she'd do anything . . ."

"Verity dear, sit down," said Gabriel, ushering her towards the chairs by the stove. The stove was unlit, but there was still some residual heat left, and Verity was trembling. "You know, I'm sure the Martins have been good to you, but sometimes good people are tempted to do very bad things. You mustn't feel—"

"When those beastly policemen took her away, I felt as though I were losing my mother a second time!" Verity cried, fighting back tears. "I know it sounds selfish, but what on earth am I to do? They're my family, and I'm going to lose them!"

"Please don't think like that," said Gabriel, sitting near her. "It may not come to that. They've been arrested, but it's not yet clear what the charges will be."

"Father, I'm not an idiot. If they had anything to do with the Nazis, they'll be disgraced. Florence would rather die than go to prison. Unless, of course—"

"Verity," Gabriel interrupted, "it's not at all clear if either of them really was involved in the death of your grandfather. Even if they were, it's difficult to see how a court could prove it unless one of them actually confesses." He hesitated, expecting Verity to interrupt, but she was staring miserably at the black, lifeless stove. "But if either of them really did kill him, they will have to answer for that."

Verity's response was little more than a murmured noise Gabriel could only just interpret as the words, "I know."

He got up and took a cup and saucer down from the dresser, pouring the tea with undue care. He braced himself. "Verity, is there something you need to tell me?"

Verity looked up sharply at him. "What do you mean?"

"I mean, is there more to your wakefulness than the thought of Florence Martin sitting in a police cell?" He held out the cup to Verity, but her hands were trembling too much to take hold of it safely, and he put it down on the kitchen table. "You said on the day of the murder that you thought you saw your grandfather leave the house. Are you sure you didn't see anyone else?"

Verity shook her head rather too quickly. "Of course not, Father. There was a thick fog, remember? I couldn't even be sure I had definitely seen Grandfather."

Gabriel sat down again, but he already had a nasty suspicion that he had lost. "You're not obliged to volunteer information, Verity. The law can't touch you for that, but there is such a thing as a sin of omission. If you know who—"

But Verity was on her feet, marching towards the kitchen door. "For your information," she snapped, turning at the door to look back at him, "the other reason I can't sleep is that the nursing home gave me a call yesterday afternoon."

"Oh Verity, I'm so sorry," Gabriel began, but he was repelled by the wall of anger he had unwittingly allowed to spring up between them, and Verity glared at him in quiet accusation. "What's happened? I should have asked."

"They told me that my mother can stay at the home for the time being, but I had to agree to them locking her in her room."

"At night?"

"*All the time*," Verity spat out. "They've turned her home into a terribly comfortable prison because she blurted out something silly. She thought she'd killed him because she wanted to, Father. That doesn't mean she did it, but she's a prisoner now. No trial. No evidence. And if the courts do decide that she killed her own father, she'll be sent straight to an asylum to rot."

Anger and sorrow were always so close with some that Gabriel was not surprised to see Verity struggling with both tears and rage at the same time. Tears won eventually, and she began sobbing uncontrollably. "Verity, sit down," Gabriel pleaded, but she refused to move, leaning back against the wall. "You know, she may not even realise she's locked in. She barely leaves that room . . ."

"She deserved better than this!" sobbed Verity, taking in great gulps of air like a drowning woman battling to keep her head above the surface of the water. "She's suffered so much! He made her suffer; she never had any freedom, and she still doesn't! She never will!"

Gabriel watched Verity's tears in silent helplessness. He

was no expert in such matters, but he suspected that the sudden, officious removal of a mother figure from the house had brought back Verity's worst memories of her own mother being carried away in the back of an ambulance. She needed someone to love her—not just to admire her or feel paternalistic affection for her but to show her that exclusive, unconditional love she had missed during those years of emerging adulthood. "Verity, would you like me to ask your young man to pay you a visit?"

But the suggestion only caused louder, more anguished weeping from Verity. She was never going to say as much, even when she was calm enough to do so, but that youthful romance was clearly petering out under the strain of a prolonged murder investigation. A shock as severe as the sudden, violent death of a loved one would have cemented a truly loving relationship, two young lovers thrown ever closer together by such a trial. But not this one. Bron would be pleased, and it would probably be for the best; but for the present, Verity needed someone to carry her through this malaise, and her allies were slipping mercilessly into oblivion.

In the end, in the absence of an obvious alternative, Gabriel led Verity back to the practice room again and waited until she had been playing for ten minutes before slipping away. It was an obsession born from a need to escape, and it had become almost pathological in its grip on her life, but music offered Verity a level of protection and comfort she could not find from any living person.

Gabriel returned to the kitchen to clear away the tea things. It was already five o'clock, and it would not be long before the house began to stir once again.

15

Breakfast was a morose affair. Verity and Gabriel were both exhausted after a sleepless night, Gabriel resisting the urge to yawn every couple of minutes, and Verity red-eyed and too emotionally drained to speak. Only Bron had any life in him, but he had the good sense to avoid any attempt at conversation, overwhelmed by the pervading sense of gloom around the table. Cook and Molly were clearly not feeling any better if the quality of the breakfast was anything to go by. Gabriel had never been overly fond of kedgeree as a child, as anything tasting fishy first thing in the morning seemed to upset the natural order, but the food on Gabriel's plate was barely edible.

It hardly helped Gabriel's mood that his head was full of massacres. As Verity stared miserably into her teacup and Bron disappeared behind his copy of the *Times*—having had to request it from Molly no fewer than three times before she remembered to bring it—Gabriel thought over and over the scene in that warehouse. He knew that there was every possibility the massacre had absolutely nothing to do with it; the thought had pestered him almost from the start. However, the overwhelming sense remained with him that Victor had inadvertently signed his own death warrant while cowering for his life in that death chamber.

There were so many other reasons why Victor Gladstone was better off dead to someone—Gabriel had had that horrific thought before; some murders are complicated to solve simply because the victim had done everything he could to tempt a wide circle of people to help him shuffle off this mortal coil. Victor was a different kind of villain to Emma, Bron, Florence and Horace. To Emma he had been the tyrannical patriarch, controlling, apparently violent and wholly unworthy of his fatherhood; to Bron he had been a different kind of tyrant, bigoted, cold, unyielding; to Florence and Horace he was a merciless blackmailer, a parasite feeding off their greed to appease his own. But to someone, he was the hapless witness to an unspeakable crime. It was just that he could think of no one left, certainly no one among the immediate circle of suspects, who could possibly want him dead for that reason.

Molly was clearing away the breakfast things and Verity had long slipped away when Gabriel's attempts at prayer were interrupted by the sound of approaching motorcars. Gabriel got up from his seat at the window and watched as Inspector Applegate and two constables got out of a car before assisting Horace Martin out onto the path. He was not handcuffed, and none of the policemen touched him as he walked to the door with excruciating slowness. There was no sign of Florence, but Gabriel suspected that he would be the only one who was not surprised. He braced himself for what was coming and moved to the door, watching as Trevelyan greeted Horace and helped him off with his coat, the two men completely ignoring the inspector and his constables.

Applegate glanced across the hall and acknowledged Gabriel before walking towards him, but Horace stepped in his path, stopping him short. "I do not recall inviting you into my home," said Horace gruffly, causing Applegate to take a step back simply to make some space between them. "You've done your job. Now get out."

Applegate regarded Horace for a moment with the glance of professional contempt to which Gabriel had been treated on a few occasions. "I'm afraid that will not be possible," he said tonelessly. "I have a warrant to search your property."

"You searched it when the body was discovered!" Horace protested, but his blustering tone betrayed more than annoyance. "There were bobbies crawling all over the house!"

"I don't remember," said Gabriel blankly.

"That's because they did us the courtesy of waiting until our honoured guests had gone!" Horace roared at him. Gabriel suspected that he made a useful conduit for the rage of a man who had been arrested, bundled into the back of a police car, taken to the station, relieved of his belt and shoelaces, fingerprinted, questioned and forced to spend the night in a cell, devoid of his pipe, smoking jacket and man-servant.

"We were gathering evidence for a different crime on that occasion, sir," Applegate explained. "Now that your wife's confessed to the murder of Victor Gladstone, we've the small matter of handling stolen goods to consider."

Gabriel stared fixedly at the frayed edge of the rug at his feet, desperately trying to conceal his dismay. He was not sure whether Applegate had hurled that bombshell into the middle of the room with the deliberate intention of shocking everyone or whether he had simply assumed that Florence Martin's failure to return home with her husband spoke for itself. The result was as ugly as Applegate could have wished it; Horace's blustering rage boiled over, and the silent Trevelyan practically had to restrain him as he escorted his master into the drawing room. Gabriel suspected that Trevelyan had intervened on many occasions over the years to prevent Horace from making a scene and accepted this role as one of many he performed when keeping the peace in a household such as this.

Verity had been in her room but had come running down the stairs when she had heard the screech of the police car, expecting to greet Florence on her triumphant return home. Verity's face bore the ludicrous signs of a woman who had been interrupted in the midst of applying her makeup, giving her the look of a half-painted porcelain doll. Rouge had been amply applied, but only one set of eyelashes had been blackened with mascara. At the news that Florence had confessed to the murder, Verity attempted to reach Horace, but Bron came marching down the stairs, demanding that Verity stay where she was.

Gabriel knew that this was Verity's worst nightmare, the loss she had wept over in the early hours of the morning. "Bron . . . ," Gabriel began, but he swallowed his words and left Bron to hustle Verity back upstairs. Gabriel knew when he was unwelcome, and if Bron could only rise to the challenge, he was more than capable of providing Verity with the comfort she needed now.

He stood alone in the hall, suddenly at a loss as to what to do. Gabriel knew he really ought to leave, but he retained a residual hope that his plan might still be rescued, and he was unwilling to go until the murder charge had been handed to the right person. In the other room, Gabriel could hear Horace and Applegate engaged in an explosive argument, Horace's rounded vowels competing against Applegate's clipped, mercenary tone. It was like listening to two worlds clashing against one another, the sharper, younger, more forceful power effortlessly asserting its authority. Gabriel liked to believe that he was shielded from the comings and goings of national class wars and international political struggles, protected by the ancient and eternal truth he pursued. However, he could not help feeling a little lost himself, caught on the fringes of a battle that was not his own but which he could hardly ignore.

Gabriel waited until the sounds of the argument began to subside before it occurred to him that he might look as though he were eavesdropping if anyone passed his way. He had just ducked behind the curtain concealing the telephone when Applegate and Horace walked back into the hall, Gabriel catching Applegate uttering the words, "I think it would be better for both of us if you were to confine yourself to one of the upstairs rooms. As soon as we have finished searching your study, you may return there."

"This is a damned cheek; it's my house!" Horace again. Unmistakably Horace. "If a man cannot move freely in his own house, I'm not sure what we fought for!"

"If you'd prefer to cool your heels in cells, I'm more than happy to arrange it. One of the constables can take you there now. He can even provide you with a nice set of bracelets to wear for the journey."

Gabriel heard the thud of footsteps retreating up the stairs, complete with much wordless harrumphing. He counted to ten before pulling the curtain back as quietly as possible, only to find himself standing directly in front of Applegate. "I wasn't eavesdropping," promised Gabriel, which was about as convincing as a child with sugar around his mouth claiming he has not been anywhere near the sweetie jar.

"What are you up to?" demanded Applegate. "I thought you'd left."

Gabriel came out of his hiding place. "I thought I should wait until everything was settled," he explained. "I'm afraid it's all a bit of a mess, isn't it?"

"Not sure I know what you mean," Applegate replied, moving towards the drawing room in the expectation that Gabriel would trot along beside him. "A woman has confessed to murder; I can put a little line through that task. Now I just have to nail the husband. Not sure I'd call this a mess."

"Inspector . . ."

Applegate shook his head at Gabriel. "She had motive, she had opportunity, she's confessed. Case closed." He allowed himself an unprofessional smirk. "You didn't expect her to confess, did you?"

"I didn't expect her to confess, because I don't believe she did it!" Gabriel protested. "I thought if you arrested her on a charge of murder, the real murderer might have a crisis of conscience."

Applegate treated Gabriel to a long, incredulous look before his rugged face cracked into a grin. He gave into a burst of jarringly nasal laughter that echoed about like a set of rusting organ pipes being tortured back to life by an inexpert musician. "Dear oh dear!" he spluttered, shaking his head in a gesture as irritating as the noise he was making. "I suppose you expected our coldblooded murderer to be terribly sorry about it all!"

Gabriel waited for Applegate's forced merriment to subside before responding. "It may not have been coldblooded, and I'm not sure our killer is so terribly sorry. But condemning a second person to death might be beyond his capabilities."

Applegate patted Gabriel on the shoulder, skilfully drawing attention to his superior stature. "Don't lose any sleep over it, Father. You may have blundered a bit, but you've given me my murderer, and I'm grateful."

"Inspector—"

"If you don't mind, I've one or two other details to attend to," Applegate cut in, turning his back on Gabriel and walking away, leaving him feeling like the unwelcome guest at the wedding feast. Gabriel swallowed what little of his pride remained and went upstairs. Sending himself to his bedroom was an old reflex. It was not of course his room, and he had no belongings to pack, but he thought he ought at least to tidy the room and make the bed to spare Molly the inconvenience.

As he walked along the corridor approaching the guest room, Gabriel suddenly remembered the linen cupboard and his suspicion that something had been hidden there. He knew he was clutching at straws, but he had very little left to do, and he hurried back down the stairs to the kitchen to find Molly.

The girl in question glanced up at Gabriel in weary resignation as he stepped through the door. Her reaction was a great deal worse than he had expected. If she had jumped with fright, Gabriel would at least have had the satisfaction of knowing she held out some hope of escape from the retribution that was coming. Instead, her sad, exhausted demeanour made it quite obvious that she had given up any belief she might be spared. Molly was a very different woman to the relentlessly cheerful girl who had brought him his morning tea shortly before a man's life had been cut off by a person he had trusted.

"Will they hang me, Father?" she asked blandly, as though the answer to the question were completely irrelevant. "They won't hang me, will they?"

Gabriel reached out a hand to her, but she threw herself at his feet. "No one's going to hang you for this, Molly," he said, placing a hand on her white starched cap. "But you do know that you are in very serious trouble, don't you?"

Very serious trouble was the most heartless of euphemisms. Molly was in a great deal more than serious trouble. Gabriel knew she was facing a lengthy prison sentence with hard labour and that she was very unlikely to marry the fine young man with whom she had hoped to share her life. "Please help me, Father," she sobbed, refusing to look up at him. "If God is my witness, I had no idea what it was all about!"

Gabriel took Molly's hands and forced her to her feet, leading her to the chair by the stove, which was burning nicely if a little smokily. The stove's glass panes were so blackened with soot that it was almost impossible to see the flames within, but it was pleasingly hot, and Molly needed warming up. He sat down opposite her and tried to make eye contact, but she looked steadfastly down at her lap, tears dropping softly on her apron. "Molly, it is very likely that you will be charged as an accomplice to murder. It was you who destroyed the evidence, wasn't it? You didn't just lie to me when you said that there was no one in this house who wore green. Mrs Martin told you to destroy those clothes."

Molly nodded almost imperceptibly. "I didn't know there'd been a murder! Surely that counts for something? How can I be an . . . an accomplice . . . if I didn't know?"

"Molly, that's not quite true, is it? I will do everything I can to help you, but you must be honest with me. When Mrs Martin told you to destroy those clothes, you didn't know that Victor Gladstone had been murdered. But you didn't destroy them immediately, did you? You hid them in that cupboard."

Molly looked up at Gabriel for the first time. Her eyes and nose were red and streaming. He pulled out a handkerchief and handed it to her, awaiting her reply. "I couldn't bear to destroy good clothes, Father. It seemed so wicked when there are so many cold, hungry people in the world. And they were good clothes. A lovely thick, warm green frock made from some posh wool. I thought she wouldn't notice if I just hid it away. I share a room with Cook, and I worried she'd notice; that's why I hid it in the cupboard. I meant to take it to my mother next time I had leave. She is about the same size, and it would have been such a treat for her. But when you noticed the sheets were ruckled last night, I got scared."

Gabriel stared at the soot-covered panes of the stove, the orange flames flashing in the background, tearing at a good-quality woollen dress, reducing it to ashes, fibre by incriminating fibre. The moment Applegate had told Gabriel that Florence Martin had confessed to the murder, Gabriel had known that Florence was protecting someone, and the possibility of a reprieve for Molly began to shape itself in Gabriel's mind. If Florence were to plead guilty to the murder of Victor Gladstone when she appeared in court, the trial would be an uncomplicated one, as would the job of the police and the counsel for the prosecution. There would be much less need to prove that Florence had committed a crime to which she was prepared to admit under oath, and if the police had failed to notice Florence's dress hidden away at the bottom of the linen cupboard, they would be unlikely to notice the fragments of it charred in the grate.

"Molly, does anyone other than Mrs Martin know that you were given the task of disposing of the evidence?"

"No one," answered Molly. "She was very careful to catch me on my own, and she made me swear not to tell a soul. Well, you know now, I suppose."

Gabriel stood up, glancing furtively at the door to ensure that no one was listening. They were quite alone. "Where's Cook?"

Molly rose to her feet, but she wobbled unsteadily and sat down again. "She always goes to shop in the village straight after breakfast. She'll be back within the hour."

"And how long has the stove been burning today?"

"Three hours, Father."

Gabriel nodded. "I'd keep the stove burning if I were you," he said with forced brightness. "It's going to be another cold day."

"Father—"

Gabriel raised a finger to his lips. "There is no law in England which obliges me to assist the police in their enquiries, as long as I do not actively hinder them. Mrs Martin had no business involving you in all this, knowing that you would feel that you had to do as you were told. She misused her authority disgracefully." He walked slowly towards the door, turning back with the words, "I have to be on my way now, Molly. Goodbye."

Molly stood up and moved slowly towards him. "What do you want me to do?" she asked. "I don't know what to do."

"Live quietly," said Gabriel. "Marry your young man and live a good life together."

There was nothing more to be said. Gabriel made his way to the telephone in the hall to let Fr Foley know that he would soon be coming home.

"You sound like you're planning your own funeral," remarked Fr Foley when the operator put the call through. Gabriel told Fr Foley what had happened. "I'd have thought you'd be glad to see the back of that house."

"I shan't be sorry to leave," admitted Gabriel, but even at Fr Foley's prompting, he could do nothing to hide the sadness in his own voice. "I'll walk home now. I left without my diary yesterday. Is there anything I have to be back for?"

"Not until the afternoon, but I shouldn't walk in the state you're in," said Fr Foley. "By the way, son, I've got Dorothy here tidying up. She wondered if you wanted to hang on to this Commie belt of yours? Should she throw it away?"

"I hadn't given it much thought," said Gabriel. "I don't suppose—" His pulse had started racing. He squeezed the telephone receiver as hard as he could. "Why did you call it that?"

Fr Foley laughed. "Because it is. You must have noticed the star on the buckle."

Gabriel floundered, his head slipping beneath an invisible wave. "Of course, that is . . . of course I did. But stars mean all sorts of things."

"Really, son, it's obviously a Soviet star! Have you been so pure in your cloister all this time that you never came across it?"

Gabriel could feel himself reddening with shame. "Whenever I think of Communism, I think of hammers and sickles. The same way I'd think of a swastika when anyone mentions the Nazis." Gabriel rested his weight against the high wooden table in front of the wall-mounted telephone. He was not just being engulfed by invisible waves, he was being churned about in a sudden, violent storm he would never have seen coming. "Fr Foley, are you quite sure that the symbol on that buckle is Communist?"

"As sure as eggs are eggs," answered Fr Foley emphatically. "Are you all right, son? You sound like you're drowning. Is it important?"

"Of course it's important!" Gabriel almost wailed. "Idiot! Imbecile!"

"I beg your pardon," Fr Foley broke in. "There's no need to be like that. How was I supposed to know it was important?"

"Not you! Me! I'm the idiot! I've made a terrible mistake, and it might be too late."

Gabriel slammed down the receiver, causing the bell to give a muffled chime on impact. He threw back the curtain, running in the direction of Verity's practice room. He could hear the piano playing softly and offered up a prayer of thanks that he might not be too late after all. He pulled open the door, freezing with shock at the sight of the silent, unattended piano, the lid pulled down over the keys, and no sign of Verity anywhere. In a corner, a gramophone played a Beethoven sonata. He turned on his heel and hurried back up the stairs, not slowing down until he had hurled himself bodily into Horace Martin's study.

Two constables were busy rummaging through drawers

full of paper, but it was Applegate who hurried over to him, too bewildered to be indignant. "Where's Verity?" demanded Gabriel, before Applegate could speak. "She's slipped out somewhere. I have to find her!"

Applegate's face took on a rare look of concern. "How should I know where she is? She is not a suspect."

"Inspector, she is about to become a victim. *Please*."

In any other situation, Applegate would have dismissed Gabriel's claims as yet more of his fanciful rantings, but he was an experienced-enough policeman to trust fear when he saw it. "Is she not at the piano? She usually is. I heard it."

"The only thing playing down there is a gramophone record."

Gabriel turned to run out of the room, realising that Applegate could not help him, but Bron had heard the sound of Gabriel's running footsteps echoing about and came to find out the cause of the commotion. Bron had to hold out his hands in front of him to stop the two men colliding. "What's this all about, Father? She wanted to go out and meet Paul, but I told her to ring his home instead. I don't like her gallivanting about like that, always chasing after him. I told her to invite him to the house and they could talk."

"Have you any idea what she wanted to say to him?" asked Gabriel. "Did she tell you anything?"

"She had arranged to meet him in the summerhouse because she wished to break things off with him. Frankly, I was rather relieved. I never thought they had a future—"

Gabriel was running towards the front door and barely heard Bron protesting in the background: "She won't be there; I told her not to go out!"

Bron might have been certain of the power of his paternalistic authority, but Applegate knew better and raced after Gabriel, catching up with him easily as he made for the back of the house. "Go ahead!" gasped Gabriel, when Applegate slowed down to avoid overtaking him. "There's no time; just go! Do you know the way?"

Applegate nodded and pressed ahead, quickly disappearing behind a row of cherry trees. Gabriel could feel a stitch stabbing him in the side, and the thudding pain of bruised ribs forced him to slow down, but the coward in him wanted Applegate to arrive at the scene first—not to have to face the scene alone, of course, but at least to be the one to throw open the door and face whatever was inside. *Grow up!* Gabriel commanded himself, but he was almost paralysed by the waves of fear and grief that were overtaking him. He gritted his teeth, hurried behind the cherry trees and over to the summerhouse, in time to see Applegate throw open the door.

"Stand back! Move away from her!" Applegate shouted, before disappearing inside the summerhouse. Gabriel arrived at the door and let out a cry of despair. Paul Ashley was moving slowly backwards, away from a small, childlike figure lying crumpled in the corner of the room. Even as a first glance, it was impossible to pretend that Verity looked peaceful curled up like that. There was a cloud of dust in the air thrown up by a struggle, and from where he was standing, Gabriel could see an abrasion making a small red, jagged mark across her pale temple.

"Paul, what have you done?" said Gabriel, but the words choked in his throat. A ghost of another woman, equally helpless, with the same childlike figure, hovered around him. Another woman to whom he had been able to offer only his impotent, futile rage. He threw himself on his knees next to Verity and searched for a pulse, but he could smell the residual odour of chloroform before he noted the strong, determined pulse beating in her wrist.

"She's not dead, Father, only sleeping," jeered Paul, offering no resistance as Applegate shackled his wrists. "You should have let me finish the job. I would have made quite sure not to hurt her."

"You have hurt her," said Gabriel simply, not bothering to turn and look at him. "You have hurt her."

"Well, the silly girl would struggle. She never did listen to me. I told her it was pointless to cut and run."

Applegate raised a hand to Gabriel to quiet him. "Paul Ashley, I'm arresting you for the murder of Victor Gladstone and for the attempted murder of Verity Caufield. You have the right to remain silent; anything you say may be recorded and given in evidence against you."

It was all so appallingly businesslike, the calm authority of the long arm of the law formally charging someone and informing him of his rights. Gabriel waited until Applegate had finished before asking, "Inspector, would you be so kind as to call a doctor when you get to the house? The effects of the chloroform will wear off soon enough, but she should be seen by a doctor."

Applegate nodded. "Leave that to me, Father. Perhaps you could stay with her for the time being."

Gabriel stood up. "Of course, Inspector. But please return as soon as Mr Ashley is safely in the hands of your constables."

With that, Applegate left the summerhouse with an uncharacteristically cooperative Paul Ashley. He expressed no fear, no regrets and no emotion whatsoever as he walked away from a young woman who had once hoped to be his wife. But whatever his confusion about the perpetrator of this crime, Gabriel had never believed that Paul's feelings for Verity were in any way comparable to hers for him. He was a man married to a set of political ideals that demanded the whole man. To that extent, Verity could never have been more to him than a mistress: attractive, engaging and personally useful to him, but nothing more.

Verity began to moan softly. Gabriel noticed her fingers starting to move, and he shifted her carefully from her side onto her back so that he would be able to see when she opened her eyes. Her brow began to furrow as consciousness slowly returned, and Verity was thrown once more back into the troubles from which she had been granted a temporary reprieve. She opened her eyes as though the lids were almost too heavy to bear and looked at Gabriel in panic. "Keep calm, Verity," said Gabriel. "He's gone. The inspector has taken him away. He can't hurt you now."

Verity's mouth opened and closed, opened and closed as though she had been struck dumb by the shock of her lover turning on her. Gabriel knew that she had everything and nothing left to say, and in her confusion, her body simply would not cooperate with her. She lay absolutely still, tears sliding sideways into her hair, waiting for the nightmare to end. "I'm sorry, Verity," said Gabriel. "I'm sorry for everything you've suffered and everything you are going to suffer. I am truly sorry."

"He was sorry too," whispered Verity, her lips barely moving. "He was so sorry it had to be this way. Couldn't have me telling the police everything I knew."

Applegate must have informed Molly of the situation when he returned to the house with Paul, because Molly arrived in the summerhouse minutes afterwards. Verity's head was a little clearer, the effects of the chloroform were beginning to wear off. She still looked deathly pale and was far too calm and subdued for a person who had been through such an ordeal. Gabriel could only guess at the terror she must have experienced when she had realised Paul's plan to silence her forever, the desperation induced by that short, hopeless struggle to escape the unforgiving pressure of a wet cotton wool pad pressed against her nose and mouth. Verity would not have had much chance to resist, the drug taking effect in the space of a single breath, but those few seconds of inhalation with the chemical odour creeping into her nostrils would have been long enough for her to comprehend that she was unlikely ever to wake up.

Molly stood in the doorway, pale and shaking. "The doctor's on his way, Father," she said.

"Help me get her to her room," said Gabriel, an instruction that gave Molly permission to approach Verity's deathlike figure. "It's all right, the effects of the chloroform wear off quite quickly, but she may be a little unsteady on her feet."

Verity was more than a little unsteady, and Gabriel struggled to escort her back to the house even with Molly assisting. Gabriel suspected that Verity was unwilling to be moved from the summerhouse for stronger reasons than shock. The realisation would be slowly dawning on her that she was unlikely to see Paul again outside a courtroom. Beyond the horror of what had just happened, there was the sad parting of ways so many young people experienced when a first romance soured. In such a context, Verity's implausible dreams of marrying a dashing young Communist seemed laughably petty. To everyone except her.

"You must rest," said Gabriel, as they stepped through the front door. The timing was unfortunate. The car bearing Paul away to custody was only just pulling away, and Verity had time to look back and glimpse Paul's head in profile through the side window. His face bore the supercilious look of a man too convinced of his place in the new order to feel any remorse whatsoever. Paul did not turn to look at Verity as the car sped away, but Gabriel was certain he must have noted her presence out of the corner of his eye.

The final insult proved too much for Verity, and she broke free of her minders, staggering ahead of them into the hall. Gabriel stopped in his tracks and watched Verity as she struggled up the stairs, clinging tightly to the banister as she ascended. He was reminded for a moment of his first sight of her—wafting down those same stairs on her way to join the party—and felt overwhelmed by that old sense of darkness descending all around him.

Molly was standing beside him as though awaiting the next instruction. "Father, are you all right? You look like you're going to be sick."

The darkness swept over Gabriel, clinging to him for a few agonised seconds before dispersing once again. "Nothing to worry about, Molly," he said quickly. "Please, would you stay with Verity until the doctor arrives? When the doctor's seen her and she's feeling strong enough, the inspector will want to speak with her."

Molly nodded wordlessly and skipped upstairs, leaving Gabriel lingering in the hall, reluctant to discuss matters with Applegate. Almost anticipating his unwillingness, Applegate came in search of Gabriel himself and stood waiting for Gabriel to turn around and acknowledge him. Applegate's patience never lasted long. "Cheer up, Father," he said, not unkindly. "If I got so down in the dumps every time I apprehended a murderer, I'd have topped myself by now."

Gabriel turned to face Applegate, managing a weak smile. "All well?"

"I've informed the accused of his rights and left a constable to take him back to the station. He says he intends to make a full confession, but he won't say a word to any of us until he's spoken with his solicitor." Applegate gave a wry smile. "And since he doesn't have anything as bourgeois as a solicitor, this may take some time."

Gabriel did not respond; he was fighting a lingering sense of lethargy. Finally, he said, "Florence Martin. She'll be encouraged to retract her confession, I presume?"

"The confession to murder, certainly. Silly of her to assume her husband was the killer. But it won't be the first time a woman's tried to protect a useless husband."

"Indeed."

Applegate appeared to be waiting for Gabriel to say something else, but he was silent. "Well," said Applegate, moving towards the drawing room, "I've a few details here to clear up, including talking to the young lady when she feels up to it." He made an elaborate gesture of waiting at the door to allow Gabriel to walk in ahead of him. Gabriel plodded through, desperate to sit down. Desperate for Applegate not to follow. "It's not particularly important if he's going to confess anyway, but I'd like to know how you worked it out."

Gabriel shrugged, sitting down heavily in an armchair as far from the door as possible. He immediately began sinking into the sagging cushions, causing him to slide backwards like a bat hibernating. "I'm afraid I was rather confused," Gabriel admitted. "You see, Paul had no reason to wish Victor dead. He might, of course, have known all along that he was to be the main beneficiary of Victor's will, but his determination to hand over the inheritance to Bron rather suggested that Paul Ashley's rejection of money was genuine. In that case, he would hardly have killed for it. And he had an interest in protecting the life of a man who had witnessed a war crime."

Applegate had seated himself on a high-backed mahogany chair that offered him every possible advantage over Gabriel, most importantly an elevated position and the ability to sit up straight. "Am I to understand that there was no crime? Was Victor Gladstone mistaken, or was it yet another fabricated atrocity story?"

Gabriel shook his head. "I'm afraid not. The massacre Victor described most definitely occurred. It's just that Paul Ashley initially made the same mistake I made. Not unreasonably, he assumed the atrocity had been carried out by the Nazis. It was only as he and Victor began to work on the book that Paul realised that those men and boys were murdered by the other side. There were, sadly, atrocities on both sides. It's just that the Soviets were on our side, and we have chosen to turn a blind eye."

Applegate frowned. "I fail to see why a man as intelligent as Victor Gladstone would have asked a Communist to help him tell a story like that. It makes no sense."

"I doubt Victor was thinking as rationally as that. Paul was an idealistic young man to whom Victor took a liking—Paul was keen that Victor should like him, after all. I imagine Victor thought that Paul would view the massacre the way he did. As a crime that needed to be exposed."

"But Paul didn't see it that way."

Gabriel stood up to avoid being swallowed by the arm-chair and leaned against the wall. "I suspect the poor boy kept convincing himself that the old man was mistaken. I'd imagine that there were a few fireworks on the subject. That was why Victor brought the broken belt to show Paul."

"Belt?" Applegate was leaning forward, looking sharply at Gabriel. "I don't recall my men finding a broken belt among the deceased's personal effects."

Gabriel, as usual, noted the danger of his position a little too late. He contemplated telling Applegate that Molly had happened to discover it in a wardrobe and it had not seemed important, but that would involve dropping someone else in it. Nor would it be strictly true. Gabriel had always suspected that the belt was significant in some way; it had just seemed too much of a red herring at the time to have any bearing on the case. "I couldn't see how it was important at the time," said Gabriel, truthfully.

"Do you know how long you can go down for concealing evidence?" demanded Applegate.

Gabriel sighed. The initial panic wore off the moment Applegate began to threaten—Applegate was the sort of man who would just get on with it and lock a man up if he thought it justified. If he was talking about it, he had no intention of carrying out the threat. In the absence of panic, Gabriel was left with the nagging sense of disappointment that they were only ever going to be adversaries. For the first few minutes of the conversation—aided perhaps by the joint effort involved in saving Verity—the two men had discussed the case like colleagues. It had not taken long for Gabriel to make a mistake and for Applegate to resume his role as interrogator.

"Well?" persisted Applegate. "Not that it matters quite so much with the man caught in the act of trying to bump off his girl."

"Oh, but it does matter," replied Gabriel. "You see, I couldn't understand why a man would have a broken belt in his wardrobe that obviously hadn't been worn in ages. Then, when Bron told me more of the details of the massacre his father witnessed, I realised that the belt had been cut from around the wrists of one of the victims. Are you still with me, Inspector?"

"Just about."

"A rather macabre trophy, I thought, but that wasn't the point at all. The belt bore Soviet insignia—I'm afraid I overlooked the star on the buckle because it didn't occur to me . . . well, I didn't imagine that there could be any question as to who was responsible." Gabriel was getting out of breath as he always did when he had information to convey to a potentially hostile party, and he inevitably spoke too fast. "He wanted Paul to see it; that was why he brought it with him. It was the only irrefutable evidence Victor had about the identity of the killers."

"So Paul silenced him—I do wish you'd sit down, Father!" exclaimed Applegate. Gabriel had not noticed that he was moving so much, shifting his weight from one foot to the other as he talked, or that it was causing Applegate so much annoyance. He stopped in his tracks. "Thank you. I take it Paul destroyed the notes himself and drew your attention to the amulet to implicate the Martins."

Gabriel sat gingerly on the edge of the armchair. "Paul had Victor silenced, certainly. I'm not convinced he was trying to pin the murder on the Martins, though. I think that was simply an attempt to expose their dirty activities."

276

Applegate looked at Gabriel in evident surprise. "Come now, Paul obviously wanted us to believe that the Martins were the killers—old man Martin at least."

It was Gabriel's turn to looked surprised. "Why would he want to pin the murder on the Martins?"

"To save his neck, of course! Why else does any killer try to pin the blame on another?"

Gabriel watched the small volcanic eruption before him in bewilderment. "Inspector, I never said Paul Ashley murdered Victor Gladstone. That he intended to murder Verity is as plain as a pikestaff. But the murder charge will have to be dropped."

Applegate lurched to his feet. If he were not a guardian of the law, he might be quite a dangerous man, Gabriel suspected—dangerous certainly to him at that precise second. The sight of Applegate bearing down on Gabriel made it impossible for him to rise from his chair, which would have been the sensible course of action under the circumstances. "Why are you looking at me like that?" asked Gabriel. "Wasn't it obvious?"

"He's admitted to the crime! He's going to confess!"

"But he didn't do it!" blustered Gabriel. "I mean, he didn't *literally* do it. Morally, he's guilty of murder. That's probably why he's going to plead guilty. He knows it's his fault."

Applegate's face was an unsavoury combination of confusion and anger. "Get up," he ordered Gabriel, having only just demanded that he sit down. "I've had enough of this. This is murder, not a game of chess."

Gabriel scrambled to his feet, shrinking away from Applegate since he refused to step back and give Gabriel enough space to stand up comfortably. "I'm not wasting your time,

Inspector," Gabriel protested, but Applegate was advancing on him, forcing him to take rapid steps back in the direction of the door. "It's just that it was all so complicated. There was more than one possible motive for Victor's murder, but what if more than one motive . . ." He trailed off. It was impossible not to feel like a naughty boy being turfed out of class by the sort of schoolmaster who made a child fear for his life. Gabriel turned his back on Applegate and hurried out into the hall.

"Just give me an answer," said Applegate. "If Paul Ashley is not the guilty man, you'd better tell me who really did it before he condemns himself to the gallows."

Gabriel's foot was on the stair. "I'll take you to her," he said simply.

16

Verity was sitting up in bed when Gabriel and Applegate cautiously entered. She was fully dressed but had removed her thick blue cardigan, which hung limply over the end of the bed frame. The doctor, a middle-aged man from the village, was packing up his bag and turned to look at them at the sound of the door opening. Verity glanced at them in weary resignation, no doubt anticipating the long string of questions she would be expected to answer. "How does your patient, Doctor?" asked Applegate, closing the door behind him. "Well enough to fight another day, I hope."

"Fit as a fiddle," replied the doctor, removing his half-moon spectacles. He slipped them mechanically into the breast pocket of his tweed jacket. "Nasty shock, of course. A bit of peace and quiet mightn't go amiss, but no harm done."

"I'm afraid it might be a while before this young lady has any peace and quiet to speak of," answered Applegate, looking steadily at her. Verity immediately began to tense. Gabriel noted her hands curling into fists over the edge of the quilted blanket and the tightening of the muscles of her face as she clenched her teeth. "You know why we're here, don't you, miss?"

Verity nodded slowly before turning to the doctor, who was looking solicitously at her as though trying to determine if she was in some sort of danger. "Thank you, Doctor, you may leave now," she said, with remarkable dignity. "I'll be all right."

The doctor turned to Applegate. "Inspector, I'm not sure this is really the moment for a lengthy—"

"This won't take very long at all, Doctor," answered Applegate more gently than Gabriel was used to hearing, but it was the first time Gabriel had had the feeling that Applegate found the weight of the truth as wearisome to bear as he did. "If she is well enough to speak with me, I need to ask you to leave."

The doctor hesitated at the door, held back by some powerful professional impulse to protect a young woman from a man who could not help but exude a sense of threat. Verity was still trembling, but she managed to make eye contact with the doctor and said, as firmly as she could manage, "I think I need to speak to the inspector, Doctor. My head's perfectly clear. I should have spoken to him a long time ago."

The doctor nodded reluctantly before picking up his bag and opening the door. "Well, if you need me again, you know where to find me. I'll come again tomorrow and pay you a visit."

"I shan't be here tomorrow, Doctor," Verity replied, her voice breaking. "I think you must go."

Verity waited until the doctor had closed the door behind him before turning to look at Gabriel. It did not take long for her to get her emotions under control, but she preferred to speak to Gabriel and blocked Applegate from view as far as possible. "Will they hang me, Father?" she asked, in the tone of a child asking if she is to be sent to bed without supper. There was an almost singsong quality to her voice now. "You knew it was me all along, didn't you? You both did."

"If I'd known you killed off your grandfather," Applegate put in, causing her to flinch, "I'd have arrested you at the scene."

"You really did hate him, didn't you, Verity?" said Gabriel, sitting at her bedside to draw her attention away from Applegate. "Or rather, your mother did. She hated him with every fibre of her being."

Verity nodded. "She had every reason to hate him, Father! He was a monster!"

"So she told you. Again and again and again. In fact, I don't imagine a day went by in your home when she did not feel the need to tell you how evil your grandfather was. When hatred is so relentless, it becomes contagious."

Verity's face blazed with sudden anger. Gabriel had never seen her so angry before, but he was distracted by the thought of how very like Emma she looked. "It was not her fault!" she cried. "He ruined her life! She had no one else to talk to except for me." She turned abruptly to Applegate. "Don't listen to Paul; let him go. You know now he didn't kill my grandfather."

"But he did try to kill you," Applegate pointed out, "and he will face trial on a charge of attempted murder."

"It was mercy," said Verity. "I told him I was going to confess, tell you everything. When he asked to meet, I thought he wanted to say goodbye."

"There's nothing merciful about murder, Verity," said Gabriel, because Verity's anger had given way predictably to the tears of a woman battling to justify a man's ultimate act of betrayal. "He wanted to kill you because you were no longer of any use to him. You had done what he wanted, and he couldn't risk you confessing everything to the police and being put on trial. All the details he was trying to suppress in doing away with Victor might have been publicly exposed."

"He said it was more merciful than dying at the end of a rope," she insisted, holding her head in her hand as though she was trying to hold her sanity together. "He said he'd do it as humanely as possible. Put me to sleep and I wouldn't feel a thing. Wouldn't even know I was being killed."

"But you struggled," said Gabriel. "You didn't want his mercy."

"Of course I struggled; I didn't want to die!" Verity exclaimed, looking up at Gabriel in undisguised horror. "I don't want to die! They'll hang me as a common murderer for acting justly! Why should the old man have lived when he murdered my mother in all but name?" She was whimpering and crying like a little girl, so much so that Gabriel wished—wished so much that it almost hurt—that he could bring Verity's mother to her to offer her comfort no one else could give. But he suspected that the flow of comfort and love in that relationship had only ever moved in one direction, even when Emma had been well.

Gabriel motioned for Applegate to move to the door. They were both well within earshot of Verity, even speaking very quietly, but the move had a touch of professional courtesy about it. "Do you have to arrest her from her sickbed?" asked Gabriel. "She's not going to run anywhere. Let her rest a little first."

"I want him to take me now," declared Verity, a shade too loudly. "I think I shall feel better when there's no going back." The attempt at asserting some authority over the situation fell apart the moment Verity looked uncertainly in Applegate's direction. "Inspector, I've never been arrested before. I'm not sure what I'm meant to do. Do I need to pack anything?"

Applegate smiled at the innocence of the question, but Gabriel found himself looking away, unable to share the inspector's apparent amusement. "Your coat and hat will be sufficient," Applegate instructed her, not unkindly. "When we get to the station, you can speak to a lawyer, and he can advise you."

"Thank you," came the quavering reply. "I don't suppose I might ask you a favour before we go?"

"You may."

"Might I play the piano? It's just, I've . . . . well, I've just realised I probably . . . well, I won't ever play it again."

Applegate escorted Verity to the fine concert grand where she had performed her recital on the night before the murder. She played Beethoven's "Moonlight" Sonata, becoming so happily absorbed in her playing that she seemed quite unaware of Applegate and Gabriel standing near the door, watching and listening in silence. Gabriel wondered, as the ache in his chest spread throughout his being, whether it would have made a difference to Verity if she had been made aware of her grandfather's evident pride as she had played for them all in this very room. Would it have been enough to cut through the years of hateful indoctrination that had slowly worn her down? Might it have been enough for Verity to know that—for all his many faults, for all his cruelty and selfishness—she had perhaps been the one person in this sad world whom Victor Gladstone had come close to loving?

Perhaps not. In any case, it was far too late. Victor was dead, and as for Verity . . . Gabriel shuddered, willing himself to be lost in the dolorous melody of a great composer who knew what it meant to slip slowly and painfully into a world of silence.

The cell was a good deal more comfortable than Gabriel's morbid imagination had imagined. When he peered through the spy hole in the heavy iron door, Gabriel found himself looking into a room not much smaller or more spartan than his own cell back at the abbey. Like in his room, there was a bed against the wall and room for a chair, though he had never inhabited a room with just one narrow, barred window right up at the top of the wall or bare brick walls covered in a single grey coat of paint. And Gabriel had not been locked up in a confined space since he was a child. He could not begin to imagine how it felt to be Verity, snatched from a world of comfort and relative freedom, into a clean, warm but barely disguised cage.

Verity looked surprisingly composed in spite of her environment, perched on her bed with a book in one hand. She was plainly but smartly dressed, reassuring Gabriel that someone was keeping her well supplied with fresh clothes, books and other creature comforts.

It was only when the constable unlocked the door to let Gabriel in that the true effects of Verity's incarceration revealed themselves. At the sight of company, Verity immediately jumped to her feet, the excitement of another human presence in the room outweighing any embarrassment she might have felt at meeting a person connected with the life from which she had been so recently removed. She waited until the constable had left them alone before speaking. "Father, what a pleasant surprise!" she trilled, taking his hand.

Gabriel handed her the Madeira cake Fr Foley's housekeeper had insisted on baking for her. Dorothy had wrapped it carefully in parchment paper, but the constable had insisted on tearing it open to examine the contents, leaving the offering looking a little less appetising now. "Sorry about the state of it," said Gabriel apologetically. "PC Ward wanted to make sure it wasn't a grenade."

Verity giggled, a little too loudly. She bore all the hallmarks of a young woman struggling to cope with the long empty hours, devoid of distractions or company. As though reading his mind, Verity said, "If I could only fit a piano in here, I shouldn't mind being locked up forever."

Gabriel waited for Verity to put the cake down on the table and sit down before seating himself in the chair. With nothing to occupy her hands, Verity's fingers fluttered constantly, marking out some concerto or other that resonated only in her head. "You must be relieved the first court appearance is over," he said.

Verity nodded eagerly. "Rather! It wasn't at all as frightening as I'd expected, but then, not much happens the first time."

"You're pleading guilty to manslaughter, I see," said Gabriel, as tonelessly as he could manage.

"Yes," answered Verity cheerfully. "My lawyers are wonderful. Mr Vine is an old chum of Uncle Bron's from London. It is a very good case, he said. They are going to press for the lightest possible sentence on the grounds that I never meant to kill him. I saw him going out on his walk and decided to follow him to confront him about his treatment of my poor mother. There was an argument, then a scuffle; then when I hit him, I couldn't possibly have known he was going to fall so far. It was all a terrible accident, really." She glanced at Gabriel for some kind of reassurance and seemed to notice for the first time that he might not be entirely on her side. "Mr Vine said that a girl like me doesn't look like a murderess, and I'll have no trouble convincing a jury. I might . . . well, I might . . . I might not even have to sit very long in prison. Uncle Bron has written to the college, explaining the situation, and they've been ever so understanding." She gave a giggle which might have been caused by nervousness or a gleeful sense of relief.

"I see."

Gabriel looked steadily at her as she got up and went over to the desk to unwrap his gift. "Why don't we have some cake?" she suggested, breaking it into large pieces as delicately as she could. "I'm afraid they won't let me have a knife," she said with a soft laugh. "They think I might top myself or try to use a cake knife to fight my way out, no doubt. It's all so silly. They even took my shoelaces. Uncle Bron had to send me some other shoes."

That was life for Verity Caufield, Gabriel thought wearily, as he accepted the squashed rectangle of cake from Verity's sticky hand. She was the spoilt, shallow child of a privileged elite who were carried through life in comfort, knowing that they could always rely on the services of others to rescue them from their own mistakes and sins. Gabriel had hoped that Verity might be an exception, afflicted with a troubled

286

mother and blessed with great talent, but she was no different to the others. The glimmer of nobility that had insisted upon taking responsibility for her actions when Applegate had come to arrest her had fizzled out after a few days of the mildest possible penance. Now, all that concerned her was getting her life back as quickly as she could and having as few interruptions to the pursuit of her musical career as her uncle was able to arrange. The seriousness of what she had done seemed to elude Verity completely.

"Verity, if you'll forgive me, I'm not sure that's quite what you said when you were arrested," said Gabriel, as delicately as it was possible to accuse a person of murder. "You hated him. You didn't believe he deserved to live."

Verity flushed, and for the first time, Gabriel noticed the beginnings of uncertainty creeping over her. "One may hate a man and wish him dead without plotting murder, Father," she answered, in words that did not sound like her own. She had already been well coached by her lawyers.

"You went to considerable lengths to conceal what you had done: getting Florence Martin to take away the clothes you'd been wearing in case they linked you to the body; making it look as though you had never left that music room; pretending you had no idea what had happened to your grandfather; making quite sure that I witnessed you discovering his body."

"I was frightened," Verity began, but her words stumbled on their own uncertainty. She was skating on thin ice and knew the danger she was in. "Look here, Father, I'm not supposed to talk about it! I was told—"

"Yes, any good lawyer would have told you to keep your mouth shut," said Gabriel, standing up as though he meant to leave. "And so you should, perhaps. But since I am not obliged to shut my mouth, I should probably warn you."

"Warn me?" echoed Verity, squeezing her hands together, which at least had the effect of stilling her fidgeting fingers. "There's nothing . . ."

"You were gravely sinned against, Verity," he continued, stepping back so that his back touched the door of the cell. "Your mother brought you up to commit that crime, forcing you to listen to all those horror stories, though I suspect all she really wanted was to be pitied. She schooled you in the art of hate when you were barely out of infancy. When she screamed that she had killed her father, she spoke the truth without knowing it. In a sense, she had killed him, even though it was only a cruel coincidence that she wandered off on that morning of all mornings and stumbled upon his dead body."

"That's not true . . ."

"A dangerous thing, hate," continued Gabriel, ignoring her interruption. "It brings only disaster. Then Paul Ashley needed Victor Gladstone out of the way. I daresay you'd poured out your heart to him about your evil grandfather, and Paul saw an opportunity. He probably told you some lie that he'd discovered your grandfather was a war criminal or something. Or perhaps he simply stoked the fires your mother had lit years ago. He'd have told you anything to get what he—"

"Father, I think you should leave," said Verity curtly. She was on her feet, her hands clenched behind her back, but her voice trembled. "I should like you to leave now. Please."

"I'll leave you alone now, Verity," Gabriel promised. "If you'd rather I did not return—"

"Thank you, I would prefer not to see you again," answered Verity, so quickly that another man might have felt affronted. "I'm not sure we have much more to say to one another."

Gabriel nodded resignedly. "It's all right, you don't have to say anything else," he said gently, "but I do have to say something."

"Father . . ."

"Only this. When they put you on trial, you will have to put your hand on the Holy Bible and swear to tell the truth. Only you can say what really went through your mind when you saw your grandfather from your window, walking out into the fog; when you took it upon yourself to slip out through the window after him; when you dealt him that terrible blow from behind. Only you can say honestly whether or not you fully intended to kill your grandfather that morning. Or whether it really was a confrontation that turned ugly."

"My lawyers . . . ," Verity persisted, but she shrank back from Gabriel, sitting back onto the bed as though her knees were buckling under her own weight.

"Your lawyers do not have to account for your crime," said Gabriel, turning to face the door. He knocked loudly three times to inform the constable that he wished to leave. "You do."

"They don't have to hang either," came the breathy reply, and Gabriel turned back to Verity to find her sitting with her knees drawn up to her chest as though trying to protect herself from a coming attack. "If I change my plea, I'll hang. You can't ask me to do that."

Any chance of a response was lost in the jarring screech

of metal on metal, as the door was unlocked and opened with an ignominious whine. Gabriel looked at Verity one last time to offer her a blessing, but she had turned her back on him, and he doubted she would ever speak to him again.

EPILOGUE

Gabriel sat in the far corner of the public gallery, discreetly tucked away behind a pillar. He had a visceral dislike of courtrooms—those dour, faceless buildings where the accused men and women of the realm fought for their liberty. Or their lives. Contrary to the depiction of court cases in the popular imagination, there was little drama to be had in the prosaic recalling of events, however grotesque, while the rituals and protocols of the English courts of justice were designed to keep emotions in check and wayward personalities in their proper places.

Gabriel was a great believer in an Englishman's right to a fair trial, but it did not stop him hoping fervently that he would never be called to exercise that right. There was something both comforting and soul destroying about the place and all its paraphernalia: the judge in his wig and gown seated below the royal crest to remind everyone in whose name judgement was passed; the witness box, the barred dock where the accused could stand, not quite caged but in an ignominious-enough position to feel the full threat of what might come to him if the weight of evidence was against him; the other players in this sad little drama—the clerk of the court, the stenographers busily taking down every single word spoken during the trial, the journalists gawping at the accused, scribbling away in shorthand the basis of what they hoped would be a juicy story. The defence counsel, the prosecution, the twelve members of the jury: *twelve good men and true*.

This was the second and final day of Verity's trial. Thanks to her decision to change her plea, it had been a mercifully short affair. Gabriel had felt the need to attend the trial and had crept into this dingy little corner, carefully avoiding Verity's friends and family. Not that Gabriel needed to make much effort in that quarter, since no one was talking to him, including Bron. Bron had known that Gabriel was behind Verity's decision to change her plea—had known it on instinct—and might never forgive Gabriel the peril in which his beloved niece now found herself.

Verity was in the dock, standing up on the orders of the judge. From where Gabriel was sitting, she seemed a good deal older than her twenty-one years, dressed in a long black gown as though mourning her own inevitable demise from the world. Her hair was scraped back to reveal a pale, pensive face, much thinner than Gabriel remembered it, her eyes staring glassily at the judge with the exhaustion of a person who has not slept or eaten well in a very long time. Her hands clenched the bar in front of her so tightly that Gabriel was sure the slender bones must be visible, and she made no response of any kind as the judge admonished her for her wickedness in ending the life of her own flesh and blood. Not only a blood relative but an elderly man who had trusted and loved her.

Judge McGrath was a diminutive man in his seventies, whose wig framed a mild, lined face which bore an expression of disappointment more than the indignation Gabriel might have expected from such a figure. He spoke to Verity with the tone of a battle-weary headmaster explaining to an incorrigible reprobate that she has earned herself a rap over the knuckles. Gabriel was so troubled by the tableau before him that he caught only snatches of what the judge was now saying, but what he did hear would always haunt him. *I am well aware of your youth, young lady. It seems to me that you are not only very young but a rather foolish and ignorant little thing, easily led and easily corrupted. It is a cruelty of fate perhaps that if you had committed this heinous crime only three months earlier, you might have escaped the fate that must now befall you.*

There was an audible gasp around the court as Judge McGrath put on his black silk cap. Gabriel noticed Bron averting his eyes. Verity did not move a muscle, looking the judge in the eye as he calmly condemned her. *Verity Elisabeth Caufield, you will be taken hence to a lawful prison and from there to a place of execution where you will suffer death by hanging and thereafter your body buried within the precincts of the prison. And may the Lord have mercy upon your soul.*

Gabriel found himself whispering *Amen* under his breath, his eyes closed and his head resting on his clasped hands, so that an onlooker might have seen a man praying fervently for the redemption of a condemned killer. But Gabriel was distracted by a thumping ache in his temples that was spreading itself like a thundercloud over his head. He felt tears welling up under his eyelids and bowed his head even further in case they escaped; he pressed his heels into the floor with all his strength, bracing himself against the savage roar of his own emotions.

"Take her down," said Judge McGrath, breaking the

deathly silence in the room. Gabriel risked opening his eyes and saw Verity, flanked by two female police constables, about to be led from the dock. She looked up at the public gallery, searching the rows of faces until her gaze rested on Gabriel. Verity may have appeared eerily placid during a trial in which she had confessed everything—her hatred of her grandfather for his mistreatment of her mother, her determination to do whatever necessary to please a lover who needed the old man out of the way—every admission spoken with an invisible noose tightening around her neck. But the spell was breaking. With the sentence passed and two uniformed officials about to lock her up again, Verity looked neither frightened nor angry as she looked across at the man she might have held responsible for the predicament in which she now found herself. If anything, she seemed uncertain, searching for reassurance that she had completed a task satisfactorily. Gabriel nodded slowly.

A moment later, Verity was out of sight.

It was late by the time Gabriel arrived back at the presbytery. He had attempted to speak with Bron on the steps of the court, but Gabriel had been the wrong person to offer comfort at the wrong time and in the wrong place. Perhaps not unreasonably, thought Gabriel, Bron had turned his back on him, and Gabriel had travelled home in low spirits, sitting in the church for over two hours before he could bring himself to speak to another human being.

Gabriel was so distracted as he crossed the courtyard between the church and the presbytery that he barely noticed the stiffness in his joints where the cold had leached its way into his marrow as he had knelt in the half light. He had only ever felt so numb, so disconnected from the world around him, on one previous occasion, and that had been on account of a truly innocent woman. He had forgotten quite how like a living death it felt. Gabriel was walking, but he could not feel his feet treading carefully across the icy paving stones; he knew that there was a faint drizzle causing raindrops to land in a light mist on his face, but he could feel nothing.

Gabriel let himself into the house and was immediately greeted by Fr Foley walking nervously towards him. Gabriel's desolation was complete; Fr Foley had been waiting for him, and not merely out of concern for his feelings. Gabriel could sense the tension in the room, but it felt like the discordant murmur of background noise when walking down a busy street. Gabriel was too distracted by the events of the day to listen to the nagging voice in his head, warning him to prepare himself for worse.

"I heard the news," said Fr Foley as Gabriel removed his coat. "I'm sorry."

"News travels fast in these parts," answered Gabriel without humour.

"You travel very slowly. Why don't you sit down; you look awful."

Gabriel walked stiffly to the armchair by the fire, unable to raise his head or respond to the comforting effects of the heat and Fr Foley's kindness. "There's a chance her life may be spared," said Gabriel, tonelessly, "a good chance. I heard talk outside the courtroom that they are going to appeal to the home secretary for clemency."

"I'm sure they'll save her," said Fr Foley. "That lassie must have clever lawyers. And she is very young, even if she has reached her majority." Gabriel still did not move or respond to the words of comfort. When he looked into the fire, all he could see was the spectre of Judge McGrath in that black silk square cap, telling a pale-faced girl in black that she was going to be killed. English justice was so perfunctory, so unfeeling . . . so *polite*. That was almost what haunted him the most. The judge had spoken so softly and courteously, as though the worst he could do to her was to send her to bed without supper. "Gabriel? Wake up, son!"

Gabriel turned very slowly in Fr Foley's direction. "I'm adrift, Father," he said, sounding to all intents and purposes as though he was about to fall asleep. "What if she loses that appeal? Are they really going to tie her up, put a noose over her head and let her drop to her death? Are they truly going to do that to her?"

Fr Foley folded his arms in front of him, a gesture which should have warned Gabriel that the old man was climbing onto a war path. "She's too rich to hang," he said tersely. "A common labourer who kills a man in a brawl may hang; a well-spoken girly will be shown mercy. Mark my words."

Gabriel winced but gave no answer. He was well versed in Fr Foley's political sympathies by now and had no energy to argue with him. He let his head drop into his hands.

"Gabriel, whatever happens to her, it is not on your conscience," said Fr Foley, with more severity than Gabriel was used to hearing. "She wasn't so young and stupid that she didn't know it was wrong to bash an old man over the head."

"She was manipulated."

"She didn't have to do it. She had free will," said Fr Foley. "In any case, whatever the rights and wrongs of it, her fate is not your responsibility. A court judged her; she had . . ."

"If it's not my responsibility, then what . . ."

"She committed a crime; she had the chance to defend herself in court. She must now face the consequences of her actions."

"Easy enough to say that," murmured Gabriel, his words muffled because he did not have the presence of mind to remove his hands from his face. "I could have let well alone."

"Yes, you could," Fr Foley conceded, sitting down with some hesitation. "You could have stood back and offered her no counsel as she perjured herself before a judge, jury and Almighty God. You've done your job; leave her lawyers to do theirs." Gabriel answered him with a barely audible whimper. "Gabriel, you're going to have to pull yourself together, you know. There's something else I need to tell you."

Five minutes later, Gabriel was storming up the narrow stairs and hurling himself bodily into his room. By the time Fr Foley had succeeded in following him, Gabriel had already dropped his knapsack onto the bed and begun pulling his meagre belongings out of the wardrobe. "I thought you wanted to go home," gasped Fr Foley; the short dash up a flight of steps had left him out of breath. He leaned on the door frame for support. "You've always been homesick for the abbey."

"I had rather imagined . . . ," said Gabriel, stuffing several pairs of much-darned socks into the knapsack. "Well, I had hoped I might be sent back to the abbey when Father Abbot thought me worthy to return. Not because I've been more of a walking disaster in a parish than I was in community!"

Fr Foley did not venture into the room, taken aback by Gabriel's distress. He was packing his bag as though every object he placed in it were a personal danger to him and needed to be subdued. "It's not forever," Fr Foley promised. "Abbot Ambrose said you'd be away a month. For your own . . . well . . ."

"Safety," Gabriel finished. He reached into the top drawer of his bedside table and took out his purple velvet keepsake bag, treating it with a tenderness and care that stood in stark contrast to his rough handling of everything else in his possession. Purple velvet with embroidered gold lettering. He sat down on the bed and let his fingers brush against the soft, inviting fibres.

"Gabriel, he must have been worried enough after you were beaten up. He heard about the court case and . . ." There was no need for him to say anything else. Both men knew that Abbot Ambrose was hardly being overcautious in recalling Gabriel to the sanctuary of the abbey. Gabriel's name had not appeared in the papers, but in a small town, the major players in such a titillating little drama were easily identified and turned into the targets of gossip. All the more so when the drama in question had culminated in no fewer than four separate trials. It might be many months before Horace and Florence Martin accounted for their criminal activities in court, but the details of their arrests had been widely circulated. Ironically, Paul's intended victim might not survive long enough to see justice done on her behalf . . .

"What about you?" demanded Gabriel, his hands still cradling the purple keepsake bag. "How will you manage?"

Fr Foley smiled but said nothing. He did not need to. Gabriel knew painfully well that an elderly priest recovering from a heart attack could live without the ministrations of a curate who attracted murder and mayhem at every possible opportunity. "I shall miss the pleasure of your company," Fr Foley assured him, "that I will. Until you return."

"Am I coming back?" asked Gabriel, wishing the question did not sound quite so desperate. "Is that what the abbot said?"

Fr Foley shook his head sadly. "Afraid not. He just said that someone would drive over tomorrow morning to take you back to the abbey for a month until the hue and cry has died down a little. I took it to mean you would be returning, but anything can happen in a month."

Gabriel nodded resignedly. He waited until he stopped hearing Fr Foley's footsteps lumbering down the stairs before he kissed the purple bag lightly and packed it away. He had been desperate to return to the abbey for months, but he felt appalled by the thought that he was being rescued from the possible repercussions of his own actions. Would he ever return? If not, who would minister to Verity if her appeal for clemency were thrown out and she had to face the hangman?

Gabriel closed his eyes to pray, but the only words that came to mind were the cry of desperation he remembered repeating over and over again in the darkest hour he was ever forced to endure. *Out of the depths I cry to thee, O Lord . . .*

He had lived to see a better day. He would live to see another.